Roke Elm

CHRISTINE HOLMES

Published by
Robert Boyd Publications
on behalf of Keith Holmes
3 Capel Close, Oxford OX2 7LA
kdhox@hotmail.com
from whom copies can be obtained

First published 2011

Copyright © Keith Holmes

ISBN: 978 1 899246 51 9

All rights reserved. No part of this
publication may be reproduced, stored
in a retrieval system, or transmitted in
any form or by any means without
prior written permission of
Keith Holmes.

Printed and bound by TJ International Ltd
Padstow, Cornwall PL28 8RW

About the Author

Christine Holmes was a New Zealand historian who settled in England in 1977. Over the next two decades she developed a deep interest in the landscape and history of the area between the Chiltern Hills and Oxford, where she lived. In 1995 she began a Masters degree in Local History at Kellogg College, in Oxford, at the same time as her husband, Keith, was posted to Brazil. For two years she thus spent half her time in Brazil and the rest in Oxford, completing a thesis on the Anglo-Saxon and Early Medieval history of the area surrounding Benson, which, in 1998, was awarded the Oxbow Prize For Local History.

In 1999, she contributed three chapters to a book about Benson, edited by her former supervisor and published by the Bensington Society to mark the millennium. At the same time, she turned her hand to creative writing and produced this manuscript, the first of three novels completed before her untimely death from cancer in 2010, four weeks short of her sixty-sixth birthday.

The story overtly incorporates much of the joy, excitement, and intellectual curiosity which the author herself had while researching her thesis, as well as her delight in Oxford life. It also exudes the gentle love and affection she had for her many friends and her family by transposing aspects of many of them into characters in the novel. More cleverly, she weaves a romantic plot and a scientific mystery into a story that steadily reveals the very unusual and significant early history of the village of Benson.

Benson; A Village Through Its History, Edited by Kate Tiller, was published in 1999 by Pie Powder Press for the Bensington Society. Further information may be found on two websites; www.spanglefish.com/thebensingtonsociety and www.benson-village.co.uk

'the garden was enclosed on all sides with air as though it were ringed with iron, so that nothing could enter except at one single place. And there were flowers and ripe fruit all summer and all winter, and the fruit had the peculiar property that although it could be eaten therein, it could not be carried out: anyone who tried to take some away could never discover how to get out again, for he could not discover the exit until he put the fruit back in its place.'

Chretien de Troyes, 'Eric and Eneide', *Arthurian Romances*, Penguin Books, London, 1991, p.107

Roke Elm

1

Katherine's letter arrived the day before Christmas. She read it and smiled, and lay it triumphantly in the centre of her desk. She made an extravagant detour around Oxford on the way in to the Gallery. On the top of Wittenham Clumps, far above her parked car, she looked out over the wide curve of the Thames, black and dull, the old Roman town, and the patchwork of the old territory, dotted with villages. The Chilterns stretched out to the horizon. She breathed heavily, smoky rings in the cold. I have to remember how wonderful this is, she said aloud. Think about it before I get stuck in the details and lose perspective. Look at it, spread out there. The circle of trees blew around her, scruffy in midwinter.

Dear Ms Laidlaw,

We are happy to tell you that next year's publishing programme has been finalised, and we are ready to go ahead with the book on Benson and Chiltern history which we have discussed with you. We hope to have your manuscript in hand in time for pre-Millennium publication. Please could you sign and return the enclosed form outlining this agreement, and our first quarterly advance can then be made.

    Can I say personally how much I look forward to working with you on this project?

Yours sincerely,
Tim Rothwell,
Editor.

'He can say absolutely what he likes', Katherine said later in the morning. 'Even personally. It means I can stay in Oxford for another year - well, I would have anyway, of course - but for sure. And be paid for the work, which I've started already.' Olivia, the owner of the Gallery, watched Katherine's absent-minded, erratic movements, and the high-cheekboned bright face. Her hair was in a very thick, loose, plait as usual, particularly untidy today.

'Have you told Orlando?' They were unpacking jugs and bowls from a potter in North Wales.

'I'll ring him.' Katherine folded the blister pack into squashy squares. 'But it is the job I'm really pleased about, not only staying with Orlando.'

Last year she had spent Christmas in Rio with Orlando; this year he had gone alone. 'These are wonderful', she said, stroking one of the smooth-sided white bowls. 'They'll go quickly.'

The High Street Gallery specialised in studio pottery. Shelves and windows were bright and serene with graceful shapes and idiosyncratic glazes in colours and stipples, and the company of Olivia and her other colleague made the minuscule part-time salary bearable. She was entirely inartistic herself, Katherine knew, but she loved being with people who were, and were beautiful and elegant and practical. Otherwise, she imagined, she might think of nothing but history, ever. Saxon records, early Norman records, the detective work of them, they were absorbing. Why don't you toss in your scrappy-sounding documents and rolls and parchments, Orlando once asked? Not worry about the gaps and forgeries and indecipherable records, and do archaeology instead? Oh no, she had answered. There have to be some people in the picture, not just objects, or bodies. Some names. Once you get to the later centuries, you have too many people; it's not different enough from now. There are a few centuries on the cusp, just around Domesday, just after, when it's perfect.

'We'll start the occasional bottle of wine today,' Olivia said. 'Customers too. Make up for sparse decorations' She looked festive enough herself, with bright orange beads dangling over the black dress, and very high heeled shoes. They sold quite briskly, including three of the new Alun Palmer pots, and Olivia told ludicrous and indiscreet stories about the Christmas rush in Joe's Accident and Emergency department - people doing unimaginable things with fairy lights, and super glue and pine cones. She waved her hands demonstratively, and let the punch lines come with panache. Katherine loved her stories. Before she left - her last shift till after Boxing Day - she handed over her presents to Olivia and to Dawn, the other part-timer. History books of a kind, of course, but light. One was called *'Queens in the Kitchen: Recipes from Lost Royal Palaces'* and the other was a square glossy book about erotic pictures on pots since prehistory, called *'Ceramic Lovers.'* A bit obvious, but the pictures were beautiful, and some of the pots now museum pieces.

'Good bye, and have a lovely London Christmas,' Olivia said, getting a beautifully wrapped parcel from her bag. 'Give my love to your mother and the gorgeous City Suit.' Olivia had a lively telephone relationship with Katherine's brother, James.

'Send positive thoughts and help me', Katherine said, and kissed her. Outside in the High Street tinsel decorations dangled above the traffic lights, and traditional academic gowns on display in a shop window across the road had sparkly parcels littered around their hems. She made her way to the car park and left the town through traffic queues and lost drivers crawling towards the London motorway. When she reached the roundabout, on a sudden impulse, she turned off and headed south on the smaller road. She wanted to go through Benson again.

Down through the Oxfordshire countryside, along the Thames, its route marked across the flat meadow by willows, still sprouting in neat sprays from pollarding long ago. How can you travel here without noticing the evocative names, settlers looking for water? Britwell, Brightwell, Cadwell, Adwell, Mongewell. A straight run of Roman road from Dorchester, and then too much water - Rokemarsh, Crowmarsh.

She drove the haphazard lines of Benson's central streets. Castle Square, but there never had been a castle. So where had the battles of the *Anglo-Saxon Chronicles* been fought in Benson? Where had the great kings Ceawlin and Offa fortified their armies? Where were the boundaries of this old land? In Mill Street she got out and walked to the weir, and leaned over it, her mind on records seven centuries old. A man once paid six sticks of eels to rent this mill pond. A woman called Agnella married three successive millers. Simon the miller was taken to court for cheating on weights. Katherine was preoccupied and deeply happy. Only she knew all these people, in this other world.

She drifted back to her car, and then stopped at a pub for coffee and food to annul the last effects of Olivia's wine. The King's Head lay on a second stretch of Roman road, south of the village. Cars were parked against the single line of outdoor tables. The puny trees in tubs beside them were ringed untidily with coloured lights, already turned on in the dim afternoon. Inside, festive groups from local offices and from the air force base were finishing prolonged pre-Christmas lunch gatherings. Paper hats littered one corner. Katherine pulled her coat off and slowly unwound her scarf. 'Are you still doing sandwiches?' she said to the barman. 'Could I have tomato? Just tomato.' She sat down, and her coat trailed to the floor.

'Here it is,' said a man at the next table, and put it on the chair beside her. He had thick almost colourless hair, and a heavy dark green jersey. 'Thank you,' Katherine said, and they laughed when it slithered to the floor, and with a quick movement he reached for it again. She glanced at him, and then anchored her coat more carefully, and threw her scarf on top of it. She reached into her bag for her present from Olivia, and unwrapped it carefully. Out of the soft paper and the mass of ribbons came a sleek watch, silver and green, with a smooth convex face rising from the strap. She lay it on the table, curving her hand over it. It filled her palm.

'That's nice', the man said. He stood up, and. she sensed him for a moment beside her.

'Isn't it! From a friend who always chooses wonderful presents'

'It's a time bubble.'

They smiled at each other as he left. He had clear, light eyes. Outside the pub he stood still momentarily, hand on the door. Then, quite slowly, he moved away.

Back in the car, Katherine thought of ringing Orlando, and even got her phone out. But he and Rio de Janeiro seemed unreal, not in co-existence with her anymore. After a minute she put the phone away, and drove off, through Ewelme and Nettlebed and Henley, to London.

Katherine arrived at her mother's house, in a small square off Kensington High Street, and edged into a parking place, one wheel up on the kerb. She glanced at the white house fronts with pleasant strips of garden at basement level, and tubs of trees chained to fence railings, and felt tired. Her mother and aunt appeared at the top of the steps, waving.

'Hallo, darling' said Elizabeth, her mother, chic and graceful in grey and yellow.

Diane appeared beside her, her aunt. When Katherine and James's father had died seven years ago, his sister had come to comfort Elizabeth, and never left. James frequently referred unkindly to them as The Keepers, keepers of the flame of Peter Laidlaw's memory.

Katherine kissed them both, suppressing instant claustrophobia in the small rooms. Even the air seemed pastel coloured, not quite clear.

'James here yet?' she said, hopefully.

Elizabeth shook her head. 'Is that all your luggage?'

'You want me to have brought velvet and tiaras, don't you? Well, you'll be surprised. I have got a new dress.' Elizabeth looked impressed.

In her room she unpacked it, a silvery Ghost dress, protected in a plastic bag from the ceramic edges of the Gallery pots her family were getting for Christmas. There was the bright cover of a Brazilian book called '*Gabriela, Clove and Cinnamon*' she had promised Orlando she would read, and on top of them all were folders of Benson notes, a photocopied manuscript, and a dictionary of medieval Latin.

Elizabeth had cooked what she called a midwinter stew, tangy with bay leaf and orange peel. With surprising speed, Diane opened two bottles of Australian shiraz. James arrived only slightly late, and took two phone calls on his mobile before they could begin. At last Elizabeth raised her glass to Katherine. 'Your last singleton Christmas, darling. Maybe your last one in England.'

'But we mightn't even live in Rio. And guess what? Much before that - I'm going to publish a book in the autumn. 'A lost Saxon kingdom,' or 'The history of Benson,' or 'The Chilterns.' Something like that, it will be called.'

Her mother and aunt were delighted.

'Money?' said James, sounding surprised. 'I don't believe it.'

'Well, a bit. Publishers are keen on history because of the millennium. Specially stuff round about the last millennium. There are grants aplenty, for once.'

'Your father would be so delighted'

'Orlando will be pleased' Elizabeth and Diane spoke together.

'If it's all right', she said, standing up, 'I might try to ring Orlando, actually, and tell him now.' She left the room and then felt ungracious and put her head back around the door.

'I'll be back for coffee.'

Orlando was a medical sociologist, at home in Rio de Janeiro for a few summer weeks. As the phone rang, Katherine envisaged the Moraes family flat in Ipanema, with a long balcony looking onto the sea. If there was no answer, it probably meant he was out playing volleyball on whichever stretch of the beach was fashionable that season. He only reverted to outdoor fitness and ball games on his visits home, and she imagined him puffing and hot on the crowded beach, with the little planes flying low overhead, towing advertisements. She was glad the maid, Elena, was not answering, and she was spared from trying out her shaky Portuguese. Just as she was about to hang up, the light voice of his mother answered. 'Katerina! He is not here, I'm so sorry,' she said in her quick heavily-accented English. 'On the beach, very hot today. Snow in Oxford? Not yet. I will tell Orlando, and he will ... Ciao, Katerina. Embraces.' Katherine returned to the table and found James hastily rewrapping something he had been showing the others.

'Didn't I stay away long enough?' she asked hopefully. 'No answer in Rio, Orlando is out. Christmas is just us, now.'

2

The weather changed on the last day of the year. A pale yellow sun overcame the clouds and rain which had hung over Oxford's marshy scenery for days, like a depressing low level fever. Blue sky lit up the shallow lakes covering the flood plains fingering into the city on all sides. Katherine looked out over Port Meadow from her kitchen window, and saw the horses standing herded together on protruding tongues of damp land, while flocks of white geese took over their water-covered territory. The whole meadow glittered in the sharp winter light. She was on the phone, listening to Olivia.

'Christmas was great, because Joe was on duty - a fiasco with a complete family, all drunk, I must tell you about it - and we missed everything and had a quiet dinner ourselves on Boxing Day. Well, just us and two of his medical mates. He gave me the most gorgeous pair of eighteenth century glasses. Wine, I mean, not reading. Everyone in the village seems to have gone to ground, but ... oh, hell, someone's come in.' Katherine remembered that Olivia was speaking from the Gallery. 'I'll ring you back because we're getting some people together tonight. Ciao.'

Ciao, that's what Orlando says, Katherine thought. And everyone else in Brazil. She unpacked her London luggage and shopping while she waited. She moved around her flat, enjoying its silence. It was the upper floor of a Victorian house, the largest in the row. Her kitchen, bathroom, and bedroom shared the huge southerly view over Port Meadow, where she could watch the horses and cows carry on their lives like creatures in a safari scene, and see the weather roll in above them. In the front, from the sitting room, all was domestic, urban - the scruffy central green of Wolvercote, plastic swings and seesaws, terraced brick houses, and cars wedged in untidy parks, half on and off the footpaths. Inside, her computer was marooned among books and papers on her desk, and some unopened mail, probably late Christmas cards, still lay on the floor. She put *'Gabriela, Clove and Cinnamon'* on top of them. Matters to be attended to. It was hard to believe in that hot, exotic, world.

Olivia quite often 'got people together', usually at short notice because of Joe's hospital hours. They lived in Beckley, five miles away, in a thatched cottage, remarkably small, and very beautiful. I'll make something to take, Katherine thought, and looked at the waxy small potatoes and smoked salmon lying on the bench. The phone went again. She lifted it. Olivia again, she presumed.

'Hi. You were saying?'

'Katherine? Hallo. Are you home?'

'Orlando! Of course I'm home. And glad to be. How are you?'

'What were you saying?'

'I thought you were Olivia.'

'Well, I'm not'

'No, you're certainly not. I was just thinking about you saying 'Ciao.''

'I'm not saying ciao.'

'No. But you do. When you do. Never mind! Yes, I am at home, probably going to Joe and Olivia's tonight. What are you doing?'

He talked for a minute. He was near confirmation of a major research grant. They would be at Copacabana beach for the New Year fireworks tonight. He sounded as near as if he were next door.

'Phone calls are very unsatisfactory' she said.

'They are, beautiful Katherine. Give my love to Olivia and Joe, but not too much. Ciao.'

She wandered restlessly to her mirror. Beautiful Katherine? I look about twenty-eight, she said aloud.

Exactly what I am. She leant towards it, framed by the reflection of the wintry blue sky. Lots of thick hair, rarely cut. Good big eyes. Wonderful when animated, I'm told, she said to the serious reflection. I hope so. She wandered towards the kitchen again, and looked at the food on the bench. Little pancakes, *blinis*. Thick and light. Joe will love them.

'Icy roads.'

'Yes, Dr Ash. I drove slowly.'

Joe was waiting just inside, greeting guests with mulled red wine. The room was full of people and talk. Clove-filled fumes floated in the air, mixing with vapours from the scented candles which stood about, flames wavering as he opened and closed the door.

'I brought these.'

'In the kitchen thank you, darling Kathy. No, give me a sample first.' He put his jug down and took one of the little pink-covered pancakes. 'Gorgeous. Do you remember our ... '

'Smoked salmon picnic. Punt not included,' she chorused with him. Joe and Katherine and Orlando had been freshers in the same college, thrown together by staircase allocation.

'You always were a great cook. Fussy, though.'

'You always were a great eater. Fussy, though.'

'That was a serious scientific diet.' Joe had made the college's first boat, and then the blue boat, rising through the rowing hierarchy like a star. 'I've never been the same since.' He took a second pancake before retrieving his jug. 'And here's my reward.' Olivia came towards them, one arm full of another guest's flowers. She wore, as often, different ear-rings, a gold hoop on one ear, and an arched black and gold cat on the other.

'Hallo, Katherine.' They kissed. 'You can have this to drink if you are warm enough. Doesn't have to be that one.' She waved a glass of yellow champagne at Joe's jug. He watched her for a minute before turning back to Katherine.

'Well?' he said, lifting the jug.

'Yes, I'd love your hot mull. But shall I take these to the kitchen first? Olivia, will these be all right?'

'Lovely of course. I'll be with you in a minute.' She took a swig of her drink. 'Go on. You know everyone.'

Katherine made her way to the kitchen. She recognised several of Joe's medical friends, and Olivia's sister. 'Hallo, Heather!' How could she and Olivia be sisters? 'Just passing through, to do something with these. Have one.' She lifted the cling film cover on her plate again. Heather wore a square woollen dress, brown and beige. Could one of them have been adopted? 'Back in a minute.'

In the kitchen, she had a momentary pang for Orlando. He was such fun at parties, so good to arrive with. But then, she thought, if he were here we probably wouldn't be here yet. He would be so Brazilian and be so late. We'd still be at home, and he would be on the phone to someone, keeping in touch.

'What are you smiling about?' Olivia was in the kitchen, dumping the flowers on the table. Her glass was empty.

'Complicated thoughts. About Orlando.'

'That's very suitable.'

Olivia began banging through a cupboard, looking for a vase.

'Livvy. Are you all right?'

Olivia turned round, her skirt swirling. Katherine saw there were tears in her eyes.

'No, I'm not. Well, I'm too well. I wanted not to be so well ... ' She cried in several loud sobs, and Katherine took the vase from her hands.

'Just before everyone came, and we were nearly celebrating, and then I went in the bathroom, and ... ' Katherine understood instantly. 'Oh, Livvy. I'm sorry. So sorry.' She felt helpless.

Joe and Olivia's childlessness was a rarely mentioned topic. She felt obscurely that Joe, who won everything, could surely achieve this. It must be Olivia who couldn't. Then she felt ashamed for making such assumptions, out of ignorance, and perhaps an even less honourable state - she hadn't won Joe herself; Olivia had. By the time she had shaken this thought out, and pressed it down again, Olivia was dabbing her face, and picking up the flowers.

'Okay', she said. 'Collapse over. There'll be other months.'

Katherine made a sympathetic face, and shrugged her shoulders.

The other part-timer from the Gallery, Dawn, was slightly tipsy. She had arrived with a well-known potter, and hung onto him, hoping his skills might enter her by osmosis. She had a very short green skirt, and sheer shiny tights.

'That's one of Sven's,' she advised Heather, pointing proudly to a striped bowl, like a huge and perfect nautilus shell. 'And that's one of mine.' On a lower shelf, within reach, stood a square black pot, matt and heavy.

'Oh, you're a potter, too', Heather said politely. 'Olivia always says she's just the facilitator and the agent, but she used to be quite good, once. I wish she hadn't stopped.'

'You must have known her for a long time?'

'Yes ... '

Katherine interrupted. 'Dawn! This is Olivia's sister. Heather - this is Dawn.'

Dawn's pretty face looked bewildered. 'Oh, God - really? Sorry.'

They were saved by Joe, 'Raise your glasses, everyone! Nearly midnight!' He switched on the television and a picture of Big Ben appeared, hands counting down towards the hour. It alternated with shots of heaving crowds in Trafalgar Square. 'Ready!' Joe called. 'Happy New Year!

Only one more till the big one, the Millennium!' They raised their arms. Katherine was holding Dawn's hand.

Auld Lang Syne began, raggedly.

'What a beautiful watch!' Dawn looked at Katherine's wrist.

'Olivia and Joe's present.' How could she have forgotten to thank them, Katherine thought. She would immediately.

'You must miss Orlando', Dawn shouted through the fading singing. She had dropped the potter's hand and looked at Katherine sentimentally. Orlando was wonderful, exotic, clever.

'Do you?' she persisted. 'Miss Orlando?'

Katherine was remembering unwrapping the watch, sitting in the King's Head in Benson. Olivia's beautiful packaging, and then someone saying it was pretty, a time-bubble. She tried to replay the man's face in her mind. She saw his fair, curly hair, and direct, light-eyed glance. His skin was a very even, faint tan.

'Well?' Dawn asked again.

'Orlando?' Katherine said slowly. 'Well, of course I do.'

3

Oxford took different incarnations in Katherine's mind, and each had its own time and different maps. The Oxford of her student days, the first Oxford, and her first freedom from home, had her college as its centre, and the lecture halls, libraries, clubs, and river banks. That beautiful Oxford was scattered with memories of faded student excitements and concerns. Now she worked in Oxford and lived in a flat on its edge, it had become a place of ring roads and traffic she had never noticed before. When her mother came to visit her, or friends came to stay, architectural, literary Oxford took over. Walks were guided and slow, and familiar shops and offices shrank and almost disappeared between ancient stone buildings and solemn history. The martyrs' plaque stood out in the middle of Broad Street, and philosophers walked in the quadrangles. Katherine's towns existed in different dimensions, never showed themselves in the presence of the others.

After New Year she began to switch from one vision to the other, at the end of each day. Soon even academic Oxford became a mere tunnel to lost Benson. I have to go, she said, to Olivia, or to Dawn, at the end of each of her Gallery shifts, and hurried off along the High to the Bodleian. In the late afternoons it was almost dark when she got there, and in Duke Humfrey's Library upstairs each reader sat in a private pool of pale electric light. The ceiling sheltered them all like a protective, gaudy marquee, blue and gold and red. She sat in the same seat each day, with changing piles of transcribed medieval records. Benson, she read about; Bynsingtun, the royal manor. She toiled over the Latin, and the dictionary became dog-eared. In the King's Arms or Blackwells across the road she drank coffee and ate muffins or sandwiches indifferently, thumbing through her notes. It was like a window she could look through into the past, she thought, but an opaque, frustrating one. The scenes through the window began in the year 571, when the high king Ceawlin of Wessex, and his kinsman, Cutha, capture Benson. But from whom? Were Celts still there, making a last stand in the Chiltern hills? And two centuries later it belongs to King Offa of Mercia - where was Wessex then? And where did the kings down the centuries collect their taxes and assemble their armies? What hall? What rallying point? Why can't we find it? And back to her books she would go, half guilty at her obscure passion.

Late in the month she got flu, and spent four days drooping in her flat. She lay feverishly in bed, and slept till dusk. By Friday, she was better.

'Don't come in to work, though', Olivia said. 'Have a rest and start again on Monday. Joe says the hospital's bulging with people who got up too soon. It's the annual bed crisis. Don't risk it.'

'Okay,' Katherine said. 'See you then.' She hung up the phone. She decided to put on layers of clothes, and go for a careful convalescent walk in Benson.

4

'How old, do you think?'

Katherine turned around, startled, dragging her coat across herself. It was blustery, almost raining.

'Older than its neighbour, anyway.' The man who spoke had the collar of his Barbour turned up, and a large dog on a lead. They were standing in Benson High Street, looking at a cottage with old wooden cruck timbers, like an upturned ark, embedded in later stone and brick. He was looking at the building, not at her, but Katherine felt a flicker of recognition, or memory.

'Not much timber building at all in Benson, otherwise,' she said, trying to place his voice. She thought the little house was unique. 'Fourteenth century, even ... ' There was flurry and commotion round her legs, and two dogs flew at each other.

'Bella!' The man with the Barbour pulled at his dog. He sounded severe but faintly amused. His face lit up and his teeth were white. The attacking terrier, attached to a woman loaded with shopping, drove himself at Bella again, and a bag of oranges, with rhubarb sticks poking out, crashed to the ground. As Katherine lent down to retrieve a rolling orange, Bella ran at her. The man whacked his dog across the back with her lead. 'Oh, God. Action stations,' he said. 'I'm sorry.' The terrier's owner was a woman with rather a gloomy wide face, and dyed pinkish hair dangling to her shoulders. Her dog seemed daunted by the rolling fruit and Bella's pounce, and hung back, looking away. 'That's right,' the woman said to it in a nasal voice. 'Pretend to be bored.' They collected the oranges and rhubarb and pushed them back into her bag. It began to rain, fast and heavy. 'Cup of coffee?' the man said to them both. 'We're right outside.' He gestured towards the door of a florist's, which had three or four round tables, set with cloths and cups, amongst the pails of flowers.

'Not with that', the pink haired woman said, looking at Bella. Her own terrier growled, and she added, 'Not with that either, I suppose.'

No, perhaps not,' he said, solicitously. The woman sniffed loudly, and dragged at the little dog, moving on. She raised the bag. 'It's for rhubarb crumble', she said. Katherine and the man nodded politely, and then glanced at each other. They smiled. Now he seemed familiar, and she felt her mouth go dry.

'What about us having the coffee? I'm sorry Bella pounced on you. She's a confused animal.' He had a slight accent, perhaps west country, or even American.

As she hesitated, he was already tying the dog to the single bicycle rack outside the florist. 'Been to the vet for a vaccination, and it's practically the only time she wears a lead. And,' he called over his shoulder, 'I think it might be thirteenth, actually, the house. Thirteenth century.' Katherine glanced at the cottage again, and then nodded. 'Okay.'

They sat at the window table, among the flowers. 'You could float on this smell', Katherine said, and sniffed, throwing her long plait back. 'Imagine working in this all day.' Her hair sparkled with rain drops.

'No rhubarb crumble on the menu, though.' She laughed,

and when he turned his eyes to her for a minute, she was sure.

'You were in the King's Head, on Christmas Eve. My coat kept falling.'

'Yes', he said. 'And what about your watch?'

She pulled her sleeve up. 'I wear it all the time.' They looked at it, the clear hemisphere like a pretty barnacle on her wrist.

'Actually,' he said, 'That wasn't the first time, either.'

'No?'

'You'd been into the King's Head before then. I was behind the bar. I work there on odd days. You were asking about Hollandtide Bottom, and some of the other foot paths. You had maps.'

'That's possible.' She withdrew a little. The smell of the flowers was almost over-powering.

'Some of the paths are old boundaries, and boundaries are interesting.'

'Yes, they are. Are you a historian?'

'No. Certainly not.' He gave a surprising guffaw. 'But I live here, and walk the paths very often. With Bella.'

The florist brought them thick blue-striped cups of very weak coffee. Why had she come in here, for a tasteless drink with someone who seemed to have been watching her in a pub?

'Made with old water from the vases, I suppose,' he said. 'Full of priceless herbal remedies.' His smallest movements, like lifting the cup, seemed to be full of energy.

'It's very early medieval, even pre-Conquest boundaries I'm interested in. Not necessarily parish boundaries.'

'And Hollandtide Bottom was an old boundary as well as a path?'

'Well, yes. I'm working on late Saxon Benson. Maybe early medieval. We don't know exactly what 'Benson' meant then.' How pompous she sounded. Who was 'we'? 'And the oldest boundaries would at least give us a physical vision of what we're talking about.'

'Of course. But I don't think the maps have all the oldest paths quite right.'

She looked at him, her head tilted. He swigged the last of the watery coffee and continued. 'Where I live, for example - what used to be called Roke Elm, but long since called The Sands, on modern maps. Have you counted the paths to Roke Elm?'

She was surprised to hear him use the old name.

'Yes, all five. I've walked them' she said, defensively.

'No', he shook his head. 'I think there are more than that.'

He pushed his cup away. His hands were brown, with heavily calloused palms.

'More than five?'

'I can find seven. Come and walk them with me.'

Katherine hesitated. He rubbed his hair carelessly. His rough palms reminded her of Joe's rowers' hands, incongruous sometimes now with his white medical coat. Could dragging a big dog on a lead rub your hands as much as that?

'How can you be sure of seven?'

'I live there. Bottom of Roke Hill Field, getting on to Scald Hill.'

They were obscure medieval names which had dotted her research notes for months, painstakingly gleaned from archives and record offices. Now they hung like lures between them.

'Where could I reach you if ... ?' she said, after thinking a minute.

'At the King's Head' he answered. 'On Tuesday afternoons, or Friday and Saturday evenings. Or at the timber yard at Roke, where I work.'

'The timber yard?' She had driven past it often, seen the

oblong patch of land covered with layers of grey tree trunks.
'Oh, the timber yard! Your hands ... '

He spread them out, palms up.

'This is going to sound rude. I noticed your hands. They look like a friend's. He is, well, he was, a rower, and I wondered ... '

'A rower? Of boats?' This made him laugh. 'No, these are timber yard hands.' He looked happy and amused.

'Only checking', Katherine said.

Now he held out one of the calloused hands. 'Richard Cottell. Bring your maps, even if they're not quite right.'

'Katherine Laidlaw. Maybe.'

5

Orlando arrived from Rio the following Sunday evening. It was raining and windy.

'Not very welcoming, I'm afraid,' Katherine said, as she steered her old Metro carefully from the parking building at Heathrow.

'Weather's not what we love England for.' Orlando looked tanned and somehow more foreign. Glimpses of brown scalp showed through his shiny, thinning black hair. She glanced at him affectionately. What a long time we've known each other. How clean he looks, even after a long journey. His clothes don't look quite warm enough. She lifted a hand from the steering wheel and lay it briefly on his knee. 'There's dinner in Wolvercote. Chicken in a pot - very restorative. Or would you rather go straight home?' Orlando had a college flat in St John's Street, with an inadequate kitchen, and a high-ceilinged reception room entirely turned into an untidy study. Each of them privately did not want to move in together and give up work space, and each was glad the other did not suggest it.

'Dinner with you, of course. Please. Dinner and you.'
'Really?'
'Really.'
She squeezed her hands on the wheel.

'John Davidson and I have been trying to swing this Rio-Boston link-up for a long time, and it's all come to pass. Ten-year grant, extendable to fifteen.'

They were drinking a bottle of McLaren Vale shiraz. Orlando had opened it obliviously, talking, and Katherine was fussily swirling it in her glass. It was not quite the perfect temperature. 'It will be the biggest project ever done on asthma, by far. Comparing diet, pollution, sleep patterns, wealth, domestic hygiene, smoking, weight, birth-weight, you name it, in both countries.'

'Star sign.'
'What?'
'Star sign. You could include star sign in your variables.'
' Okay. I talk too much.'
'Come and eat dinner before you fall sleep.'

Orlando had had a shower and pulled clean clothes out of his airline bag. His shirt's perfect ironing was visible, even through the fold marks - the work of the Moraes family maid in Rio. After a few days back in Oxford he would look rumpled and familiar. They sat to eat the chicken Katherine had left slowly cooking while she drove to Heathrow. It was in a heavy black casserole dish, packed around with apple slices and dark cabbage leaves.

'What do you think?' she asked.

'You know, I think this is what you are wonderful at. One of the things.' He leered obligingly, and waved around the table. 'But in Rio you won't have to do it unless you want to.'

'I know.'

They ate silently for a minute. She poured more wine.

'Now', he said, with his mouth half full. 'Tell me about the book. I want to know all the details.'

'The letters are simpler. I'll find them for you.' She crossed to her desk and rummaged for the publisher's file. 'Tim Rothwell is the editor. I've met him once.' Orlando skimmed through them, long fingers graceful. 'Commissioning ... fees ... time-frame ... Millennium ... This is great, Katherine. I congratulate you again.' She smiled at his flash of Latin formality, and he put his arm around her. 'And then the TV series?'

'But of course. You know archaeology gets all the glamorous telly time. Why not history? Detective work in documents is just as exciting as digging around. And it's got to be local history. Everyone knows the national stuff. That's public. But this is - well, it could be the history of any of us.' He pulled her down onto the arm of his chair, smiling at her intense eyes. Her breath smelled of the wine. 'It's, - it's like the tomb of the unknown soldier of history!' They both laughed, and she said, 'All right. Over the top.' She scooped her hair around her face and then let it go.

'Darling Katerina. You do history at least as well as cooking. Come and try the other thing.'

'Patronising.'

'I want to see your Port Meadow view.'

Against the bedroom window the rain came and went, and the sky was fitfully lit up by a full moon. He twined his legs heavily around hers, and talked sporadically. She lay under him and thought of Rio de Janeiro, where he had been so recently. She thought of the scarlet poinsettia outside the window where they had slept together a year ago, and the humming birds which played in it from dawn.

Then she remembered something.

'Orlando.' She nudged at him. 'Olivia isn't pregnant.'

'Isn't what?'

'Pregnant. Another month's flop. She told me at their New Year party.'

'Oh, poor Olivia.'

'And Joe. Does Joe mind so much, do you think?'

'I don't know. I suppose so.'

It was raining, quite heavily now. She thought of Benson, and the cruck cottage, hiding in the ordinary high street.

'Katerina', Orlando spoke into her ear. 'This new project will mean lots of travel.' He was talking about his asthma study. 'I'll be in Boston as often as Rio. Will you want to come? It'll be fun.'

'Sure. I'll want to come, I expect.'

'Good. It'll be good.' He was almost asleep. 'Am I going to go home tonight?'

'Doesn't look like it.'

'No.' He slept. Katherine thought about the Ash's party for a minute, and then Rio again, and Orlando's project. Between her inner mind and them all, it seemed, like a filtering screen, was her own preoccupation, stronger than ever. She would have to go back to the King's Head. What did he know about Roke Elm, Richard Cottell? Tuesday afternoons, he said. She would go on Tuesday.

6

'We're probably the biggest helicopter base in Britain.'

'Or Europe, maybe.'

On Tuesdays, Richard took over behind the bar of the King's Head from Eric, the publican. He pulled pints and half pints, and relayed food orders to the two Australian girls in the kitchen. Bella lay in front of the bar, her tail thumping under a stool.

'It's good news, isn't it? Other bases are closing down, or merging.'

On the first Tuesday in February the clients were mostly local people, gossiping over a lunch-time drink. Serious business clients were taken to grander pubs along the river, or even into Henley. Tourists out from Oxford, specially Americans, stayed in Dorchester. Richard felt simultaneously alert and distracted. He answered the couple discussing air force manoeuvres, and refilled glasses briskly, but watched the door. When Bella got up and moved towards the kitchen, shaking herself casually, he turned to pull her back in front of the bar. 'Lie completely still, or you'll be out on your neck', he said, and when he looked up, the girl was there, tall and slim, opening the door, walking to the bar, unwinding that long scarf. She had long boots on, and carried a folder awkwardly, clutched against a handbag. Her pale face looked serious. How old was she? Maybe thirty? He was bad at judging. She saw him, and her face was transformed by a smile.

'Hallo. Here I am, as you see.'

'Hallo. Are you going to have a drink?'

'Yes - maybe juice of some kind. Apple, please. Is this a busy time for you?'

'It's a very good time. Is this a Roke Elm visit?'

He poured two little bottles of apple juice into a large glass and passed it to her. She had brought a faint, flowery smell into the pub with her. She had a single ring on, a tawny coloured stone, on her right hand. She took her coat off and perched at the bar. The finest of lines edged her large dark eyes; the rest of her face was very smooth and there seemed to be no make up.

'Hallo, dog', she said, glancing down. 'Well, yes. I have been thinking about our conversation. I couldn't believe you, about seven paths converging.'

The helicopter couple got up and paid, looking undisguisedly at her.

'Are you sure this is a good time?' she asked.

'Absolutely. I was hoping you would come.' He looked directly at her. She arranged her folder carefully beside her drink on the bar.

'I do now think there might be six. So I am half-convinced.'

'What changed your mind? I haven't seen you pacing it out there in the meantime.'

'I went and found an aerial photo yesterday, in the Oxford Library. And I've brought you a copy of it. But maybe you've seen one?'

'Of course not. Let's see. Oh, hang on.' A second lot of departing customers needed attention. 'Cheers, Richard', one of them said as they left. Katherine bent her head over the photo, and smoothed the thick matt paper carefully on the bar. In a minute he joined her, peering at it. For a moment he was silent, and then let out his loud, easy laugh. 'This is wonderful. Look, not only Roke Elm, but the timber yard, and, yes, could it be Bella?' The dog lifted her head instantly.

'Bella?'

'This is my house here. Look.' He pointed to a cottage almost hidden in a patch of trees, not far from the centre of the photo. There was a black speck on the green grass behind it. She bent her head lower to look, and laughed herself. 'No. I'm afraid we have to call that non-proven. Sorry, Bella. You may or may not be starring.' The dog moved her ears hopefully.

'But look. This is what I really wanted to show you.' Not far from the timber yard the road from Roke met the main Benson road in a T-junction. Her forefinger pointed at it. Two smaller routes stretched out from it. 'These we know about. On the Ordnance Survey. But look at this - you're right.' A clear line ran north-east, heading diagonally across a ripe yellow field, towards Hollandtide Bottom and Brightwell. 'Not visible on the ground, and not on the map', she said, triumphant with discovery. He looked at it for a long time, and then moved his eyes slowly over the rest of the photo, pausing on the timber yard, and then on his own cottage.

'Well?'

His eyes lifted to her. 'I still think it might be Bella.'

'No! The path?' She couldn't help smiling.

'Yes, it is another one. And very clear. But look - this is where I think there is, or was, yet another.' Now she bent her head as he pointed, with his rough hand and very clean fingernail. 'Along here.' He traced a line north west from the T-junction. 'Up it goes, and over to Rokemarsh.'

'I can't see anything there, really. With the eye of faith, perhaps a wisp.' She looked doubtful.

'But why,' she said, 'whether or not that one is real, that's still six, anyway. Why did everyone in the Middle Ages want to go Roke Elm? There is absolutely nothing there, and I don't think ever has been. I love it', she added. 'It is so interesting.' Her voice was animated.

Richard watched her, smiling slightly. 'It is.' His voice was softer, but his movements still brisk. He stood back from the photo, and pushed some glasses around, and made a little stack of lemon slices. The lunch hour was well over, and two other groups paid, noisily calculating costs, and then left. Only one man remained, holding a newspaper close to a window to read it.

'How often did you say you work here?' she asked, suddenly self-conscious.

'The occasional evening, usually Friday and Saturday. And Tuesday afternoons. Eric, the publican, keeps a boat tied up in the boat yard here. He goes and plays with it then. He and Zinnia plan to retire on it.' Something in the way he said it made her laugh.

'Zinnia?'

'Honestly. Eric and Zinnia.'

'Don't you think they will?'

'Doubtful.'

She slowly replaced the large photo in its folder.

'Thank you for bringing it.' He touched the folder lightly.

He was as uncertain as she was, she thought; not trying a bizarre pick up at all.

'What about this walk, then?' he said. 'I need to convince you about the seventh route, I can see.'

'What about starting in the village centre - working the old paths outwards? That would be really helpful for me.'

He smiled with pleasure, crinkling his light coloured eyes.

'We could start at the florist's bad-coffee place again. How about that? Saturday?'

'That's too soon', she said, in a knee-jerk defence. Orlando's first week end back. 'Next one?'

'Next one. Ten o'clock too early?'

'Ten is fine.'

'I look forward to it. Bring your eye of faith.'

'No. I'll bring lots of maps.'

He came out from behind the bar and helped her pull her coat on, and the newspaper-reader looked up with interest. She was nearly as tall as him. 'I haven't paid', she said, anxiously.

'I will', Richard said. 'You buy that healthy coffee next time.' She held her scarf, pleating it. He looked at her hands and the brown ring.

'Good bye.'

'See you on Saturday week.'

She left, and he leaned down and rubbed Bella's ears. 'Don't you follow her', he said. 'Don't even think of it.'

He straightened up and stood by the bar, serious for a moment.

7

571 : 'In this year Cutha fought against the Britons at Biedcanford and captured four villages, Limbury, Aylesbury, Benson and Eynsham; and in the same year he passed away. That Cutha was the brother of Ceawlin.'

'Benson enters written history in the year 571', Katherine wrote. *'But this enigmatic entry in the Anglo-Saxon Chronicle raises more questions than it answers. From whom did Cutha and Ceawlin take these four townships? Were Celts still surviving in a Chiltern enclave? And if these were indeed Celtic tribal centres, why did they have Anglo-Saxon names? Is the poetic alliteration in Ceawlin and Cutha not suspiciously reminiscent of any number of Anglo-Saxon migration and settlement sagas, and does any other evidence suggest King Ceawlin was actually reigning in 571? These questions are a starting point for any history of the village of Benson ... '*

And that's before we look at archaeological evidence, she muttered, which certainly doesn't show Britons in the Chilterns then, but the dates don't fit for Anglo-Saxon migrants, either. And there are place-names - early Saxon types, but not the earliest - and beneath it all the landscape itself, mute and frustrating; the lowest level of the palimpsest.

Katherine was keyed up with a pressing energy, putting her clues together, framing the outline of her book, from the earliest records to the Middle Ages. She made charts of all her different sources, from archaeology, literature and documents, and saw with a lift of her heart the few places where they meshed together. After meticulous analysis she closed the first chapter cautiously.

'It seems best to see this 571 reference as a surviving scrap of an old settlement saga, blurred in accuracy but honed with repetition for generations before it was inserted in the Chronicle centuries later. What is important to recognise is that Benson was the central place of a recognised tributary region, dominated by an early tribal leader or king, probably already an Anglo-Saxon, but possibly a Briton. When territory changed hands in the formative years of Anglo-Saxon kingdoms, it was not the land alone that was of value, but the produce to be got from it, in the form of food renders to the ruler from those settled on his domain. Implicit in the conquest of such a central place was the assumption of widespread tributes owed to the defeated rival. In this way the structure of a ' regio' could survive conquest and changes of a ruler. The territory remained.'

She wrote the words with a flourish, and then added notes to herself.

- next ref. not for 200 years; land grant?
- still a long way till solid ground of Domesday and that not very solid.

It was the day before she was due to meet Richard. Before then, that evening, lay a College dinner, an annual celebration for graduates and guests. She and Joe and Orlando were taking Olivia, of course, and a visiting American couple known slightly to the Ashes, a rabbi and his wife. 'Not Orthodox', Olivia had said. 'So they'll be able to eat the College food. They may not like it - who does - but they can eat it.' In the event, the chef had excelled himself, and it was a notable meal. The long tables glittered with glass and silver, and subdued lights threw shadows and gleams on the hall's high panelling and the portraits of illustrious past members. The master banged his gavel and pronounced the

Latin grace, and fellows and graduates shuffled their gowns and chair backs as they sat down.

'This is good', Olivia said disbelievingly, as the first course came. She had surprised the others with a new hair cut, very short and feathery. Her ear-rings, for once, matched; green malachite on silver. 'Is it pigeon's breasts, Katherine?' She leaned forward to speak to the rabbi's wife. 'Joe's old college doesn't always delight us with its food. Wine yes, food no. Katherine will tell you - she's a champion cook herself. Wasted in history.'

Shelley Morris took her cue deftly. 'What sort of history do you do, Katherine?'

'I'm working on the early history of a village near here, on the Thames. Called Benson. It's a pretty ordinary place now.'

'Isn't it an RAF base?' Rabbi Morris said, surprisingly.

'Yes! How do you know?'

'I think my father was based there during the war. Or certainly visited.'

There were smiles at the coincidence.

'We are near separated now, because of Benson', Orlando said. 'It's a book which might take us over.'

'I wish it would take anyone over', Katherine answered. 'Early history is not always gripping for the unconverted'

'The dark, dark ages.' Joe said, blandly.

'But Benson's history is actually very unusual. The richest royal manor in Oxfordshire at Domesday, and five written references before then, which is pretty unique.'

'Either unique or not, please,' Joe interrupted again, chewing as he spoke.

'Okay. A unique number of records before Domesday, and powerful then, but what happens next? Absolutely nothing. Dorchester gets the monastery, Wallingford gets the market, Oxford becomes capital of the new shire - Benson fades to nothing.' She looked sparkling, in the silver

Ghost dress with a thin back scarf around her throat. 'But that's really enough of Benson now. You encouraged me, talking about the RAF.' She closed her mouth firmly, and looked down at her plate. Yes, pigeon breasts, she was about to say. And something in the sauce, perhaps it could be figs? But Rabbi Morris was speaking to her again.

'I'm happy it did encourage you. But why, about the RAF?' He had a pleasant, intelligent expression, and brown, pock-marked skin.

'Because I imagine it began life as a military place, all that time ago. At least fortified, and worth fighting over, and recording the battles there later. Warrior leaders like Ceawlin and Offa and Alfred thought so. So, after more than a thousand years with nothing in between, it just seems - neat - that in the last war, it became a base again.'

'Well, sure', he said, politely.

They talked about other things, about the Gallery, and the Morris's sabbatical in Oxford. He was studying isolated modern Jewish groups, and told them about the Jews of Cochin, in India, and the inscribed stones of the synagogues there. Shelley was a photographer, bright and argumentative. She and Joe had a dispute about whether you needed to say 'He or she' at every reference to an unidentified expert witness in a current court case, or whether it was acceptable in post-feminist times to use 'he' as a short cut.

'Oh, surely these old semantic battles are long won!' Katherine said. Orlando smiled at her affectionately. After the chocolates and ginger, and a mulberry mousse, the Master made a speech, full of his notorious puns. He described the college's successes of the past year, both academic and sporting, and made a light-hearted joke about the pressure of business preventing the attendance of a former member now a cabinet minister involved with education. He specially mentioned several splendid donations made. And he implied very gracefully that the college's main strength lay, as ever, in its unbroken stream of scholars and students, represented so ably towards this millennium's end by the company gathered together that night. As the guests applauded and began to drift off, Katherine noticed that she was relaxing, as if a coiled-up tension of the last few weeks had lifted off. Only much later did she think it was not because she was surrounded by her friends, but because an arc of waiting had carried her nearly to its end.

Afterwards, she and Orlando walked back to his flat in St John's Street. Outside it her car was parked, resident's visitor's sticker prominently displayed. As they went up the stairs, she said to him,

'Olivia told me her new haircut makes her feel empowered. Did you like it?'

'Olivia, need empowering?'

'That's what she said.'

'The food was better than usual.'

'I liked the Morrises. She gave Joe lots of good disagreements.'

'Mmmh.'

They made love in Orlando's elegant, untidy bedroom. There was a pile of books on respiratory diseases on the end of the bed, and Katherine kicked them off. The street light cast a familiar orange glow.

'I'm not staying the night, though. Benson tomorrow,'

'And I've got a meeting. John Radcliffe.' He sounded blurry.

At home in Wolvercote the undrawn curtains showed the Meadow, calm and dark, but still visible in the indirect lights of perimeter roads. Few places are dark enough, now, an astronomer had written in the local paper very recently. She stood at her window for several minutes, looking at it, and then got into bed. Almost immediately, she was plunged into a long and complicated dream about Richard Cottell, or maybe even a series of dreams, all night, of astonishing clarity and impact. She and Richard were in a kind of park, or arboretum, with all the trees labelled, and were walking through very quickly, checking all the names, almost running. Then another figure was with them, a girl called Sylvia. Katherine had been at school with her, but never seen nor thought of her since, yet there she was. She and Richard didn't quite trust Sylvia, and walked away from her, out of the arboretum. Then, for a long time, they were sitting very close in a bus, or even a boat - it was rocking - shoulders pressed hard together, and she didn't want to move. In the morning, while she sat and drank strong coffee, perspective seemed to have shifted slightly out of true, and the College dinner had retreated from her in time.

8

Katherine and Richard had arrived at the Benson boat yard, on the steep southern turn of the Thames, and were peering over the moored crafts. He was showing her Eric and Zinnia's vessel. Behind them, an antique shop added to the cluster of boat yard buildings and sheds, and beyond that, the yard spilled over into a caravan park. Between the river and the village traffic roared past on the new London road.

'At the far edge. Blue and yellow. Marine yellow, of course.'

He was so entirely familiar to her from her long dream-night that she had to remind herself that she hardly knew him. He had been sitting at one of the florist's tables when she arrived, looking very solid, even slightly military, with his feet among the buckets of flowers. His remarkable eyes crinkled with a smile when he saw her. They tried the florist's tea this time.

'Marginally better?' he had asked.

'Marginally. But the same water source you identified before, though, I think.' He ate shortbread. Katherine said she was still full from a festive dinner the previous night, and described it to him. They spoke little. There were silences.

'I haven't brought Bella.'

'I noticed.'

She had her ring on, he observed, and her hair in the usual long, loose single plait. She didn't touch the plait, but brushed shorter wavy strands out of her face.

'Shall we start at the river? That's why Benson's here at all, at a guess.'

'Of course', he said in his decisive way. 'We should walk outwards, from the beginning.'

And now, out on the bank, they had relaxed and were talkative.

'Is it a barge? Is it flat-bottomed?'

'Well, it's the best of all worlds, really', Richard laughed. 'Not a barge, but nearly as long. A river boat, but not very tall.'

She pointed. 'There?'

'No. Further to your right.' He took her outstretched arm in his hand, and swung it slightly. After a fraction of a second he let it go and they were both silent. Then Katherine said, 'Oh my goodness. Is that it? *Halcyon Daze?*'

'I'm afraid so.'

She spluttered, and Richard laughed his loud laugh.

'Zinnia is in charge of the colour schemes. Inside is just as - um, immaculate. I'll show you one day.'

Katherine glanced at him, but he was smiling and looking inland. She stood beside him, back to the river. His face in profile was even, regular and handsome. From the front it was not quite so perfect, a little asymmetrical, softer.

'Are you married?'

'No. What about you? No wedding ring, and free on Saturday morning, but ... ?'

'No, but sort of engaged.'

'I was married, but my wife is dead.'

It was not an answer she was ready for. He looked so cheerful and laughed so easily. He saw her hesitation. 'It was a long time ago. Believe me. I live competently by myself ... ' He smiled, and she looked at his sunny eyes.

'I'm sorry.'

'Okay. All that cleared up?'

'Cleared up.' She responded to his brisk manner. 'Now,' she said, as they crossed the road and walked up to the churchyard. 'The odd thing about this village is, the church is in a place you would expect, on a lip of gravel, just above the river.'

'It is.'

'And the earliest huts, or hall, or barn for collecting tributes at the very least, should have been right there.' They were passing four modern houses, built side by side below the church. 'And there was something actually there. But long gone, never excavated. Always referred to in old literature as ruins, or banks.'

'Or Offa's Castle.' He watched her, still smiling, and she shrugged at the popular medieval name.

'Maybe it was, at one stage? Who knows?' A slight wind blew their coats around, and her hair, and bowled clouds along. It was like a spring day, despite the bare trees.

'Okay', she went on. 'So the odd thing is not the site of the church, probably beside the founders' hall or whatever, which then collapsed and survived as a ruin. But why did the rest of the village drift away? Why don't the oldest buildings cluster around?'

'Because by the time they were putting up buildings

which have survived, stone buildings, they'd moved up along the brook, and round the mill. Like our cruck cottage had, by twelve or thirteen something.'

'You're right.' They walked around the church, which was covered in scaffolding from which flaps of tarpaulin dangled. 'The first old wooden church got beyond fixing up. And they wanted a good new stone one.'

'And the devil threw down their first efforts, every night.'

'Of course. Until they moved it a bit to where he could tolerate it - here, I presume.'

'And they worked on it for several generations. Does it belong to Dorchester Abbey?'

She was beginning to love the links his thoughts made with hers.

'No. It did, officially, for a century or two after Queen Matilda handed it over. But long before that, in the beginning, I'm sure they were part of the same holding. One for the missionary who converted the king, in the suitable nearby Roman town, and one for the king himself, here.'

'Under the same management, as it were.'

'Quite stringent management, I'd think. The early little kingdoms. More like protection rackets - call Ceawlin for all your security requirements.'

'Or else.' She laughed, and he added, 'Don't be caught off guard. Get Offa's guard!'

He watched her glowing face, and she loved his peals of laughter.

When they reached the cruck cottage again, they stood in front of it and returned to the idea of the drift of the village. 'I think its shapelessness is actually a sign of very old age', Katherine said. 'Much older than planned settlements, orderly arrangements. Just bunches of pretty basic huts and little houses, fluctuating around. By the time this was built -' she gestured towards the cottage, 'This was the part of town to be in.'

'Or where there was space for a new one that year.'

'And across the road the mill and the brook, and all the action there.'

For a few minutes they walked towards the brook, in silence. She noticed his very easy, light steps. 'You make me feel very focused on it all', she said. 'It's good for me.'

He smiled, and gave her an exaggerated polite nod, and their eyes met.

'And now I should go home and do some writing, while I feel enthusiastic.'

'This was fun,' he said, in his direct way. 'Good for me, too. But not work, of course. And I still think that watch is very pretty.' He was looking at her wrist. He touched it lightly, the face of the watch, and not her skin. 'And still Roke Elm some time?'

'Still Roke Elm. Of course.'

She set off for her car, and he wandered towards the florist's for a minute, and looked at the tables. A family was sitting around one, and a child had spilled bright orange drink on the flowery cloth. He turned away.

9

'Guess what Shelley Morris told me after the dinner? We had another drink with them after you and Orlando had gone.'

'What?'

'She didn't get pregnant until after going to analysis for a year.'

'How American can you get? That's not what causes pregnancy, I understand.'

'Now they've got three sons, all students at home. Well,

one's dropped out and gone to Panama City, but only for a while, they think.'

It was a quiet Monday in the Gallery, and Olivia had paperwork out on a desk, and Katherine perched on a low display stand, facing her. They were in the basement. Upstairs, they could hear Dawn trying out a CD for background music, which she said was essential, and had been proved to encourage sales.

'I'm not sure if she called it analysis or therapy,' Olivia added. She was in very dark bitter-chocolate brown, and her new short hair showed the incongruous childlike curve of the back of her head. Katherine thought she looked tired.

'What did Joe think about that?'

'Oh, he didn't hear her. But I can guess. You know him; it has to be the latest high-tech science, or nothing at all. It couldn't be more removed from his sort of medicine.'

'No, I suppose not.'

'So it's nothing at all. Katherine, are you listening?'

'Yes of course I am. But what can I say? I think it might be good if you could stop thinking about it. You know, people adopt a baby and then promptly get one themselves, because they've stopped concentrating on it.'

Olivia made a shrugging noise. 'Easier said than done.'

'I know. It's hard to unfocus yourself.'

The music upstairs changed from fashionable Gregorian chant to a single male voice.

'Van Morrison', Dawn called down the stairs to them. 'He's so far out of it he's in again.'

'I don't think so,' Olivia said, standing up and pushing the papers aside. 'Really I don't.'

As they went up the stairs they heard the entry bell clang. Katherine knew the customer, a man called Piers Finch. He ran a small chain of select cramming establishments, preparing those with money and needing personal attention for A-level or Baccalaureate exams. His flagship school was in Oxford. He made a beeline for her, as usual.

'How is the historian?' he asked in his well modulated voice. He had a bald head with hair swept thinly over it, starting from just above his right ear.

'I'm fine, thank you. And busy. How are you?'

'Also fine. Also busy.'

'Have you seen the new John Wards? And our solitary Janet Leach?' Piers was a serious collector of studio pottery. He studied the pots closely, lifting them up, standing back, glancing at the prices. As he looked he talked. He discovered that Katherine was working on a book.

'So no chance of you coming to us, then?' He had several times offered her a job teaching history in one of his schools.

'I'm afraid not.' Katherine had once said to Orlando that she could never bear to work for Piers Finch; he stood too close to her when they spoke, and he frequently claimed to know people intimately, including other historians, but then would say 'Just remind me of his first name again?' 'Is that such a crime?' Orlando had said. 'He buys your pottery and he pays better than other schools.' He can afford to, she thought.

'Tell me about the book', he asked now, and Katherine found herself talking about King Offa of Mercia, and how he, too, was reported in the Anglo-Saxon Chronicle to have won a critical battle at Benson.

'You know, Offa, as in Offa's Dyke.' she said, helpfully. 'He 'took the vill' it says , whatever that means - a fort, a royal residence, a village? Anyway, that's the part I'm working on now. That Chiltern area seems to have changed hands for a while then, from the kingdom of Wessex to Mercia.'

'Fascinating.' He put down the Janet Leach vase, and stood a little nearer. 'I'm sure it will be a winner. Pity for us, though.'

The music changed to a plaintive Satie piano piece. This is unbearable, she thought, so soft it aches instead of sounds.

'Sorry', she said, loudly. She turned her head, and Olivia was approaching, holding a black and white bowl forward for display, and smiling at them both.

'Hi, Piers', she said. 'Did you notice this?' Katherine took a step back, and watched Olivia sparkle, all signs of tiredness gone. Further back in the shop she gazed at them both, with her mind empty. The separate notes of the piano floated in the air.

10

The music in the King's Head was from Eric's self-assembled medley tapes. It was an eclectic collection. A few Verdi choruses alternated oddly with Pink Floyd and Abba, but the overwhelming choice was Country and Western. Richard poured drinks for the sparse number of late lunch customers and hummed sporadically. Bella lay dozing, with her back to him. 'Abilene, Abilene', he heard the Australian girls singing in the kitchen, and then it changed to Kris Kristofferson's deep voice. 'I come from just the other side of nowhere ... ' Richard mouthed, 'Heading for the light of day ... ' Before it finished, Eric appeared, looking worried.

'Could you do me a favour, Rich?'

'Try me.'

'There's been some vandalism at the boat yard. Painters cut, mostly. They tell me mine is all right - but, normally I'd be there today. I need to wait for a delivery. Could you finish early - like now? And have a look at the boat for me?'

'Sure. We'll check it out. Bella?' He nudged her with his foot.

Out in the village he breathed in the air, cold and clean.

It was a gloomy day, as though the afternoon was fading furtively into evening. He walked briskly down to the river, and as near to *Halcyon Daze* as he could get. Several cars were parked there, and owners were carrying boat fittings backwards and forwards. Eric's boat looked entirely intact, moored securely at front and back, and with the padlock fast on the hatch. Pencil-pleated curtains were pulled neatly across each porthole. Richard reached into his pocket for the padlock key, and stepped aboard to open it. All was as immaculate inside as he had promised Katherine, and he relocked it carefully. Out on the small deck again, he stood and looked inland, eyeing the site as if he were arriving at this curve of the river for the first time. After a few minutes, he jumped lightly ashore, and crossed the London road. Instead of walking directly into the village centre he turned left to the slip road that ran up to the church. He counted his steps along it, and paused to look into the gardens of the four new houses.

'What do you think, Bella?' he said. 'All covered up under there?' The dog was pleased with their detours, running ahead, and then glancing back at him, one front paw raised. Still he didn't return directly to the King's Head or to home, but crossed the village and turned down Mill Street. At the end where the little brook roared at a noisy pace beside the old mill house, he stood for a long time, leaning on the fence and gazing into the water. He looked sombre. Bella paced around him and pushed his leg as he ignored her. Slowly he turned around and ruffled her head, absently.

'Let's go and reassure Eric', he said to her.

The next Saturday morning Katherine took a last look at the aerial photo of Benson. It lay on her desk, with a magnifying glass beside it. She bent over it, concentrating on the centre. Then she breathed out hard, and turned on the radio. News and arts programmes blotted out inhibiting thoughts, and details of the coming day's sports. She drank coffee, swallowing it with a tight throat. There was a Rugby match on in London. Probably James would go. Out in her car, on the ring road, she kept the radio on and listened as if she might need the information for an exam. An American film star was interviewed; she planned to bring her infant daughter to England to be educated. The day would be mild, but windy, and there was risk of light rain later.

She turned towards the Chilterns. By half past ten she was driving slowly past the timber yard, and five minutes later she found the cottage, scarcely visible from the road, behind a high hedge and wooden gate, slightly open. In an otherwise featureless stretch of farmland, it sat in a square of its own, outlined with trees, just as in the photo. A close, she thought. Like a close off the open field. Her mouth was still dry. She put the car keys in her pocket, pushed the gate open, and walked to the door.

She knocked and he opened it almost immediately. He seemed to be in the act of putting his Barbour on, and stared, and then smiled.

'Come in.' He reached her hand, and pulled her in, and held it for a minute. 'Hallo', he said, and looked at her face intently.

She realised she still had not spoken.

'I wanted to see where you lived. You said you live competently. I thought that was such a funny word - I wanted to see ... '

'Here it is.' He spread his arms expansively. She took in a single large room, which seemed to be both kitchen and sitting room. A couch and a big chair at the other end both faced out of back windows, presumably on to the garden behind. A smaller couch stood in a corner.

For a minute, he became his brisk self. 'Coffee?'

'Oh, yes, please. I got up quite early, and ... ' She started to take her coat off, and he turned back from the bench.

'For goodness sake', he said, cheerfully, and took her coat from her. 'And my own.' He took his own Barbour off, and then put it down very forcefully on the table. He turned round and pulled her to him, and she sank against him.

'This isn't why I came.'

'No. But I wanted you to. Wanted you to so much. Are you sure it isn't?' She felt the immense knot of tension spread from her chest to each limb, even her hands, half painful, half pleasant.

'Where were you going?' she asked, into his shoulder.

'To take Bella out, of course. She didn't need it - I did.' He laughed as he said it.

'How do you make things so uncomplicated?'

'Katherine.' He held her a little away from him and looked at her. She raised one hand and felt his crisp, curly hair, touched it with her palm and her fingers. 'For me it is uncomplicated. A decision made long ago. I've been waiting for you.'

Upstairs, his bedroom had windows to both back and front. It was tidy, a large bed made with sheets and dark blue blankets. A green jumper, the one she recognised from the first time she saw him, on Christmas Eve, lay on a chair. Several wooden bowls stood along a shelf.

She stood near the door, and glanced at the back window, ready to step towards it and look out. 'No', he said. 'Not yet. Bed first.'

'But it's eleven o clock in the morning ... '

He gave a gust of laughter, and put his arms around her 'Are there special approved hours? Pretend you've been here since last night.'

After the first fierce time she burst into tears. He held her wet face against him for a long time.

Later, he lay still half on her, mouth in her neck, and mumbled, stopping and starting.

'Shush', she said. Her body was still flickering.

'Shush, I can't understand what you're saying.' She kissed the side of his face, through her hair. The sheets seemed exact body temperature, indistinguishable from her skin. A car outside turned the corner to Roke. She closed her eyes, but he was speaking again, more clearly and conversationally.

'It was odd when we met last week. I had had such a clear dream of you the night before, it made me think I knew you very well. That you had been here in this house already.'

'Really? Had you really?'

'Yes. Why is that so surprising?'

'I'd been dreaming of you, We were in a forest, or in some trees. I was so carefully telling myself it was only a dream.'

She pressed against his shoulder, remembering the dream, and sighed with pleasure.

'Do you dream often?'

'Not very.'

'I dream all the time', he said. 'Every night.'

'Do you remember them all?'

'Some. That one. I don't try to, it would be too time-consuming. I suppose it's processing stuff, ordering it.'

'But are they happy dreams?'

'Mostly, I think. But there are goodies and baddies in them sometimes. Some chases.'

'And yet all the people must be you?'

'I suppose.'

'It must be ourselves, working each side of the equation.'

'This is what you did in my dream last week. You put your arms around me, and your legs ... '

'You're making that up! For shabby purposes.'

'I am, actually. We were really drinking coffee. I had brought it upstairs, to bed. As we don't smoke. Do you?'

'No, I don't.'

When they sat up, he fetched the green jumper from his

47

chair and draped it around her shoulders, touching her breasts. She looked down at his hands, rough and calloused. They didn't seem to match his smooth skinned body.

While he was gone, she got up and walked around. The view from the back window surprised her. Within the outer fence lay what seemed to be a small farm - chickens wandered in a fenced-off area at the back, a pond filled another corner, with a neat little wooden house on stilts in its centre, and a vegetable garden was laid out with a climbing frame for beans, and rows of different small spring-sized plants. She recognised leeks and potatoes and the feathery heads of carrots. Beyond them was a greenhouse. Between the vegetables and the back of the house, and separated by a low hedge, was a lawn with a winding path through it, and a white-painted wooden table with two chairs. A length of tree trunk, presumably from the timber yard, was in the process of being sawn and shaped into a long seat. A pile of chippings lay beside it. In front of it sat Bella, looking alertly towards the house, tail swinging slowly backwards and forwards. As Katherine watched, she heard a door open, and Bella ran towards it, and disappeared inside.

She turned from the window and prowled back to the bed by a circuitous route, eyeing the shelves and walls. A cupboard for clothes, a chest of drawers with keys and a few papers lying on it, and a wooden bowl of assorted small objects, like little discs, or coins. No photos. Her eyes wandered. The wooden bowls stood along one shelf against a wall, and above them hung the only picture, a version of a well-known Breughel, with a multitude of figures in action in a rural landscape. She was looking at three men in a fruit tree, apparently spying on a tableful of diners, when Richard returned. He was carrying a tray with coffee and cups and a tubular tin in the exact form of a red digestive biscuit packet. He wore trousers and no shoes or shirt. He put the tray down carefully, and stood behind her, arms around her naked body.

'That belongs to the owner of this house', he said. 'Not mine. I left it there.'

'Do you rent this?'

'Come on, get back in bed, You'll be cold. Yes, it belongs to David Freeman, who owns the farm, and the timber yard, and a lot else here.'

'It looks so long and well-settled, by you.' She gestured towards the garden.

'About seven or eight years.'

'It is competent. Now I know. Where were you before then?'

'Chichester, near Chichester. You would like him, David Freeman. He has an antique shop in Dorchester, too, and very interesting old furniture and artefacts in his own house ... '

He seemed to have deflected her question. Perhaps he moved here when his wife died?

'We're in competition over things like these.' He reached out of bed to pick up the bowl from his dressing table. 'Look. All found on the fields around here. This even in my own garden.' He passed her the small lead disc. 'They're tokens, as you probably know. Produced by local traders as currency.'

'When the proper mint units of money were far too big, for eggs or something? This is wonderful; I don't think I've ever handled one. Look - a shoe!' The token she held had the clear outline of a high-heeled shoe on it. She rifled through the others excitedly.

'This is a good one.' He said, hunting. 'Here it is. What do you think that says?'

They leaned over the little coin together, slanting it against the light.

'Could it be - 1588?'

'That's what I think,' he answered. 'Quite an old one.'

'Richard! These are wonderful. No wonder Mr Freeman wants them.'

'He has plenty else. Believe me. Even another farm, nearer Cuxham.'

'Goodness.' She lay back against the pillows, carefully holding her cup. 'He certainly is a Freeman.'

He laughed. 'Indeed. For many generations, I think.'

'You are lovely. No one else gets my obscure medieval references.'

'You are lovely.' He pulled the sheet down a little, and looked at her.

'Come on', he said soon. 'Before it rains. Let's walk Bella into the village, and get some lunch. You're allowed to find the bathroom - it's in there', he pointed across the landing. 'But all other exploring is for next time.'

They decided against the King's Head. 'I'll be there quite soon enough, tonight.' Richard said. 'And you need to be at peak strength to meet Zinnia. Are you at peak strength?' He looked at her with his eyebrows raised. 'No', she said, holding his hand tightly. They ate a ploughman's lunch at The Lamb. The cheese was an unnatural yellow, and the onions violently pickled. 'Do you know the whole ploughman's lunch idea was dreamt up by the pub trade, a few years ago?' Katherine said, eating it hungrily. 'A committee somewhere.'

'But ploughmen did eat bread, always. Cheese was a good addition. And I think bread was more porridgy sometimes, heavy. Not always properly baked, and perfectly risen.'

'Really?' She caught his eye, and they smiled.

Bella quivered with pleasure when they emerged, and jumped up at Richard. Katherine rubbed the dog's beautiful, velvety head for a minute. 'How old is she?'

'About four. David Freeman's wife breeds them. Her

brother was even more handsome', he said. 'With a big square face. But I'm glad I didn't get him - he's turned out rather stupid and characterless. Hasn't he, Bella?' He pushed the dog down.

'I should go home. This was supposed to be a working day.'

He made a quizzical face.

'We are pretty well on Roke Elm at my house, you know. The seven paths? Next week?'

After a minute of looking at each other, she nodded. Very light heartedly, they walked back. Just before his cottage they came upon two hares, standing on their back legs like little kangaroos, and boxing dramatically, backing across a ploughed field. They watched transfixed. Even Bella seemed astonished, and whimpered slightly. Katherine heaved a sigh as they disappeared into a hedge, and turned huge eyes to Richard. They hardly spoke again. It was spitting with rain. He kissed her beside her car, and she got in and wound the window down. He leaned through it, and she touched his hair.

'Global warming', he said. 'They're a bit early.'

'You're fussy,' she answered. 'They're wonderful.'

As she started the car the rain began in earnest.

11

730 : 'Banesinga-villa. A cartulary of Abingdon Abbey records a grant of twenty six hides of land in Watchfield, Berkshire, by King Aethilbald of Mercia. King Aethilbald signed this 'in Banesinga-villa iubente rege' - in the royal villa of Benson. The official witnesses included the Bishop of Sherborne.

> *779 : 'In this year Cynewulf and Cutha contended around Benson and Offa took the vill.' (Anglo-Saxon Chronicle)*
>
> *After a silence of nearly two hundred years the eighth century brings us two more references to Benson. The royal vill is in the hands of a Mercian king in 730, but by 779 it has been lost to Wessex again - Cynewulf is a descendant of Ceawlin. King Offa of Mercia fights a battle to retrieve it, and his name is associated with the area for long afterwards. It becomes apparent not only that this is contentious border territory, disputed between Wessex and Mercia, but that, just as in the sixth century, although the walled and very visible Roman town of Dorchester lies nearby, it is Benson that is the sought-after prize. We are in a new world of kingdoms like Wessex and Mercia, written legalities about land exchange, and the powerful presence of the Christian church - but Benson and its territory survive.'*

And the central place of this central place, the hall, or palace, or fort, or barn for collecting food tributes - where was it? Surely King Aethilbald hadn't just stood out by the river, in front of his bishop and his princelings, and signed his document? Katherine put her pen down. She was in the library, and was about to finish for the morning and buy a sandwich in the Covered Market before going to the Gallery for her Thursday afternoon shift. She stretched her arms forward, flexing her elbows, and bent her head back to rest her eyes on the painted ceiling. At home she would transfer her written pages to the computer, improving them as she went. She stood a sheaf of miscellaneous notes on edge, to bounce them into tidiness, like a pack of cards, her mind on the river bank site beside the church. I want to peel back its layers, she thought, shuffling mechanically. Somewhere beside that mundane boatyard, under those four houses, below that church, Cutha and Ceawlin had arrived, Aethilbald had signed, Cynewulf and Offa had contended. Over the historical fantasies, like a double exposure, she saw Richard pointing at *Halcyon Daze*, and then it faded into Richard's bedroom at Roke Elm. All the images had become infused and overlain with emotion. She banged the notes into a file and looked around her. How could the other readers be serious and oblivious?

Her work went forward in two parallel strands. On some days, like today, she was pressing on with writing her orderly chronological account. At other times, she was accumulating the later material - notes and references and reminders to herself, letters from specialists in place-names or Domesday statistics or medieval diet - and her maps were getting more detailed, and the lists had swooping arrows at cross-reference points. The year 1485, and the arrival of the Tudors, was the cut off point agreed with Tim Rothwell. All that has to happen, she thought as she left the Bodleian, is that the first activity, the orderly writing, has to catch up and overtake the rest, and subdue it into order by about October. As if she could do it by force, she clasped the file against her and squeezed it until her ribs hurt.

By Friday night, tense with the silence of the week, it occurred to Katherine that she could, in the normal way, look him up in the phone book. Cottell, Richard, she found instantly. Oak Farm House, Benson. Of course, it had stopped being called Roke Elm about a century ago. Oak Farm House. She swallowed several times as she dialled. There was no answer, and she remembered he worked at the pub on Friday evenings. She looked up the King's Head, but then sat with the phone book in her lap, envisaging the pub and its noise and smells.

I can't do it, she said aloud. But they did have an arrangement for tomorrow, surely? She got out the current

Ordnance Survey map, a reproduction of a Victorian map of the area, too small a scale, but good for names, and her aerial photo. From her file she took her own sketch maps and notes. She put them in a neat pile on her desk, and then walked restlessly around. She needed to do something practical, she thought, and on an impulse, put her coat on and drove the car to Sainsbury's. In an hour she returned home with plastic bags of food which filled her fridge and freezer to over flowing, and stores of soap powder and bleach and mineral water. Orlando had faxed her a message. 'Where are you?' she read. 'You are elusive this week. See you tomorrow. I'll ring. Good night, darling.' She unpacked her shopping carefully, and poached one egg. She ate it on a piece of brown toast, and went to bed.

In the morning, she rang Richard again. He answered immediately.

'Katherine! Tell me you are on your way here.' She had forgotten his slight accent. 'We must have been mad last week, no phone numbers ... I'm pacing around.'

'Are we doing Roke Elm today?'

'Whatever you like today, but probably that, yes. Boots are at the ready. I miss you.'

'Okay.' Could it be so simple? 'I'll leave in ... half an hour.'

She felt hot, and changed to a thinner jumper, and looked in the freezer to remind herself what she had bought last night, and read again what she had written during the week. After twenty minutes she got in the car, and drove to Roke Elm.

He made it seem just as simple. He opened the door, Bella barked, they kissed. When they drew apart she said, shakily, 'We are going out today, to look for paths.'

'Well, of course. Did you have other ideas? I'm responsible for this large dog, you know. And I have a seventh, mystery route to persuade you of. Scholarship is uppermost in my mind.'

'Yes?' she said, flooding with confidence, and kissing him again.

'Absolutely yes. Believe me. Only after eleven o'clock, as you know, things can change.'

'Let's go while we're safe ... '

'Here we are at the central cross roads of the world,' she said, ten minutes later. 'Called The Sands on the current OS - don't know why.' The orange Ordnance Survey map flapped between them, and Richard's curly head bent over it. He had released Bella, and she was hurrying along a hedge trail with her black tail waving ecstatically.

'Probably from a quarry pit', he answered. 'There are several around here.'

'True. And from The Sands we still have the road passing from Benson to Britwell Salome. Two directions. Three, we have the path called Tidmarsh Lane, now only going to - well this road between Benson and Ewelme now. Nowhere much. But I think there is more to Tidmarsh Lane than meets the eye, but we can't talk about that now ... we're counting.'

'Certainly not.' He pulled her plait gently.

'Don't interrupt. So that's three. Four, the road to Berrick Salome. Five, the footpath still marked to Ewelme. So that's the five I first knew about, and I've walked them.'

'And?'

'Then, after we had that first talk - when you were argumentative in the flowery coffee place and the woman dropped her oranges - '

'And rhubarb.'

'Oh, you looked so nice that day; I wanted to touch you!'
'Touch me now.'

'No, Richard. We're doing work now.' Happiness lifted inside her. She pointed sternly at the aerial photo. 'You will remember that later I half agreed about a sixth one on the photo - here. So since then, I've looked again at the Enclosure map from last century in the Record Office. This point was still then called Roke Elm. Here's my effort at copying this part of it, and you're right. There was another path then, north-east towards Brightwell Baldwin, just as it looks in the photo.'

'And when you half agreed about that, I suggested, you may remember, that there is a seventh.' His sunny eyes turned from her face to the aerial photo, and he moved his hand from her back to the coloured page. 'Look, the other diagonal, north-west from here to Rokemarsh.'

She studied the photo, slanting it. 'It's just a shadow, surely? It wasn't on the Enclosure map. I searched, of course.'

'Shall we have a look?'

'Why not? I'm already puzzled about so many roads leading to Roke Elm, with nothing here. Another would add to my puzzlement very happily.'

They crossed the road and climbed into the field. Once there she realised instantly how close behind the timber yard the line of Richard's postulated path lay. They talked about his work there as they walked, about deadwood and elm disease and fulfilling orders for building planks and fencing wood. 'It's a small operation', he said. 'Not as small as it looks, because David collects timber from several other plantation areas, not just the fallen stuff you see there. But small on the scale of things.'

'Do you like it?'

'I like timber. Not so much the orders and deliveries and truck work. The forestry and the wood itself, yes. Very much.'

In a minute he said, 'It's locked up now. I've got keys, as it happens. But we don't need them. We'll head for the top corner, and you'll see what I mean.'

'Now look. I need to stand close to you for this ... ' She leant against him as he held her shoulders and directed her gaze. 'See it?'

She squinted up the field. Very possibly, she saw, there was a dip running along the middle. If it petered out, it shortly reappeared, very straight. 'Oh, Richard', she said. 'You might be right!

Could it be a drain, though, or a pipe?'

'Straight into the timber yard? Believe me, I know it's not.'

'Can we go?'

'Of course. We'll go up here, across the top of the triangle, and down the other one, if that seems all right?'

She nodded and was already ahead.

After ten minutes walking, she was convinced. 'I can feel it,' she said. 'Grown over and almost filled up. It's just the slightest indentation, but it never stops, and it's the width for normal walking, but no more. This is so exciting! Already gone by Victorian times, but we've found it again! Well, you did. How did you?'

He smiled at her pleasure, and after a minute said, 'Well, I see the field in all weathers, don't I. See the shadows. Walk the dog, that sort of thing. Where is the dog?' he added, distractedly. He shouted, and Bella appeared from scouting around the hedge far ahead of them. 'I should put a pedometer on you,' he said affectionately. 'Do you double or triple our distance?'

At the top of the field Katherine turned and surveyed their route. 'Pretty definitely', she said. 'Brilliant! Thank you,' she said, earnestly. He took her hand. His palm was as rough as ever.

'One more to go.'

The second path, visible on the aerial photo, was easier to follow, and they could walk side by side.

'But my puzzle is,' Katherine said. 'About why all these routes, seven even, meet at Roke Elm. Why?'

He was silent.

'I begin to believe something very odd.', she went on, picking a long stalk and whacking it on her leg. 'I'll try it out on you. Hundredal meetings. You know, Benson was the capital of four and a half old hundreds, Chiltern Hundreds?'

He was smiling. 'And?'

'Where did they meet? No big hall that we know of in Benson. These meetings had to go on well into medieval times; this isn't Ceawlin and Offa, or vague Dark Age business.'

'Well?'

'Could this have been the centre of all the Hundreds? Roke Elm is a funny name; 'at the oak elm' - what does that mean? Some kind of weird clump of trees, for sure, and outdoor meeting places were often at noticeable natural features. Old tumuli, high points. This isn't a high point, but the road conjunction is amazing. Do you know three parish boundaries meet here, still? ... Richard! You're being quiet. What do you think?'

'I think you're right.'

She stopped walking and stood still. 'You think I'm right? This strange idea?'

Now he stopped walking, too. 'It's not strange; it makes sense. Have you worked out your distances. Look.' He took the Ordnance Survey map in his hands, and measured roughly with his fingers. 'Benson, a mile and a half. Ewelme, a mile and a half. Berrick Salome, a mile and a half. Brightwell, just a bit more. It's bang in the middle. Of course it's where people walked, every month, or however often it was. It's a very good idea indeed.'

'I'm stunned. You look at in a library, and you come out ... and here it is. How could anyone not love it!' She threw her arms around him. 'This was great walk.'

This time he held her arms there and leaned his face on hers, eye to eye. 'It wasn't bad, was it? And good for Bella, that's the main thing. What time is it, though?'

'About ... I can't move my arms. Maybe midday? Oh, no! Lunch time, I hope you mean?'

'I do. Come home with me.'

They made sandwiches and drank beer, but before they were finished, reached the bed upstairs.

'This is a muddle,' Katherine said. 'I am so happy.'

'It will only be a muddle', he said, 'If you don't tell me where I can ring you during the week. And when.'

'I need to talk to you about all that sort of thing,' She thought confusedly about Orlando. 'But not just yet.'

12

The next Saturday they met for lunch in the pub at Britwell Salome. Its food and its chef were well-known. They faced each other across the table.

'That game you play when you're a child. Levitation. You stand in the frame of a door and push your arms hard against the sides, as if you're trying to raise them. Then when you walk away they do float up, by themselves.'

Richard watched Katherine as she spoke, moving her arms in demonstration, and glancing at him. 'That's how I felt when I arrived and saw you waiting just now. Floating up, my whole self.'

He gazed at her, and said, 'And if I'd run, really run, when I saw you coming, I would have taken off, too.'

They looked away, and swallowed drinks.

'It hurts not to touch you.'

'I know.'

Looking steadily at her face again, he felt in his pocket for his wallet. He glanced at the menu and counted out some notes.

'I'm sorry', he called to the waitress. 'We have to go now.'

'But you ordered two ... ' She looked at her notepad.

'Two Parma ham omelettes. And drank a cider and a beer. Here it is.' He put the money on the table, and pulled Katherine to her feet. As he steered her out his hand felt warm on her shoulder.

'Richard', she said, speaking very quietly. 'You are mad.' He raised his eyebrows and smiled. They got into his car and drove to his house in silence.

Bella barked as he unlocked the door.

'Ignore her', he said, and walked straight up the stairs. When they stood in the bedroom he put his arms around her from behind, and crossed them over her ribs.

'You're shaking.' Still with his wrists crossed, he opened his palms and held her breasts.

'Yes. You too.'

They lay on his bed and he arched over her. As the shuddering came, Katherine thought she was losing consciousness, and clutched him in fright, before it turned to pleasure, ripple after ripple.

'We can't ever go back to that pub', she said eventually.

'I bet we do.'

After a long time they heard Bella barking; isolated, affronted yaps.

'Don't make me do this all again', he said.

'I'm not trying to. I'm lying here keeping still.'

'But provocatively.'

'Richard. Why is it so nice for us?'

'I'm so good at it. Skill, patience, concentration, timing. I try to keep my eye on your watch whenever possible.'

She giggled.

'Are you hungry?'

'Am I hungry? I thought you would never ask. Leaving those omelettes was pretty serious.'

'I'll make us some.' She sat up and groped for her clothes. 'They'll be even better with your home grown eggs.'

'But can you cook?'

'You wait and see.'

Downstairs she hugged Bella with passion before opening the door to let her out. They ate their delayed lunch on Richard's table with the sun streaming over it and their shoulders touching.

'Levitation must be real', she said.

'Of course. Anything can be.'

As the winter turned into spring, and a pattern of week end meetings developed, it became their code word for feeling high with emotion. 'Levitation?' he would ask, when he noticed her looking at his hands instead of a map, or when she went silent in the middle of a conversation. 'Just a spot of levitation', he would say, stroking her hair on the tow-path beside the river, or once after he had watched her make a difficult parallel car park in Benson High Street.

But on another occasion, when she asked again, like someone marvelling at a new possession, 'Why is it so good?', he was impatient.

'This is not a recipe, you know, or a history text. Believe me, it's just us, Kathy. Think less, could you!'

13

At Easter, Orlando and Katherine went to London. The Boat Race was on Saturday, and Joe was arranging suitable parties. When they arrived Elizabeth took Katherine to the attic floor of the house and showed her the double room there, made ready for visitors. It was warm, and a vase of stargazer lilies gave the whole floor an exotic, musky smell. 'I've put you both here.' She looked pleased and expectant.

Katherine's stomach churned. Her mother's bold new arrangement was a sign of approval of Orlando and impending marriage. Katherine realised she had been counting on the old system, of separate rooms, and, if essential, creeping night visitations. She had not planned any night time visits. In Oxford it had been relatively easy to devise excuses the last few weeks.

'Well?'

'A bit of a surprise.' This is cowardice, her mind told her, while she spoke. It has to come sooner or later. 'The room looks lovely.'

They had an excellent dinner of lamb with a haricot bean sauce and sweet potatoes. 'I noticed they were grown in Brazil', Diane said. 'So we had to have them. Would you like to pour, Orlando?' She passed him the wine.

Orlando was charming company, and described his research project with enthusiasm and modesty. 'We hope it will mean some periods of living in Boston over the next few years. I think Katherine will enjoy it. Rio can be a bit rich without some occasional rigour ... '

'My book's going well,' Katherine said suddenly. 'It'll have to be finished before ... well, before anything really.'

Of course. They looked at her with interest and pleasure. 'How are you getting on?' her mother asked.

'It's absorbing her' Orlando said, proudly. 'Progress report in the College Year Book.'

'Is that true, Orlando?' Katherine asked promptly. 'Who wrote that?'

'Don't sound so defensive. I can't remember. I've got it to show you, in my bag somewhere.'

'I hate it when they write things without letting you check it.'

He looked surprised. 'It's very polite, as I recall.'

Later in the evening she said brightly to him, 'I don't think I've ever slept in this bedroom before. Not officially.'

He was unpacking books and getting out his diary. 'No? It's the power of my - what do you call it? Propriety? Look, I want to fit in one visit to King's College on Sunday; someone's coming in to meet me there. Can we do that?'

'Whatever you like.'

In a minute he said, 'Well, are you getting into this previously forbidden bed with me?'

She looked at him, filled with discomfort, and then thought, but this is kind Orlando, not a stranger.

She lay beside him in an uneasy sleep, scarcely touching. In the morning the sun was shining on Kensington, and they made conversation.

Returning to Oxford in the car, it was not the nights he commented on. 'I talked to your mother about your sister.'

Katherine was driving, and kept her eyes on the road.

'She said she worried occasionally it had saddened your childhood'

Katherine's older sister had been run over and killed, aged three.

'Saddened is too strong a word, I think. I had no memory of her. But I think they were sad, and that must have affected me. People stopped talking when I came into a room. I used to think they were full of secrets. Or even that she was a secret.'

He nodded. After a few more miles, she said, 'But James didn't suffer! Anyone less sad than James I have yet to meet. So it might have been me being a bit touchy.'

'Yes,' Orlando said. 'You are a bit touchy, on your home ground.'

Back in Wolvercote, Katherine threw open her windows and filled the rooms with cold air. She sat at her desk and pulled the papers towards her. But then she lifted the phone and dialled. 'Orlando', she said. 'You were right - I was a bit touchy, at home. I'm going to write to them now, and thank them for our nice Easter.'

'Well done.'

She thought she might say something else, but in the end only said, 'I'm unsettled just now. Will you be patient?'

'I noticed. Yes, for a while. Write to your mother. Ciao, Katerina.'

'Orlando. Ciao.'

After resting for a moment, hand still on the phone, she opened her files and spread her maps all over the desk, edge to edge. In the middle was the aerial photo, and in the middle of it was the suspect speck behind a house. She craned down at it. 'Hi, Bella!' she said, and tapped her finger on it.

14

'Now here's a tricky thing!' Olivia came into the Gallery slightly late, trailing the smell of 'Eternity.'

'What?'

'Heather has moved in with Sven.'

'What!'

'Left the London job, moved to Winchcombe. Radiant with happiness et cetera.'

'What ... '

'Don't keep saying that. I asked about Dawn, and she says he says that was never the least serious, Dawn is twenty years old, what sort of paedophile did we think he was?'

'I'm simply astonished.' She thought of Olivia's sister at the New Year's Eve party, square and beige.

'And Sven also says, she reports, that one potter in any

couple is enough. That's what was the problem with his wife.'

'Last wife. He's had two, remember. Was that the first time they met, at your party?'

'Yes. It's all happened since then. She's kept very quiet about it, and just given us the *fait accomplit*. As long as he still brings his pots to us, I said.' Sven Hansen was a valuable client. 'She sounded absolutely sparkling, for Heather.'

Katherine took this in silently for a moment. Olivia filled the electric kettle for their first coffee of the day.

'While we're at it, what about you?' Olivia swept on. She was looking much revived herself this week, less tired, somehow shiny. One ear-ring was a star, and the other a sickle moon. They were much more obvious with her shorter hair. 'We'll deal with Dawn later. You're quite bubbly yourself, but I haven't seen Orlando in here for ages. Is all well with Orlando?'

Perceptive Olivia. Katherine thought for a minute before answering.

'I don't know, Livvy. I've got so engrossed with this writing I'm doing, in all sorts of ways ... I haven't been nice enough to him, to be truthful. My mind is elsewhere. Easter in London didn't go well ... no, it's not perfect.'

'Temporary and passing?'

'Maybe not.' Her world with Richard was so far from this daily and familiar one, she couldn't think how they could ever be brought together. 'We could all be stressed together when Dawn comes in.'

'Not me! I started the therapy we talked about, and I feel soothed and positive.'

'Really? Tell me about it. Where do you go? What happens?'

'A man in Iffley Road. Don't tell Joe - he doesn't know. His name is Meredith Baker-Lynn. Isn't that a good start - 'Meredith?' You go through to a sort of conservatory at the back of his house, except it's covered in curtains. He's got strange teeth, like very bad false teeth, and you pass certificates along the wall as you go in. Also photos of small children, so that's a good sign.'

'Is he a cognitive therapist, or what? Are people still Freudians?'

'He's an idiosyncratic analyst, he told me. Several people recommended him; he's not just from the Yellow Pages. Although he is in the Yellow Pages, I checked.'

Tactful as ever, Olivia chattered on about Meredith Baker-Lynn until it was time to focus on the first customer, and on logistics for their major autumn exhibition. But she watched Katherine's face and expression. Orlando was Joe's oldest friend, and she worried for him as well as Katherine.

15

887 : 'The Readanora Charter. In this year Ethelred of Mercia, son-in-law of King Alfred, gave fourteen hides of land in Brightwell and Watlington to the Bishop of Worcester. This Chiltern land grant, which included woodland, also conveyed six slaves to the Bishop, 'from the royal vill at Benson.' They were called Ahlmund, Tidulf, Tidheh, Lull, Eadwulf and another Lull.

'This rare glimpse of the lowest social class gives us the first named residents of Benson. In later records slaves are usually associated with work on the manorial lord's home farm. Benson is still a royal vill, in the orbit of the kingdom of Mercia, but it is now more than merely a tribute-collecting centre, or the focus of a large and diverse royal territory. We can begin to see it as an agricultural unit, with more intensive farming giving rise to a settled community.

Within a few weeks more, Katherine had brought her history almost to the end of the ninth century. For the first time, that century, she knew she might have recognised a more permanent village, a Benson. She wrote about the break up of the founders' great territory into the smaller estates which prefigured the manors of the middle ages, and began to struggle in her mind with what might have persuaded these embryonic communities to pool their farming lands into huge open fields.

The fascinating thing about this area where the Thames runs near the foothills of the Chilterns' , she wrote one evening in late April, *'Is that, as with political boundaries, this is border country. The riverside estates, like Benson, later in history reveal themselves to have become open field strip-farming country, while those in the hills remain partially or entirely farmed in individual small holdings. The two landscapes, so close together, would have looked very different. Woodland and common grazing grounds were shared among all these communities, still locally governed by Benson.'*

She put down her pen, and paced into her kitchen. Port Meadow lay in evening darkness, but she could hear voices and make out a group of people on its edge. The weather was mild enough to bring night time walkers on to it. She made coffee, grinding the beans and trickling boiling water on to them, and turned on the radio. A discussion of Darwin and the widening applications of his theories was in progress.

'Come in, chattering classes', she said to the radio. 'All your voices are familiar.' In a minute she realised she actually did know one of the speakers, a biologist acquaintance of Orlando's. The woman had unmistakable voice, slightly Scottish. She switched it off.

Coffee in hand, she returned to her desk and wrote fluently for a moment.

'There is century of silence before we have another document from Benson. In the year 996 King Ethelred granted two hides of land 'in Bynsingtun' to three brothers, Eadric, Eadwig, and Ealdred. The boundaries of this land are set out step by step in a surviving charter, but tracing them on the ground has so far proved impossible.'

They had tried on a cold day, the Sunday after Easter. The first white cherries were in blossom, edging the woods, and the oaks and beeches were hazy green. Richard had pushed a thermos of soup into his pocket, and she wore gloves. They bent their heads over the Old English of the boundary description, and Katherine had a scribbled translation they compared it with. 'We need a spring, and a mound, and several different valleys, allegedly. This *'fildena wudu weg'*, she pointed out. 'Field path to the wood, roughly. That's the only sure point, we know it from another charter. It's Rumbold's Lane, today.'

'As you mentioned to Eric in the pub, the first time I ever saw you. Rumbold's Lane and Hollandtide Bottom.'

They grinned at each other.

'I would love to know who Mr Rumbold was. I get plenty of names in old records, but not him.'

'He'll appear.'

The three brothers' plot of land defied tracing. 'We've got some of the features,' Katherine said while they drank the soup, leaning on a stile to pass the flask back and forward. 'But jumbled up, in no logical order. We need a woad valley, for goodness sake. They grew woad in 996, it seems.'

'Woad is easy. We've passed some already today.'

'We've passed woad plants? Real woad, as in blue dye?'

'And pink, too, if you treat it differently.'
'Really?'
'Believe me. Between here and home.'

Back towards the Roke Elm crossroad, he detoured slightly near a stile and showed her a single clump of three or four tall stems, each with leafy heads of tight yellow buds. They crouched over it, and Katherine held Bella off as she tried to press herself into the centre of their attention. 'This is it, then. Woad? It's so ordinary looking. Tall and thin. How do you make the dye?'

'With the leaves, I think. Fermenting and boiling and everything smells.'

'You are a wonderful source of information, Richard Cottell. I want to take just a few leaves, if you say it's common enough.'

She took off her gloves and picked a long, spiky leaf from each stem, and straightened up.

'You take a few leaves, Katherine Laidlaw.' He took her in his arms. 'Whatever I can find for you, I will.' His serious voice was so unusual that she looked deeply into his light eyes. They kissed for a long moment, with Bella in eager attendance. Katherine had her gloves in one hand and the woad leaves held delicately in the other, dangling.

They came in from the cold and put the thermos and the leaves on the table, with maps and papers.

'Fire, I think.' He lit matches and bent by the fire place until the kindling caught and flamed. Katherine sank into the couch and looked out onto the orderly, divided expanses of the back garden.

'This is a close, you know, medievally speaking, or even a messuage.'

'A mess, actually, in places. The pond is filthy, for instance, but it's full of frog spawn, so I'm leaving it.'

She looked out at Bella, running busily round her

borders, checking that nothing had changed during her morning's absence.

'You could get territorial about this, Richard. It does feel good and self-contained and private.'

'You still haven't seen the fun bit. Come.'

He reached out and pulled her off the couch, and into the kitchen. They stepped through a narrow door on the far side into a light workshop with a long bench underlying a window on to the same garden view. Under it lay a basket made of bark, full of logs and odd-shaped wooden off-cuts. The sweet smell of wood-cutting infused the room.

'Richard!' She stepped towards the wall of tools, hanging tidily on racks. 'Your dark secret.'

'All cast-offs from the timber yard, of course. Even these.' He touched a heavy vice and a lathe. Beside the lathe stood a solid square of wood, and she fingered it. 'What's it for?'

'It's going to be for Prue Freeman, when I get to it. That's pear wood.'

When she still looked uncertain he pointed to the shelf behind her. She turned and saw two smooth glowing bowls like those which stood in his bedroom.

'You make those?' Her voice rose.

'Prue wants one for a friend's fiftieth. Pear tree from the Freemans' own garden, of course.'

'But I assumed you'd got the ones upstairs from a Gallery, or ... '

'All made on the premises. You look very tempting when surprised.'

'Let go, because I haven't finished thinking about this.'

'I'll make you a historic one. We'll find an ancient piece of wood and carbon date it before I start.'

'But do you sell them, or show them, at least?'

'Of course not! They're fun, not a job.'

She rubbed his hair and brushed her lips over his mouth

and chin. 'They are very beautiful. They shouldn't just be hidden here.'

He held her harder. 'Should we have some lunch before we ... miss our moment?'

'Good idea. Could I watch you, later?'

'I beg your pardon? Is this a fetish of yours I don't know about?'

'Wood carving.'

'Oh, wood carving? It depends. On how long everything takes.'

'Let's add some vegetables to the remains of that soup we took with us', Katherine said, and proceeded to cut fine cubes of carrot and potato and leek, very quickly. While they cooked she wandered in the cold garden and picked a handful of parsley and mint, and a few tiny grey thyme leaves. At the last minute, she plunged the herbs into the hot soup and their scent rose. He spread a tray with bread and cheeses.

They ate in front of the fire. 'Thank goodness you're so competent in the kitchen,' Richard said. 'I thought you were just beautiful and knew a bit of history. I was prepared to put up with it, but really ... '

When he pushed her slightly down on the couch, she said, 'Is this something you're supposed to do straight after eating?'

'Very possibly not. You wear a lot of layers, for charter-boundary walking, don't you?'

'Warm in here, though.'

'Luckily.'

'I love doing this with you.'

'I quite like it, too.'

They spent the rest of the day together. While she watched him make a start on the pear wood bowl, setting the wood on the lathe and showing her the chuck that would hold it in place, they talked about Orlando. She sat on a stool and watched his hands and his face, intent on the wood and the machine. 'I think we ... drifted together.' He had commented that she no longer wore the topaz ring. It was a Brazilian stone, she had told him. 'He came back to England, after years away, and found most of our old friends scattered. But Joe still in Oxford, married. And me. Maybe that's what happened.'

'And where had you been, in the meantime?' He had taken the wood off the lathe, and was fitting on a stone grinder, instead. He didn't look at her.

'In London. Teaching. I had a long sort of ... affair with a man who had been my history teacher at school. Not till after I left school, though. Quite proper.' As she told him, the dream of checking trees in a forest floated into her mind, because of the school friend, Sylvia, who had appeared in it. Sylvia had once, briefly, also loved the history teacher. 'It went on for years, on and off.' Off for the phases when she had thought Joe within her reach. 'But it fizzled out, and deserved to.'

'Move back, now, my darling, drifted-into Katherine. This is a hot bit. Tools are safer kept very sharp. You don't push so hard.'

He put on clear plastic goggles, and switched the lathe on. The stone grinder spun, and when he held first one chisel against it, and then another, a firework of golden sparks flew out. When he stopped he took the goggles off and tested the blades on his finger, gently. He removed the grinder and picked up the piece of pear wood again. 'We do the outside first.'

As he fastened it on to the lathe, she said, 'It's sort of ... on hold, with Orlando. I haven't wanted to ... sleep with him. He says that's okay, for a while ... that's what I meant once by a muddle.'

Richard adjusted the piece of wood carefully, and then the chuck which held it in place.

'If I were in his place,' he said, 'I don't think I would like that arrangement.'

He switched the lathe on, and held his chisel against the turning wood. She looked at his serious profile, turned away from her, eyes slightly slitted. 'No, I don't think you would,' she said, but the noise of the lathe covered her voice.

As she drove home to Wolvercote, she thought of his wooden bowls. They were rarely offered any as perfect as his for display in the Gallery.

Last thing in the evening, she took *Flora Britannica* from her shelf. 'Woad', she read. *'Isatis tinctoria'* The ancient dye plant has long stems and sword-shaped blue-green leaves. Its yellow heads blossom into foamy clusters of small yellow flowers. The fermentation process was so disgusting that Elizabeth I forbad its production in any town she was passing through. Katherine spread the four long leaves on her desk and stroked them, gently.

16

Richard's bathroom was a mirror image of the bedroom across the landing, a large room with windows on two sides, and the walls painted a dark, clear green. There was an old armchair in one corner, and a chest of drawers with shaving gear and a few spare soaps on top. Along one wall ran a rail where some of his clothes hung, mostly slatey-blue or sombre green. Katherine was lying in the bath watching him install a new piece of railing. With some splashing, she changed ends so she faced him. It was the following Saturday, and they had been down to the river, walking upstream, and talking about where a ford might have been at Shillingford, and exactly where the ferry ran at Benson.

'Do you ever do things that are not practical?' she asked, idly, as he measured a piece of rail against the distance from wrist to elbow. His hair was still wet from the bath, and curled very nicely on his neck.

'Spent a lot of time in bed lately', he said, holding a screw between his teeth.

'That's true.' She trailed her hands in the water.

He took the screw out of his mouth. 'If you would stay the night sometimes, I could spend even more. That's what this extra rail is, clothes space for you.'

'But you are out on Friday and Saturday.' She felt immediately uneasy.

'Only till about eleven thirty. And there are other nights.'

She ran more hot water, but then got out of the bath and pulled the plug. She put a towel around herself and stood close to him.

'I do want to stay with you.'

'But?'

'But my computer and all my notes ... and the Gallery ...'

'That sounds a bit weak. But -' he put his arm around her and rubbed the towel around on her wet shoulders. 'I do actually know you have another world there. And we both may be not sure how to play this, yet.'

'Really?' She seized on that.

'Really. I'm talking about the occasional bold night. Like a Thursday, for instance. A Sunday. Or tonight.'

She kissed him with relief. Oxford and Benson, public and secret; she needed the indecision to last longer.

'Would I meet Zinnia, if I came to the pub late tonight - just before you come home?'

'You would indeed. Now that might make the whole exercise worth it ... '

The King's Head on a Saturday night was very different from the daytime. The tables were all full, and standing room around the bar was crowded. Patsy Cline could only just be heard above the hubub. Richard's face lit up when Katherine entered, and he smiled and shrugged impatiently. A very fat couple were perched dangerously on bar stools, with much overhang, talking to someone beside him who could only be Zinnia. He introduced her. Zinnia was like a negative image of Dolly Parton, black long curls instead of white, and a ghostly, made up face with red mouth. Black strings of beads dangled over the low opening of her jacket and very white throat. Beneath the trouser suit were white, fringed boots.

She was open and friendly and curious, and focused on Katherine immediately. 'He's a dark horse', she nodded towards Richard. 'Do you live near here, or where?'

'In Oxford.'

'We hardly ever go, although it's so near. We have a boat on the river, and spend most of our time with that.'

'Yes. So Richard says. In fact, he showed me it.'

'You've been down the river with him, have you? We often take it out on a Sunday. Perhaps he could bring you? Do you play cards?'

'Not much. Or not very well. My mother and aunt ... Does Richard?'

'Oh, yes. He's a bully at cards, although he always says he's reluctant. Sometimes we only get half a mile down the river and Eric decides something needs fixing, or we stop for a cup of tea, or in summer we make Pimms. I always take it all on board, the cucumber and mint and everything. So once we've stopped we don't always get started again, and then we have a game or two. Such nice company Richard is, although it's sad. What do you do, Kathleen?'

'Katherine. I work in the Gallery, in Oxford. We sell a few pictures and some jewellery. But mostly pots ... '

'Is it in the High Street?'

'Yes, actually, near - '

'I think I know it, near the Market. I got an Indian jacket next door, once, embroidered with tiny mirrors in an elephant pattern, or maybe it was birds? I must have a proper look. That might have been the last time we were in Oxford. So how did you meet Richard?'

'We're both interested in history, the history of Benson ...'

'Oh, yes?' Her eyes glazed slightly.

'What did you mean, sad about him?'

'About his wife. You know, he doesn't talk about it much, but he must be lonely. Eric reckons that's why he works in here; he doesn't really need to. He brings Bella. Well, there's no one but him, is there?'

She looked hopefully at Katherine.

'No.'

'You know,' Zinnia went on. 'You need someone behind you, batting for your side, sort of thing. Specially if you don't have children, like we don't.'

'Of course.' Katherine looked at her small concerned eyes, surrounded by heavily blue-covered lines. Richard with children had never crossed her mind. Zinnia was kinder than she was.

'I would like to see inside your boat,' she said.

'We'll get Richard to bring you', Zinnia said, confidently. 'And here is Eric, finished out the back.' A small, neat looking man with glasses had emerged behind the bar. Patsy Cline suddenly got louder. 'Stop, look and listen!' she sang, 'You may be missin' kissin' ... ' The fat couple joined in. Richard introduced her to Eric, who shook hands formally.

He had a tweed tie with the National Trust oak leaf on it. Five minutes later, out the back again, he said to Zinnia, 'That's the girl who came in here last year, with a load of maps. I knew he fancied her then.'

'Well, it's about time, isn't it?' his wife said.

'Nothing matched', Katherine said an hour later, when Eric had locked up and they were outside. 'Not Zinnia and Eric to each other, or what she looks like and quite sensible things she says, and what he looks like and his music.'

'If I hear Patsy Cline again I might give in my notice.'

'I rather liked it. Everyone else did.'

'Mmmh. But every Saturday?'

She thought of Zinnia's theories about why he was there every Saturday. Now seemed not the right time to ask him. 'Do you realise this is the first time we have been together at night?' he had said as the pub closed. 'Let's look at the sky, if it's visible. And the river at least.' Now they were walking towards the boat yard. She hummed, 'Stop, look and listen!' and he laughed, his teeth showing white. They crossed the London road and sat on a bench on the scrappy lawn by the boat yard.

'Look', he said, his head turned back. 'So few stars. Too much light now.'

'Light pollution.' She quoted the newspaper astronomer.

'You used to be able to see more, so many more', he said, dreamily.

'When?'

'Well, in the country.'

'Where you last lived?'

'In Sussex? Yes, I believe so.'

'Where did you live before then?'

He put his head sharply upright, and turned to look at her. 'Why?'

She rubbed her face on his shoulder. 'I can't help needing chronologies. It's an addiction.'

'Dorset before that. A place called Gillingham, near Sherborne.'

'Dorset. Your accent?'

'Have I got an accent?'

'Slight. Were you born there?'

'Very probably yes, my obsessive person', he said, lightly, and kissed her.

'We smell of smoke', she said, pulling away from him.

'We do', he said, relaxedly. 'It's awful.'

For a moment they watched the river and the boats in silence. Voices carried from the caravan park. A car arrived at a farmhouse across the river, and in the distance they saw lights go on in the windows.

'I didn't know you played cards.'

'I only ever do with Eric and Zinnia. Sign of my wasted past. Darts, too ... Hell!' he shouted, ' Leave that alone!'

He was on his feet and running towards the water's edge. Katherine saw a line of three or four dark figures jump from one moored boat to another, and heard a splash as something fell into the water. Then the figures were on the short pier and then on the bank, running towards Richard. One swerved towards him and slipped in the mud and swore. Almost before she had grasped what was happening in the dark, they reached her, in a cloud of sweat and alcohol, and then were past. She saw a leather jacket glint in the street light, and heard them one of them calling to the others as they disappeared across the road and up towards the village, into the darkness.

'Richard!' She ran after him, dragging wildly at her scarf which was stuck around one end of the bench. 'Are you all right?'

'Yes, okay,' he called over his shoulder, but he continued

on to the small pier. 'Buggers', she heard him mutter, and he crouched down by the middle boat. 'Look.'

With difficulty she made out the that the heavy rope tying the boat to the iron ring on the pier had been slashed, and the boat was drifting and about to swing into its neighbour.

On the other side of it was *Halcyon Daze*. Richard jumped aboard it where he could reach the drifting boat and push it back to the pier. 'Hold it, could you', he called, and brushed at his hair and forehead. In a minute he was back beside her, and reached down into the water and felt around until his hand closed on the floating shorn off rope still attached to it. He pulled it up. For a moment then he was still, and Katherine could look at him as they knelt on the pier. 'Richard!' she said in horror. 'You're covered in blood!'

'He swiped me as they ran past.' He wiped at his forehead again with his free hand. 'It's only a scrape. The knife was in the water by then. But he was wearing rings.' He was breathing heavily, but seemed quite calm. Katherine was shaking.

'Are you sure?'

'Let's get this tied up. Then you can look at my forehead for as long as you like.' There was enough rope to tie the floating middle boat not to its ring again, but to *Halcyon Daze's* own mooring line. Richard satisfied himself that his knot held, and fed the loose end through one last time. They sat there for a minute, and Katherine felt very cold. 'For goodness sake' she said, and found a wad of clean tissues in her coat pocket. He pressed it on his right eyebrow. 'Okay', he said. 'The police can check the rest. Let's go.'

'Can you drive?' Katherine asked, as they reached the King's Head again. They each had a car there, after their separate arrivals. They were the last two cars in the car park, lit by the street light and a security light. She examined his head, removing the sodden red tissues. It was a clean looking cut across one brow, with the blood already slowing to a seep.

'Everything bleeds a lot there,' he said, and bent to look in the car wing mirror. 'I'll be fine.'

'You'll look like a boxer.'

They were home in five minutes, and Bella emerged, looking benign but tired, disturbed in an important sleep. Richard rang the boatyard owner, and got no answer. 'Can I be bothered ringing the police?' he thought aloud. 'No, they'll be full of questions. We don't want to share our night with them. Tomorrow will do.'

'I completely forgot,' Katherine said. 'I made us a pizza. It was all the ingredients I could find in your cupboards this evening. It seems ages ago. Do you still want it?'

'Absolutely yes. And we'll open a bottle.'

'Actually', she said. 'I really would like a cup of tea. And you should be having a sugary one. For shock.'

In the end she washed his cut with care, and sat on his knee, facing him, to dress it. She made an efficient cross over pattern with two strips of plaster. 'As good as stitches,' she said. 'We won't have to take you to my friend Joe in casualty.'

'The whole idea of tonight is that we go hardly anywhere.'

She remained sitting on his knee. In a minute she ran her fingers over his mouth, and he bit them, lightly.

'It's too late to go to bed early.'

'But shall we?'

In bed she shook again. 'I hated those men.'

'But they aren't here. We are.'

'Are you all right?'

'Well, what do you think? Am I all right?'

'Nothing special ... '

They woke just before dawn, and Katherine reached out to him. 'You have to lie very still,' she said. 'Because of your cut.'

'I was dreaming, that I was in Dorset, I think. Bella was there, which she wasn't really, of course. And some other people.'

'You're always dreaming.'

'Yes, aren't you?'

'Not as much. Or I don't remember as much. You're very warm.'

In a minute they slept again.

17

'The King holds BENSON. 12 hides less 1 virgate of land. Before 1066, 50 ploughs.

Now in lordship 8 ploughs: 5 slaves.

32 villagers with 29 smallholders have 24 ploughs.

2 mills at 40 shillings; from meadows and pastures, fisheries and woodlands come £18.15s.5d a year; from church-tax 11 shillings; from a year's corn £30.

The jurisdiction of four and a half Hundreds belongs to this manor.

In total, it pays £80 and 100 shillings a year.'

After the random glimpses afforded by the chronicles and charters of previous centuries, Domesday Book of 1086 brings Benson into clearer view at last ... the richest royal manor in Oxfordshire ... a population of sixty six villein and slave families ... mills and fishponds, pasture and woodland ...

In May, while the fruit trees in Richard's orchard blossomed in heavy bunches of pink and white, Tim

Rothwell wrote to Katherine to remind her that the draft of the first half of her book was now due, and that he awaited it with interest. If she could send it soon, he suggested, perhaps they could thereafter meet for lunch to discuss it? Unless she was going to be in London shortly, he concluded, he was more than willing to meet her in, say, Henley.

'There have been unforeseen distractions,' Katherine said to Richard. 'But I think I'll make it.'

Domesday Book's terse information on Benson could be unpacked in a dozen different ways, and Katherine spent engrossed days working out whether ploughs represented actual working land or mere fiscal units, and if so, in either way, how big Benson might actually be? She knew that several other unnamed townships, including Tim Rothwell's Henley, were included under Benson's heading, but how many, exactly? If a Chiltern village was not mentioned, did that mean it was not there at all? This is all for the king's tax purposes, she reminded herself. If a question didn't need a money answer, it wasn't asked. Benson paid a church tax to the king, therefore St Helen's Church was there, uncited. Only the earliest missionary churches still paid church taxes; therefore St Helen's Church was very old. As old as a Celtic Christian church? She was back with the question of who Ceawlin and Cutha might have conquered there, five hundred years before. And the corn tax, the oldest tax of all, a conversion of the food render of the earliest kingdoms - still there, in Benson, in 1086.

She became absent minded during her hours in the Gallery. 'Oh God, I'm sorry, Livvy,' she said, when she had forgotten to liaise with a potter new to their artists' list, a young woman in Staffordshire. 'We were going to include her in the autumn show. Sorry, sorry; I will ring as well as write, now!' Dawn was downcast after Sven Hansen's defection, and disappeared to the back of the shop when he once arrived, tactfully without Heather, to talk with Olivia. Her misery played well on creativity, however, and Olivia gave two of her newest works, highly-glazed, narrow-neck bottles, pride of place in the window, and arranged the 'Dawn Hammond' labels clearly beside the price tags.

'I really like them,' Katherine told her honestly, and was reminded. 'I met someone who makes remarkable wooden bowls recently. He uses all sorts of hardwoods, mostly local Chiltern wood. Would we be interested?'

'Very likely', Olivia said. 'If they are really one-offs. They can be wildly successful. Get him to bring some in, if you meet him again.'

'Maybe I will.' Later, she asked Olivia, 'How are you getting on with the Iffley man? Dr Meredith Double-Barrel'

'Baker-Lynn. I'm going twice a week. It's costing hell. But I am relaxing and calm, and we visualise things together.'

'Visualise?'

'Visualisation. It can be very positive. You envisage the outcomes you want.'

Katherine raised her eyebrows and hoped she looked encouraging. Olivia was very charming and half-amused at herself, even in solemn moments. 'And we're thinking bravely about hypnotism', she went on. 'He's thinking and I'm being brave.' Katherine pulled a hopeful face, and nodded vigorously.

But Orlando was not so easily assuaged. He stormed into the Gallery and spoke to her in an icy intense whisper. 'I ring in the evenings, you're at the library. Week ends you're God knows where, but rarely at home. Shall I come and visit you at midnight? Three in the morning? It's a long time since we had a meal together, let alone ... I know you have a deadline; we all have deadlines. Is this a rational way to deal with it? I must have been mad to be pleased about this book of yours. What's happened to you, Katerina? How long did you mean this 'being patient' to last?'

'I am very sorry, Orlando', she said, feeling distraught. 'I haven't been ... direct with you. I've been strange even to myself. I don't know if I will ever ... change back ... '

'What is it?'

'I don't know. I'm obsessed ... with the book, I think.'

'How the hell can you be this obsessed with a book, a piece of work?'

'This isn't a good place to talk about it.'

'There isn't going to be another place for a while. I'm going to America tomorrow, to Boston. It might be a few weeks. You may have been too ... absorbed ... to remember, but I did tell you, a while ago, I have a possibility.'

A rare English mistake. Dawn pranced up to them, looking pretty and alert. Katherine saw Orlando make an effort. 'I like your bright blue bottles in the window,' he said. 'Something new for you?'

'Quite a departure,' she said. 'I seem to have got out of my black phase.' She waited for further response, but they were silent. 'I'll leave you to it, then. Nice to see you, Orlando.' She pattered away, long legs under her usual very short skirt.

'Tonight?' Orlando said to Katherine.

'Okay.' She forced a smile. He left the shop, and she saw him glance at Dawn's bottles as he passed the window.

They had an uncomfortable short meal at Brown's, around the corner from St John's Street.

Katherine sipped glass after glass of water, with a dry mouth. They talked about Orlando's asthma project and the three full-time statisticians they planned to employ, and the candidates John Davidson had already interviewed, in Boston. 'We'll do the short-list together, while I'm there', Orlando said, starting on a steak and kidney pie. In a minute he put his knife and fork down. 'Now. What about you? Why are you in such a rush?'

She played with fish on her plate. 'I'm up to Domesday,' she said eventually. 'It's quite different in nature and ... texture, to all the conjectural stuff earlier.'

' So, good. And?'

'And I've had some luck with boundaries.'

'With boundaries?'

'In Benson's case certain old boundaries, paths now, often, might be the limits of a kingdom ... '

She trailed off. This felt, ridiculously, like private territory.

'This isn't working, is it?'

'Not just now, no.'

They both stopped the pretence of eating.

After a long silence, Orlando said, 'I'll see you when I get back.'

She was very pale. 'Okay.'

When they left the restaurant it was still light. 'Ciao', she said, and leaned to kiss him.

'Don't do that!' he said, with real anger.

When she got home she pulled on old shoes and walked on Port Meadow until the light was fading. She felt guilty, and relieved, and guilty again to find herself straying into more absorbing thoughts about Benson at Domesday. She let them come, and made notes at home until late in the night. In the morning she got to her computer early, and began writing with a new surge of energy.

> *Domesday provides us with the first explicit description of the linked hundreds so interesting as a possible survival of a core part of the old royal territory, or 'Bynsingtun land.' Benson has the soke - that is, the jurisdiction, and the valuable profits of jurisdiction - over 4 ½ hundreds. These*

Oxfordshire Chiltern Hundreds were Binfield, Lewknor, Langtree, Pyrton, and the half-hundred, Benson itself. Somewhere on this territory the hundredal court met regularly, supervised by the king's reeve, to deal with matters of public order, taxation and certain crimes. Meeting places for such courts were sometimes large manorial halls or barns, or the local church, or, very commonly, an outdoor site. Such sites were often marked by a prominent feature like a natural hill or artificial tumulus, a marker stone, or a grove of trees. A number of surviving place-names mark these significant ancient sites, usually found now on boundaries where several modern parishes meet.

An outstanding puzzle about the Benson Hundreds, a territorial unit with a record of continuity from pre-Conquest to medieval times hard to equal in England, is that we do not know where the hundredal meeting place was. There is no record, archaeological or historical, of a central hall or manor. There is, however, one place on the map to which many clues draw us. Today this is an insignificant T-junction on a minor road. Once it was called Roke Elm ... '

18

On the last Friday of the month, after laboriously checking footnotes one last time, Katherine posted off her first six chapters. She sent them from the post office shop in Wolvercote, and gave a great sigh as she pushed the parcel through. Then she walked a little further. Wind was blowing blossom petals into untidy fringes around the trees, and a group of geese patrolled the shallow edges of a flooded dip in the meadow. In its middle a pair of swans floated as serenely as if they occupied a private lake. She walked slowly, looking with heightened vision at everything familiar, back from an absence. Leaves were every shade of green from palest lime to very dark, and the seesaw in the children's playground was a lurid, glowing orange. Her own front door was scruffy and peeling, but the Victorian bricks around it made a perfect, soft red frame.

She bounded up the stairs and, for the first time, rang Richard at the timber yard.

'Could I invite myself for the week end? Two whole nights?'

'Don't go in the workshop. There's a secret developing.'

She drove via Sainsbury's, and filled the trolley with fruit and fish, meat and cheese, wine and olive oil and dips and bread rolls for couch-side eating. At the last minute she added the most expensive foaming bath oil the shelves offered. Richard's green bathroom was bereft of cosmetics.

At Oak Farm House she inspected the garden and picked some vegetables. Venturing into the hens' far corner, she located three eggs, and then sat on the new log seat to admire the scene. It was still rough and unsanded, and she moved again, careful to avoid splinters. She was sitting on the back step, beside the little pile of potatoes, carrots and eggs, when Richard arrived, Bella galloping around his feet.

'This is very domestic', he said, and kissed her. He smelt of sawn wood. 'Mmmh, better than the pub', she said, breathing it in. Very domestic, she thought, and yet the great absence of a family? No photos, no letters lying around, no childish works of art. It had suited her, because of Orlando, not quite to know. Zinnia had made her see that.

'Hey, your head', she said, examining his brow for last week's damage. 'It's almost completely healed. Amazing. There will hardly be a scar.' She touched it with the back of her fingers. Only a thin line above his eyebrow showed where the bleeding slash had been.

He had a bath, and she sat in the bathroom and talked. 'Don't you dare!' he said, when she threatened him with the rose and cinnamon bath oil.

'Okay, it's for me. Later. Listen, what this week end is celebrating is, I sent off the first half today. Finished. With all our Roke Elm ideas, and our charter boundary efforts properly included.'

'Your ideas. I only need extravagant thanks.'

'You have to do much more medieval work yet, in that case. We're up to about 1100, I suppose.'

'1100.' He repeated it thoughtfully, as though inspiration might come.

'I resisted going into your workshop.'

'Good. There could possibly be a present for you there. It depends. I'll show you the pear wood bowl, if you remind me. Prue Freeman's. You're not the only one to finish something this week.'

With a surge of water, he stood up, and she passed him a towel.

'I won't come to the King's Head with you. I'll do some cooking. Would you like beef or monk-fish for a midnight feast tonight? Whatever you don't have tonight will be for tomorrow.'

'Fish. It's Friday.'

She glanced at him, but before she could make a remark, he had pulled her to him, and kissed her, against his still wet chest.

'I'm going to leave Bella here with you. And I'll be back as soon as I can escape.'

'I live by myself, you know. I'll be fine. Tomorrow I'll come with you, but tonight I would love to read the papers, and lie around, and cook. And talk to Bella, yes please.'

Before he left he showed her the pear wood bowl, a wide curving dish with a lip turning slightly out. The fine grain of the wood was so warmly brown it was almost pink.

Katherine held it in delight. 'Would you bring it, or some of them, to the Gallery? Olivia would love to see them. I know you don't want to make them feel anything like work, but this is a serious ... It's a beautiful object, Richard.' He looked at her standing in his kitchen, stroking the bowl. He loved the way her focus jumped so passionately from one pursuit to another. Her clear pale skin was slightly flushed. 'I can't believe you got this out of that lump of wood.'

'I might.'

He pulled on his jacket and she walked out to his car with him. It was a rusted old Saab, 1980. 'Believe me, an excellent year', he had told her. It had a succession of stickers on it showing the concerns of past owners.

'Enjoy Patsy Kline.'

'Or Tammy Wynette. Or Waylon.'

Bella whimpered slightly as he drove away, but returned obediently inside with Katherine. There, in protest, she made straight up the stairs, forbidden to her, and into the bedroom.

'You come right out of here,' Katherine laughed, following the dog and pulling her out. 'Although it can be very nice sleeping on that bed, I know.'

They went down the stairs together, and sat in the garden, companionably.

When he got home they went to bed even before eating the monk fish brochettes. 'It was knowing you were here while I was there', Richard said. 'It was domesticity run riot. That and thinking of your bath foam, or oil, or whatever it is.'

Later, after they had made love again, and he was nearly asleep, she said, 'I don't know how old you are.'

'No, you don't. How old do you think?'

'About ... maybe forty-two?'

'Right first time.'

'Forty-two?'

'Is that a good number?'

'Excellent.' She kissed his shoulder.

In a few minutes her mind had strayed again. 'Richard?'

He groaned.

'Do you think the king's reeve might have held court somewhere here all through the middle ages? People summoned and sentenced and sent to war ... just where we are in this bed?'

'No, a little to the east I think. Under my workshop.'

She prodded him, and smiled in the dark.

'But really?'

'Yes, really. Absolutely. Four or five times a year. Turn your active brain off, darling. Think about cooking. That calms you.'

'I love you, Richard.'

'I love you, too.'

It was the first time they had said it.

19

'I had ducks here last year,' Richard said the next day. 'The blighters flew away without consultation. I thought they might be back this nesting season, but not a sign.' They were looking at the pond in his garden. 'They were messy, actually. It's cleaner without them.'

'It seems unappreciative, though.'

'Exactly. I provide water and plants and a bit of a fence against foxes, and it is scorned.'

They had had an extensive slow breakfast and were planning to visit Dorchester to hand over the pear wood bowl to Prue Freeman, in her antique shop. A history-free day, Katherine had decreed. 'This is my half-way point holiday.'

'Oh, yes,' Richard had said, sceptically.

They went in his car, with Bella looking proprietary in the back. 'This is not an outing on foot today', Richard warned her as she jumped in, avoiding the word walk. 'You'll have to wait here.' Katherine held the bowl on her lap. She looked at his profile as he drove, and his hands on the wheel. She had noticed that the soles of his feet were as calloused as his palms, hardened as though he worked barefooted, instead of with heavy protective boots. The rest of his skin, all over his body, was smooth and flawless, like a much younger man's. 'What are you smiling about?' he said, without seeming to glance away from the road.

'I'm thinking. But certainly not about levitation,' she said, untruthfully.

'That's all right, then,' he said, and rested his hand on her knee.

Even on a Saturday, they parked easily in Dorchester's curving main street. It was a sultry day, cloudy but warm. There was clearly going to be a wedding later in the Abbey, and a florist's van was parked across the road in front of the George Inn. 'Not ours', said Katherine, checking the name on the van. 'Seems to be a very superior establishment from Henley.'

'Very superior wedding venue.' He gestured at the Abbey.

'Beautiful. All given to them by a king in Benson, of course ... '

'Kathy ... ' he said warningly, and she stopped, laughing.

'Okay. History-free. How can you help it, though?'

Prue Freeman was dressed as elegantly as if for a day at the races, rather than an afternoon in a shop. She was slim and high-heeled, and wore a mulberry coloured jacket with perfectly cut linen trousers. Her blonded hair swung in a thick curve as she greeted Richard.

'This is Katherine Laidlaw', he said.

'Hallo, Katherine,' she said and shook hands warmly. Katherine looked around the shop as she and Richard spoke. Items of polished furniture, desks and chests and dining tables, were placed artfully between display cabinets of smaller items. A tapestry hung on the back wall, showing a fragile looking virgin taming a unicorn in a dark oak forest. It was a shop for serious furnishers of enviable homes.

'Oh, Richard!' she heard Prue say, as she drew the bowl from its box. 'This is going to be perfect. She will love it.' She ran expert hands over the contours of Richard's bowl, and stood it on a low table for them to admire it.

'I think he should show them', said Katherine, emboldened by her enthusiasm.

'Well, I have thought so, too', Prue said. 'But I know he is reluctant, and it is nice for me to have a secret source to use occasionally. They are such unique presents.'

Richard shrugged. 'I'm busy elsewhere. Its optional, this way.'

Prue chattered on, assuming that Katherine would recognise her reference points - local occasions and places and people. She told them about the wedding to be held in the Abbey later; the groom, but not the bride, lived locally. Several people had bought wedding presents from her.

Before they left the shop, Katherine and Richard peered into the display cases. Between a shelf of blue and white willow pattern pieces of china, and another holding glistening paste buckles, in sinuous art nouveau shapes, were trays of coins. 'And look', Richard pointed. Below the coins was a small cluster of lead tokens.

'I like them so much,' Katherine said. 'I can imagine real

people using them. Coming back over the fields with milk or eggs or bread.'

'Dropping them sometimes, fortunately. The tokens, I mean. For me to find.'

They farewelled Prue, and left the shop.

'Will she pay you?' Katherine said worriedly, feeling inquisitive.

'A generous lot will be discreetly added to my next timber pay, going by past events. Remember the lathes and all the gear are technically theirs.' He seemed relaxed, and she said no more.

20

The sky had blackened dramatically while they were in Prue's shop, and within minutes of emerging big splatters of rain began to fall, and there was a thunder burst and then a crackling flash of lightening. The rain fell in dense sheets, with furious, tropical intensity. Figures vanished from the street, holding ineffectual cardigans and jackets above their heads. Katherine and Richard ran for the Abbey. In the porch Richard trampled his feet, and said 'Surely the George would have been a better refuge?'

'But we've had so much food and drink already today', Katherine answered, thinking of their prolonged breakfast. 'This will be interesting. Poor wedding, though. I hope it clears.'

In they went, to the austere People's Chapel, and gravitated instinctively towards the spreading light of the sanctuary end, and the huge window covering the east wall. The rattle of the heavy rain was dimmed, and even the thunder crashes were hushed through the thick, ancient roof.

'The Green Man is my favourite,' she said, and took him to see the plant-covered head, high but not quite hidden, in the corner of a wall of sculpture. 'Do you know this church?'

'Yes', said Richard. 'I've been here.' He didn't sound affectionate.

'St Birinus has been carried away altogether.' They looked at the six carved figures designed to carry the saint's absent coffin. 'This all dates from about 1320', she summarised, skimming through a leaflet thoughtfully provided for visitors, and waving around the eastern end where they stood. 'Part of the massive restoration and extension work carried out in the fourteenth century after papal indulgences were granted for work on it after 1293.'

'Et nunc, et semper, et in saecula saeculorum.'

'What's that?'

'Something about now and ever shall be, isn't it? World without end, and nothing changes.'

'Are you a Catholic?' she asked, thinking, Zinnia probably knows this, too.

'If anything', he said. 'Nothing much, though.'

The florists were fastening white roses with big floppy white bows to the aisle end of each pew. Briskly, they moved down the church. The altar was resplendent in green and white ranks of roses, lilies, orange blossom, and early sweet peas, with pink, spotted centres.

'Now this is interesting', Richard said. He was bending over a low tomb chest. 'The Stonor arms, I think. I wonder if that's the notorious judge?'

Katherine looked at the effigy of the dour figure in legal robes, contrasting with the military regalia of surrounding knights' tombs.

'What judge?'

'Another fourteenth century one, I guess. A Stonor, anyway.'

'You are surprising,' she said. 'I've never noticed him.'

There was a loud crash of thunder. 'Bella will be miserable.'

They made their way slowly towards the door. They paused and studied another tomb, where it was just possible to make out little figures in descending size kneeling in line on the carved stone side, representing the large family of the burgher buried there, and Richard took her hand. His rough palm was as warm as ever. As they looked at it, she said, 'Richard, I've got very ... extremely ... late, with this question, but - have you got children?'

He continued to look at the tidy carved family. She stood holding his relaxed hand, and waiting for him to speak. At last he said,

'No, I haven't. I had three, though, at one time.'

'Three? What do you mean - what happened?' Wild thoughts of baby-snatchings and broken families flew through her mind.

'They died.' His face was fixed on the little kneeling figures. This is grotesque, she thought frantically, and I don't know how to respond.

After another silence he said. 'At the same time as my wife. They all - caught an infection, and died.'

She was stunned. 'But that doesn't happen ... '

'It did happen', he said, conclusively, turning to look at her.

'I don't know what to say.'

'Nothing much good to say', he spoke in his usual brisk tone, and she held his hand as though it were she who needed support.

They stood in the porch. The rain was visibly weakening, and in the west the sky was brighter.

'Can I ask you anything more?' she said, still shocked. He waited. 'Were they boys, or girls ... ?' She needed to envisage these children, these children with no pictures in their father's house.

'A boy, then a girl, then another boy. Our baby, Thomas,' he answered instantly.

'Richard. I'm so sorry,' she said. She had never felt so helplessly inadequate. 'How can you bear me chattering on about ... place-names, and King Offa, and boundaries, and ... ?'

'And food, and recipes, and Brazil, and your friend Olivia's therapy? I love it, of course. That was the past, Kathy. We have to live it as it comes.'

But that is nearly too much, she thought. Too much for anyone to survive. She felt a little frightened of him. One of the florists edged past them with a tray of orange blossom, a large woman with a green overall over jeans. Across her square bosom, on the overall, it said: 'Flowers make my day, too.'

'Scusi me,' she said cheerfully. 'Work must go on!'

'We've been haunted by keen florists since day one' Richard said to Katherine, equally cheerfully.

Something about the calm way he said 'we' and his brisk, ordinary voice reassured her, and she smiled at him, and leant her head for an instant on his shoulder.

'Come on!' he said. 'Rain's stopping. Let's rescue Bella. She'll be beside herself.'

But when they reached the car, and she saw him get the dog out, and rub her ears hard, and tell her to run around before they set off home again, she knew her view of him had shifted slightly. It was as if he had, in the meantime, been somewhere else.

21

Eric nodded courteously when she arrived at the King's Head that evening, and Zinnia greeted her like a long-expected fixture on the scene. 'Hallo, Katherine', she called. 'What are you having? This man Richard might get it for you.' Zinnia wore the red suit and white boots again, but her hair was piled up in loopy, escaping curls on her head. Around her white throat hung a miniature guitar, with shiny gold strings. Eric Clapton was playing a real guitar on the tape. There had been a local cricket fixture, and the game was still being relived along the bar. Two uncomfortably well-dressed couples looked as if they might have attended a wedding earlier in the day, and pushed Dorchester Abbey immediately into the front of Katherine's mind again. She had brought Bella with her, and the dog hurried confidently behind the bar to find Richard.

'Hallo, you', he said, and without asking slid a glass of wine across the bar to Katherine. 'You just missed David Freeman', he said. 'But you'll meet him sooner or later.'

'Is he pleased with your bowl?'

'Apparently.'

They held each other's eyes for an instant. The rush of passion after only a few hours' separation was becoming familiar to Katherine, but tonight it felt almost violent, like the sensation of shock at a sudden noise, or relief after an accident avoided.

'Not long now', he said to her, in a conversational voice, and she looked around, faintly embarrassed and blushing when he laughed.

Zinnia introduced her to the very fat man she recognised from her previous evening visit, once more overhanging a bar stool, but this time with a different woman, thinner and older.

'I've only heard you singing along to Patsy Cline before.' Katherine said to him.

'Well, you're close,' he said, in a surprising public school accent, 'I am a music teacher, but unfortunately we don't usually stray anywhere near Patsy Cline.' His wife, sitting next to him, taught art at the same well-known school a few miles away. She knew Olivia's Gallery well, and several of its artists. Her husband's companion the previous week had been his sister, visiting from Wales. Zinnia smiled from behind the bar, happy at having arranged an excellent small party, and Katherine enjoyed herself, acutely conscious of Richard nearby, occasionally joining them, sometimes moving off elsewhere. Bella flattered her by searching her out and leaning heavily against her legs.

'It was almost ...', she said to him as they arrived home, 'almost domestic, to use your word.'

As soon as the door closed behind them, before switching on the light, he pulled her against him. For once without talking, they kissed and she felt him hard against her. Staggering slightly, they lowered themselves without separating onto the bottom stair. She walked her hands up his back, under the dark green jumper, and held his shoulders. In a minute he said, his voice slightly thick, 'We could be more domestic than this. If I don't lie down with you, I might die.' He gave a laugh at his own remark, but Katherine said,

'So might I. Die if you don't.'

She cried again afterwards. 'This is completely ungrateful,' he whispered, brushing her hair off her forehead and holding his hand against her wet face. 'Tell me I didn't hurt you?'

'No. I thought I was rough with you.'

'You were, a bit.'

They lay on his bed a little longer, in a debris of clothes.

Before they slept, she told him about her sister, Julia, and how that death had coloured her childhood. 'I couldn't be sad for her myself, really', she said. 'I hardly remember her. Just one or two images. We played with a scooter, I remember. And our father showed us a baby horse, and I didn't think she, Julia, was nearly impressed enough by it. She wanted to hurry; I wanted to touch it. But I think I knew my parents were sad, and made an effort not to talk about her too much, so then they seemed secretive. And in petulant moments I imagined they were wishing she was there, and not me. Now, I don't think that was necessarily true at all, but it was my childish perception of it.'

Richard moved her on his arm, and turned half away, pressing his side against her, and looking up towards the ceiling. His eyes were open in the dark. 'No one could wish you not here', he said. And then, as though answering a request, he added, 'I will tell you properly, about my children. And Ellen. Of course you should know.' He was quiet again for a minute, and she waited.

When his silence had grown so long she was about to speak, he said, 'But it's tied up with so many other things. Can it wait a while?'

'Of course,' she said, relieved.

22

'You haven't seen my flat, yet,' she said to him the next morning. It was a perfect day, warm from dawn, and with a gentle, lustrous light on Richard's garden and the flat fields beyond his fence. 'What about coming in to Oxford, and we could do non-Benson activities all day? I wouldn't show you my maps and photos, although they are all there ... we could go for a picnic!' She distracted herself inspiredly.

'Fine', said Richard. 'Bella?'
'Bring her.'
'We'll have to go in convoy.'
'Unless you stay with me tonight.'
'Bank Holidays mean nothing to Freeman. I'm working tomorrow.'
'So will I, then. It will make me.'

Outside her flat the Wolvercote streets were busy with families enjoying the early summer day. The playground was loud with seesaw negotiations, and several youths had chosen to take a motor-bike to pieces in it, and had an audience of small children watching them. They parked with difficulty, and when Richard walked back from his car he found Katherine looking up at her own window. 'It's open,' she worried. 'I never leave it open.' He looked up at the top floor of the small brick house.

'You could have, just once. There's an inside lock too, I suppose?' She nodded. 'Come on, then. Let's look.'

She let them in at the front door, and they walked up the narrow flight of stairs, Bella behind them. On the top landing, Katherine put her key into a white door, and turned it, once.

'Seems all ... '

'No, I always turn the key twice.' He pushed past her and opened the door. 'Hallo!' he called. At the same moment, Katherine said behind him, 'There's one person who ... ', and a man's voice inside the flat answered.

'Hallo to you! Hell, a dog'

A figure appeared in front of them in boxer shorts and with messy hair standing up on his head. He held a towel, and blinked as if the light was painful. He had muscular arms, and the faint beginnings of a pot stomach. Katherine's face broke into a smile. 'James! Why are you here? This is my brother, James. Richard, Richard Cottell.'

'Hallo, Richard.' James transferred the towel to his left hand, and the two men shook hands. 'Your dog? She's beautiful.' He turned back to Katherine. 'What do you mean, why am I here? Eights, of course. Where were you, is the question?'

He sat down suddenly, as if the effort of getting up had absorbed current energy supplies.

'Oh, no! The final day of Eights. I completely forgot, James. How could I? I've been so engrossed in work recently that all our usual things have ... left my mind. James always comes up for the rowing,' she explained to Richard.

'And a major boat club party. Major.' James groaned slightly. 'Joe asked about you.' What Joe had said was that Orlando was in America and possibly in some kind of distress over Katherine. Even in James's tired state, he connected this with the man who had just arrived with his sister. Katherine had taken his hand, lightly. She looked sparkling, somehow taller than before. Richard was looking at James with a pleasant, interested, unsympathetic expression. He looked a bit older than her, very fit. He reached out and pushed his dog into a sitting position.

'So how did it go, the rowing? What about our boat? The Bartholomew boat', she explained to Richard.

'All interrupted by a mighty thunderstorm. Race cancelled, everything off for half an hour, then re-rowed. Where were you, not even in Oxford?'

Richard and Katherine looked at each other. 'No,' Richard said. 'We did notice the storm. We had to shelter for a while.'

James felt sceptical; he guessed they had been in a bedroom somewhere. It was a new image of Katherine. 'Anyway,' he continued. 'We bumped Saints. It was a great race when it got going.'

'I completely forgot,' his sister repeated, sounding

surprised. 'Have you had some breakfast? Shall I get you something? We might go out for lunch later. A picnic even; it's so gorgeous.'

'Coffee would be about it, thank you. You'll see I helped myself a bit last night. Only a cup of tea, which was sad.'

'Come and see my view.'

With a humorous shrug of obedience towards James, Richard followed her into the kitchen. James heard Katherine laugh, still sounding surprised, and then Richard's voice, teasing her.

He clicked his fingers hopefully at the retriever, and she crossed the room to him, looking alert.

'You're very beautiful,' he said to her, feeling her thick fur with pleasure. 'Could you fill me in on any of the details of this? What exactly is going on?' He nodded towards the kitchen. Bella looked willing and knowledgeable, and waved her tail encouragingly. 'Are there things we would all like to know? There are? I'm just too tired now, though.' He stood up, and called out, 'I'll be in the shower.'

Richard and James got on very well. Katherine heard their relaxed voices while she stood in the kitchen filling bread rolls with bacon and tomato, and packing cheeses and apples. James had declined their invitation to join them, and was heading for a lunch party back in London. 'God knows how I'll eat,' he said, chewing his way through digestive biscuits.

'You'll manage. I thought we might walk to Godstow.' She looked at Richard. One arm trailed over the end of her couch; he wore an old green shirt with the sleeves rolled to his elbows.

'Godstow?' He sounded intensely surprised.

'Why not? It's very near, hardly a walk at all. A very traditional Sunday picnic place.'

'I suppose it is', he said, thoughtfully. He stood up and walked to her window. 'Yes, I'd like that.'

James surprised Katherine by kissing her when he left. 'See you this time next year.'

'Don't be ridiculous. It will be before then. I'm so sorry I forgot.'

He shook Richard's hand again. 'Hang on to it,' he said. 'They haven't made a better one yet.'

'I will - no option, really. Good bye, James.'

'What was he talking about?' she asked.

'The Saab, 1980. I told you so!'

'There is something about the wiring of men's brains ... '

'Correct. There is.'

He embraced her and rubbed her back in soothing circles.

'You know', she said, touching his eyebrow. 'That scar has pretty well completely gone. It's remarkable.'

'I liked meeting James.'

'Did you? It wasn't part of a plan, as you could see. I'm glad, though'

23

The long grass brushed against Katherine's bare legs as they walked. She wore a linen shift, reaching just above her knees. Bella ran ecstatically ahead, and then back to round them up. It was the first day of real heat. 'There should be lizards basking on these warm stones', Katherine said, as they wandered the remains of Godstow nunnery. 'Hard to believe all that rain yesterday.' Richard nodded. He was absorbed in the ruins, standing on a stone every now and then to find an overall view.

'I've never been here before,' he said, twice.

Seeing that he was so engrossed, Katherine said 'I know that this is supposed to be a Benson-free day, but - the

Abbess of Godstow was a big landholder there, before the Dissolution.'

'So you said. Around Shillingford, specially.'

'Your memory is amazing, and I get over-enthusiastic. You should stop me.'

'It's fascinating. Think of them riding down there on her business, setting out from here. Horses, carts, parchments to record the money, most of all.'

'And her battles with the Abbot of Oseney over property and mills and fishing rights. Endless.

At least as interesting as Fair Rosamund.'

'Fill me in', he said, and put the picnic bag down in a sheltered corner off the path. They lay in the sun and Katherine talked about King Henry's twelfth century mistress, hidden at Godstow as a nun.

'That's ancient history', Richard said eventually, pouring cider into a mug.

'But it is good, though.'

'It is, quite', he said, lying down and closing his eyes. 'This whole weekend was a good idea.'

In a minute he added, 'If I go to sleep, will you stay awake and make sure Bella doesn't go in the river?'

'No.'

She held her head up on one bent arm, and looked over his face and down the line of his shirt to below his throat. With his eyes still closed, he reached up and pulled her head down to his shoulder.

'Shall we go for another picnic?' he asked. 'Midsummer day?'

'Wonderful.'

'I'll take you to a great Chiltern place. One we haven't been to.'

'Yes, please.'

That evening Katherine's phone went twice. The first was

Richard, home in Oak Farm House. 'I've got a calendar in front of me', he said in his usual brisk way. 'Midsummer Day is a Monday this year. So perhaps the Sunday before would do, three weeks today?'

'Absolutely. I would love it.'

'I have to work on your surprise before then. Secretly, of course. So if you disturb me one evening this week, which I hope you do, ring me before you disturb me.'

'I'll disturb you. Happily.'

When they finished speaking, she sat by the phone, thinking about him. When it rang again, she was still absent minded. It was James.

'I liked the man,' he said. 'But what's with Orlando? Which is serious, if either? Our mother was mentally prepared for a wedding, you know.'

'Perhaps you could arrange one for her? I don't know, James. It's confusing. No, he's not an academic. But yes, we talk about the book. No, he doesn't live in Oxford. Yes, he's fun. I feel bad about Orlando; it happened out of the blue. It's - blown me away.'

After she said goodbye to James she stood at her bedroom window, looking out on to Port Meadow. The horses were standing in sociable groups in the last yellow evening light.

24

'From 1279 comes one of the most remarkable documents of the early Middle Ages - the Hundred Roll. This enquiry into his prerogatives was instigated by Edward I, amassing his resources for war against Scotland. For Benson it is a record unexcelled in detail until modern times. Every tenant of the

village is named, and we know the size of his landholding, his legal obligations and status, and the nature of his church attendance. His rent to the lord of his manor is broken down into cash payments, regular work obligations, and renders in kind, from eggs and cheese and livestock, to hunting dogs or gauntlet gloves. We know his individual taxes, from swingeing death duties, to payments on the marriage of daughters or the education of sons, and, always, tithes to the church. We know if he may graze cows on the meadow, or run pigs in the woodland. We know if he may fish in the millpond or gather firewood for fuel. We know if he may brew beer and we know if he may rest on Sundays and Holy Days. It is a zoom-lens picture of a community more than seven hundred years ago.'

Zoom-lens is a bit colloquial, Katherine thought, and stopped writing. She gazed into space. In a minute she left her desk altogether, and lay on the couch. James's question of yesterday drifted unclearly in her mind, and Zinnia's remarks about loneliness, and images of a wife and three small children. She thought of the little kneeling figures in the church carving. A baby, Thomas. Then, making her slowly swallow, came images of Richard's face, looking down at her in bed, his lips slightly drawn back, and teeth white. He was glad to have met James, he said. James liked him. The telephone rang, and with a jump she stood up and stumbled as she went towards it. It was Orlando.

In Benson, late in the afternoon, Eric and Zinnia tied their boat up at its appointed mooring. They had actually taken it out and had a pleasant two hours afloat, with Eric steering while Zinnia sat out and polished cutlery, ready for summer visitors aboard. Eric was playing a tape, one of his regular Kristofferson favourites, and the music emerged from his two speakers, one at each end of *Halcyon Daze*. He wore beige trousers over nautical deck shoes with safe soles, and a white polo shirt, neatly tucked in at the waist. After the boat was fastened, they continued to sit awhile.

'Turn that sound down a bit', Zinnia suggested. 'Everyone mightn't like it.'

'It's already pretty quiet. Okay' He reached inside to the controls of his player. As he did so, he heard Zinnia say 'Hallo! Nice day for it!'

He emerged and saw Richard walking towards them from up river. Bella was beside him, looking wet, muddy and triumphant.

'Not bad', Richard answered, reaching them. 'Yesterday was better, though. Hotter. Garden party weather.'

Zinnia looked at him, standing with his hands in his pockets. He looked brown, had got a touch of the sun. No sign of the girl, Katherine, today.

'Been far?' Eric said, wondering if there was enough beer in his Vacuum-Pak bag.

'Only to Shillingford. I was at work most of the day, but it seemed too nice to go straight home.'

'Beautiful stretch there, Shillingford.'

'It is, both the river and the village. Even the bridge.'

'I always think the bridge makes it more interesting,' Zinnia said. 'Eric, are you going to offer us a drink? Richard?'

'I won't, thank you. Plenty of things to do at home today.'

'Visitors?'

He shook his head. She looked inquisitive, and he laughed. 'Not today. You have to allow some thinking-time, too, Zinnia ... '

Eric was relieved about his supplies. 'See you tomorrow, then, Richard. And you, Bella. But you'll need a shampoo before you cross my pub door.'

'She'll get a hose, at least. See you!'

Zinnia watched him go for a minute, and then said, 'Thinking-time.' She shook her head. 'I'll have a drink, anyway, please. A shandy.'

'He's keen enough. Give him time. He's quiet.'

'He's had years. She's very nice. Wants to see him play cards.'

'I bet.'

'Eric! She is all eyes for him, I'll give you that.'

The Kristofferson tape ended, and Eric reached inside and switched it off. They sat comfortably together in the silence. The boat rocked slightly.

'It's a waste,' Zinnia said. 'With him looking the way he does.'

25

The following week Olivia watched Katherine move around the Gallery, straightening pictures, moving pots a few centimetres on their stands, placing pieces of jewellery square on their coloured background. Then she returned to the desk and sat behind it, bending her head over the still hand-written listings for the autumn exhibition. She looked like an advertisement for an affair, Olivia thought - blossoming, but inward-looking. Her skin was tanned, and she touched her hair, untidying it and then smoothing it. Her clothes, a loose cream top over a sarong-like skirt today, seemed as mildly neglectful as ever, but wrapped themselves gracefully around her.

She laughed with delight at Olivia's remarks, but asked few questions. Olivia thought of Orlando, and sighed. He had rung Joe to say he would be longer yet in America, and visit Rio, too, before returning to Oxford.

Now Katherine looked up from the exhibition list, and

stretched her arms above her head, pulling the loose plait up, and letting it flop back. 'What about this music, Liv? It's repeating itself.'

'So it is.' Olivia removed the plainsong tape, and replaced it with Vaughan Williams.

'You missed Piers Finch yesterday. As urbane as ever. Is that what urbane means?'

'Oh, yes. I think Piers is urbane, definitely. Is that where the blue jug has gone?' Katherine gestured towards a newly arranged shelf, and Olivia nodded. 'That's good!' Piers Finch had bought an expensive jug, of impeccable taste.

'And, yes, he asked after you', Olivia went on. They groaned simultaneously, and then laughed. 'Your book.'

'I've finished the first half, and posted it off. The editor may even buy me lunch in Henley very soon.' She looked so suddenly animated that Olivia said, hopefully,

'Is this editor a man?'

Katherine stared at her for a moment, and then laughed and shrugged. 'Oh, Livvy. Yes, Tim is a man, but I hardly know him. Gay, possibly, now I give the matter thought. Yes, probably.'

Any time now, she would tell Olivia what was happening. James meeting Richard had made a first crack in a wall.

She went to the back of the shop, and down the basement stairs, walking as though every movement pleased her.

For a minute Olivia watched her. She had been going announce that she was starting hypnotherapy tomorrow, with Meredith, but it would have to wait. The door bell clanged, and a middle-aged man came in. Dawn turned off the footpath close behind him, and he caught the door behind him and held it for her. Olivia noticed Dawn give him a long glance as she thanked him, before he strolled towards a shelf and bent over a bowl, and looked up again, at a collage on the wall above it. He had wide, relaxed shoulders. Dawn walked past him, and spoke to Olivia without moving her lips. 'Who is the beautiful man?'

'I've no idea', Olivia muttered, about to go and greet him. 'Probably a potter, though. Look at his hands.' The man had picked up a wooden dish, and was carefully turning it over.

At the moment she said 'Are you looking for something special, or ... ?', she glanced around. Katherine had appeared at the top of the stairs, and was looking at the man with radiant surprise. 'Why are you here?' she said, moving towards him. The man nodded politely to Olivia, but spoke to Katherine. 'I thought you might be finishing about now. Are you?'

'Well, yes.'

She stood close to him, not quite touching. 'Yes, I am. Dawn has just arrived ... ' She gestured towards Dawn and Olivia. 'This is Richard,' she said, as though everything was explained.

'It seems he had a day off in lieu of the Bank Holiday,' Olivia told Joe that evening. 'Decided to come and see specially the wooden pieces we've got at the moment. I vaguely remember her saying she had met someone who works with wood.'

'Where does he live, did you say?' Joe was reading the sports section of the newspaper as well as conversing.

'Benson, where else? He really came to see her, of course. But we did talk for a while, before they disappeared off.'

'And?'

'I liked him. He couldn't be more opposite to Orlando, though. Fair not dark, older, more outdoorsy, less academic, feet on the ground up to the thighs, I'd say. I was surprised. You could tell they were waiting to be alone, but enjoying the postponement, too.'

'Your over-lively imagination.'

'He was very funny about the eclipse, and some of the things people in his pub say will happen.'

'Is it serious?'

'Serious for Orlando, I think.'

Joe shrugged, and returned to the paper. Olivia poured herself more wine, and thought briefly about Katherine and Richard looking at each other in her Gallery, and then about Orlando. He and Katherine had always seemed equally matched in academic abstraction, but perhaps that didn't work, such a balance. She and Joe were very different. Then she thought about Meredith Baker-Lynn, and beginning hypnosis therapy tomorrow.

26

'Are you going to make a regular thing of this?' the archivist complained, in a friendly voice. She was carrying a long wooden box on her shoulder, and lowered it on to several reading tables pushed together. Katherine had asked to see the same map on two consecutive days, and was waiting with protective white gloves already on. 'Here we go then.'

Between them, they lifted the map out, and unrolled it gently.

'Thank you, again.'

Katherine smiled with pleasure at it. She held the edges down with the smooth leather weights, and bent over the faded, beautiful colours. After her first excited survey yesterday, she had rushed away to the telephone. Today she had hours in hand, and was going to be methodical. She forgot everything else, and moved from chair to chair around the table as she studied it. When she got to the crossroad labelled Roke Elm, she counted the routes aloud.

' ... five, six, seven. Yes!'

She got out paper and pencil, and made a rough copy of it.

When she got home to Wolvercote she looked at her sketch again, and shuffled her notes for a brief instant before beginning writing.

> *'A beautiful map of Benson parish survives from 1788. It is by the noted cartographer Richard Davis, and was commissioned to show ' the open fields of Benson in which the pieces of land titheable to Berwick lay intermingled with those of Benson and Ewelme.' The strips of land owing a tenth of their produce to each parish are colour-coded, and their intricate patch-work pattern is clear topographic proof of the ancient unity of this area, and the primacy of Benson within the territory. Davis's map names fields, furlongs and closes, and these names are a rich source of historical extrapolation, from family names familiar from medieval sources (Cadwells' Field or Moggeput Wood) to names reminding us of the hard work of generations of farmers: Clay Field, Stoney Lands, Foul Slough Field. His map also shows trees, hedges, boundaries, roads and lanes. Most interesting in this respect is the unexplained meeting place of seven routes called Roke Elm ... '*

Later in the day, after frowning at her own sketch again, Katherine rang the library.

'Would it be possible to get a copy of such a big map?'

The archivist sounded doubtful. 'Some of our maps have been photographed before, and we keep negatives in the file, of course. Not this one. Why don't you come in and speak to our photographic department about it? See what they might do.'

Simon from photography was a large man with sausage-like fingers and an Australian accent. He had Davis's map out and was measuring it when Katherine arrived.

'This is going to be a tricky number,' he said. 'I presume you want the colour? So it'll have to be slides, not photos. Okay? In that case ... ' He blocked out patches along the map. 'We could take ten slides for you. That would cover it, five down and two across. Get what I mean?'

She nodded.

'That's the good news,' Simon said. 'Bad news is that we've got a backlog and someone on maternity leave and summer coming up. Might be as long as two months, even more. Do you still want it?'

She counted on her fingers. 'I might need it for illustrating a book. Could I have it by October, at the latest?'

'Sure. Easily.'

They filled in the form together, with Simon dictating the exact photographic requirements.

'Will you be using the map any more today?' he said, when they had finished. His friendly manner made him seem familiar.

'No', she answered. 'I need a change of gear now. I'm going to go shopping for midsummer clothes, whatever they are ... '

'Warm ones, in this climate,' he said, and watched her admiringly as she went.

27

She drove to Oak Farm House in the early evening, with her Roke Elm sketch beside her. It's a different country, she thought, comparing the drive with her winter journeys along the same road. Chestnuts were glamorously white and pink, and the river was invisible behind hedges solid with leaf and clusters of trees. The pale yellows and limes of early summer were turning a darker green. The village names had new, sensual associations. The sun had come out after a cloudy day, and threw long shadows across the road.

Richard was in his workshop when she arrived, and came out shutting the door firmly behind him. 'Hallo,' she said, drawing in the smell of wood and sawdust from him.

'Hallo.' He looked at her in the intent way he had, as if she might have changed infinitesimally since he last held her.

'You were right about the paths.'

'I know. You rang me yesterday.'

She bit him gently. 'Now I can show you my drawing.'

'I'd love you to show me your artistic work. Beer? Food?'

They sat in the garden.

'They all had names then,' she said, passing him her sketch of the Roke Elm portion of the map. 'Except the only one which does have a name now, on the Ordnance Survey. Tidmarsh Lane.'

On Davis's map, she recalled, the unnamed lane ran between two hedgerows, drawn as dense lines of curly trees, nearly touching across the narrow path.

'Shimming Lane,' Richard said. He was watching swallows swoop above them.

'Shimming? I wish it were called something more significant, like Silchester Road. You know I believe it's a lost bit of Roman road. Or Courthouse Way would be nice for my even newer theory. Where did you get that name from?'

'I thought it was you,' he said, turning from the swallows.

'I'm afraid not.'

He poured her some more beer.

'Don't', she said. 'I have to drive back.' But she took the glass, and held it. The air was so mild it seemed almost to have substance, to add an opaque sheen to the garden colours. The strong spicy smell of mock orange floated from the untidy bush by the door, and Bella lolled behind Richard's chair.

'You don't, actually.' Richard trapped her ankle with his feet, legs stretched out.

'I have to open up the Gallery tomorrow morning, so I can't be late. But maybe ... Olivia has started hypnosis therapy, for goodness sake. With Dr Baker-Lynn. That's where she will be first thing tomorrow. When she is completely relaxed they talk about Olivia's past, which seems to have been perfectly happy and ordinary, so I can't imagine how they spin that out. Then they visualise conception.'

Richard laughed. 'I'm trying, really trying, not to make any obvious suggestions.'

'Thank you. But Olivia is so funny about it herself. And she is happier, and looks well.'

'So it might all happen, and then he can take the credit.'

'Who cares, if it's happened?'

'Isn't she married to a doctor?'

'She is. Joe.'

'So what does he think?'

'He doesn't know. I have a theory that it might be him, the problem, but he doesn't want to have the tests here in the town where he knows all the medics, so he's leaving it.'

'Yes, I can imagine that.'

Something made Katherine think of his children, and she was silent for a minute. For the first time in her life, she envisaged herself pregnant, walking slowly.

Richard got up with a single energetic movement. Bella lifted her head to watch him. 'What about this?' he said, taking her hand to pull her to her feet. 'We go inside. We make very unhealthy bacon and eggs and tomatoes. You okay my shopping list for the picnic next Sunday. We go to bed early. We get up early enough tomorrow for you to go back to Oxford and open up the Gallery while Olivia goes to Iffley.'

'How on earth did you remember it is Iffley?' Katherine put her arms around him inside the kitchen. 'You never forget anything.'

28

James and Katherine took their mother out to lunch on Saturday, her birthday.

'Any decisions?' James asked her when they met.

'Yes, maybe,' said Katherine. 'Please, please don't say anything to these two yet,' she pointed to Elizabeth and Diane, walking ahead of them on a Kensington footpath. 'I can't face the post-mortems, and anyway, it's her day.'

'Okay, message received.' She still looked glowing and tanned.

At the end of the afternoon they returned to Elizabeth's house, and Katherine prepared to leave.

'Thank you, darling,' her mother said. 'I always had the best parties. It's the time of year.'

'It is a great time of year,' Katherine agreed. 'I love it.'

She took the train back to Oxford, and collected her car from the station car park, and drove to Benson once more.

It was nearly ten o'clock when she arrived at Oak Farm House, but still very light. She parked outside, and carried her bags in. She heard running footsteps inside as she turned the key in the door, and then a bark.

'Hallo! Did he leave you here to wait for me? That was nice of him, wasn't it.' She bent down and rubbed the dog's warm head. 'You are the most cheerful person I know. Boringly, predictably cheerful. No, you don't!' She pulled Bella away from the bag of parcels from the Kensington delicatessen, and moved it into the kitchen. On the bench she found a note from Richard. 'Don't start without me. Love you. Look after our dog.' His writing was big and untidy.

She walked to the end of the garden. It smelled wonderful after London. After some moments there, she went inside and started a bath.

'I've got a present for you,' Richard said, after he hugged her, with his usual intent glance.

'But it isn't as I promised, carbon dated and historic. It's new.' He smelled of smoke and the pub, and threw his shirt off into the wash. 'That's it, until Tuesday. Good!' He pulled on a clean shirt, but left it unbuttoned.

'Wait there', he said, and went out of the room. His persistent calm seemed altered; he seemed faintly - Katherine felt for the word - faintly glittery. When he came back both hands were behind his back.

'Choose one.'

'Left.'

He pulled his left arm round, and gave her a small bowl. It was of pale fawn wood, as thin as porcelain, with a fine black line running all over it, like a beautiful, erratic spider's web. On the rim a knot in the wood had broken out, leaving a hole picked out of the edge like a small hook. She took it from him, and it felt like a smooth egg shell in her hand.

'Richard. I don't know what to say. This is the nicest bowl I have ever seen ... '

'Now the other hand.'

He brought his right arm round and opened his hand. There was a second bowl, in the same pale black-lined wood. It was slightly larger, and had a coin-sized untidy edged gap on the rim.

'This is what it's supposed to do.'

He took the smaller bowl, and sat it inside the other, and turned it a few degrees. With a small hollow click, the hook on the rim of one fitted into the hook of the other, linking them.

'There you are', he said. 'Need I comment on symbolism, and things like that? Or of course, they are good at standing on their own, too.' He separated them and passed them back to her.

She held one in each hand, and then put them together.

'I love them. I absolutely love them. I've never seen anything like them.' She kissed him. 'Thank you very much. They are just ... spectacularly nice.' She kissed him again.

'Beech', he said. 'Local Chiltern wood. It's specially knotty, so I thought it might work.'

She put them on a shelf beside them, and when they moved upstairs she took them to the bedroom and stood them beside his other bowls, close together. In bed, though, she still felt his slight edge of sharpness, and he made love to her without saying a word. Afterwards, he stroked her hair and looked at her eyes and mouth, and said, 'Kathy, darling. I'm sorry. I took my eye off your watch. I didn't ... '

'I haven't even got my damn watch on. Nothing matters. Come here.' She held him, and said, 'Promise to tell me some of your best dreams in the morning?' Richard's reliable dreams had become regular stories to start the day.

She nuzzled his neck, and turned on her side. Soon she dozed, and then was properly asleep. Richard lay separating pieces of her long unplaited hair, and trailing them through his fingers. Just before the early dawn, a few hours later, he fell asleep.

29

'Welcome to midsummer!' Katherine pulled the curtains open the next morning. It was raining.

Richard came and stood beside her. 'Not real midsummer until tomorrow. This will be all right', he said, looking at the sky. 'It's passing stuff.' He looked calm and relaxed again, and his hands were warm on her shoulders.

By late in the morning patches of blue sky interrupted the rain, and they arrived in Swyncombe, high in the Chilterns.

'Near here,' he said, 'Was a customary high point for midsummer fires.'

'If you say so ... '

'So where else can I bring an obsessive historian?'

'Can we look in the church first?'

'If you insist.'

'I do.'

He had a rucksack of food and drink, and heaved it on to one shoulder as they entered the little flint building. Katherine looked around with pleasure. 'The oldest and the least messed around with in the Hundreds', she said. Richard rolled his eyes in pretend boredom, but looked briefly around the small plain interior. He looked more often at Katherine, glancing at the roof, and touching the pew ends affectionately. She caught his eyes, and said, 'You're supposed to be thinking about architecture.'

'I am.' he said. 'Believe me.'

Out in the fitful sun they walked side by side along the ancient Ridgeway path out into the hills.

'Wait,' Katherine said. 'Slow down.' He walked as effortlessly as if the ground were flat. She got her sunglasses out and put them on, and took his hand again. Every now and then he paused to scoop a handful of twigs and branches from the path's edge. Bella ran ahead and returned to check on them. In a few minutes they had reached the high point and the round tumulus of the earthwork.

'This'll do,' he said, and threw the rucksack down. The Chilterns stretched in all directions around them. They could see the spires of village churches, separated by green hill tops and damp patches of woodland. Farms were laid out like children's pictures, neat houses with symmetrical outbuildings, circled by white fences. Between them and Benson lay the bare steep sides of Sliding Hill, and a pig farm, with individual houses for each occupant lined up like suburban streets.

'That is just so satisfactory, on *Swyn*combe.'

Richard nodded and smiled.

While she sat on a rug and watched, he made a hearth circle of stones, and then a mound of twigs and scraps of wood. After some searching, he found two bigger broken branches, and perched them on the top. Bella joined in.

'No, Bella. Your pieces are much too wet, but thank you all the same.' In a minute, he knelt back. 'The whole thing's a bit damp, actually. It will be smoky, but it'll go. It needs to be hot enough to cook lamb chops so they don't kill us.'

As the fire started, the sun above them grew steadily warmer, and the clouds drifted away.

'It's doing the fire magic, exactly as it should.' Katherine said. The fire made her feel elated. A group of walkers passed a little distance away, with heavy boots and maps in plastic envelopes dangling around their necks. She set out plates and bread and a bottle of wine and glasses, balancing them carefully. She stood up to pass him some wine.

'The view is amazing,' she said, looking around again. 'And I have never been here. I should have.'

He was turning the lamb carefully, prodding at the fire and waving smoke from his eyes. She held his glass for a moment longer, watching his hands.

'There's an unidentified part of Benson called Fernfield in Domesday Book, and it was probably somewhere here on Swyncombe Down. Here's your glass.'

For a moment she thought he hadn't heard. When he turned she saw instantly that the tension of last night had returned to his eyes. He took the wine and swallowed half and set the glass down carefully.

He reached up and pulled her sunglasses off. 'I can't see your eyes with those things on', he said, and threw them towards the rug. He kissed her roughly, pressing her teeth hard against her lips. Then with great deliberation he sat her down and sat beside her. Again he was silent, and Katherine felt uneasy. The voices of the walkers floated back, retreating towards Sliding Hill. She turned to look at them, and he spoke.

'Plenty of bracken around. Not a puzzle.'

After an instant of confusion she realised he was referring to the name, Fernfield.

Before she could respond, he spoke again.

'I was going to talk about this last night, but the moment didn't come.'

She thought of him last night, and felt a wave of affection roll powerfully over her, mingling now with her own tension. She reached out to touch his face, and he put her hand aside and almost shouted. 'Katherine!'

There was such anger and sadness in his face that she pulled back. A ball of fright arrived in her chest from nowhere, pumping. Then the words poured out.

'How do you think I know the things we talk about? About whether this was Fernfield, for God's sake. Of course it was wretched Fernfield. About Roke Elm, about the ruins by the church, about the ... I don't know, the ferry, anything!' He leapt to his feet, and she shrank back, but he went to the fire and pulled the meat off it, talking all the time. 'Do you think I read your documents and sit in your libraries? You know I don't. I work in a timber yard, remember?' He was wildly wrapping the chops in newspaper, dragged from the bag.

'Can't Bella eat them, if you don't want them?' Katherine said, timidly. Her throat was dry. He ignored her.

'Didn't you know? There were some days I was so sure you knew ... We talked about Ellen and our children, and I thought ... how I used to be able to see more stars ... ' He plunged the newspaper parcel into the rucksack, breathing heavily. 'This is where I was born, Katherine! How do you think I know about working on Benson Church?' He had fat on his hands and wiped them on the grass with big swiping movements.

'Plenty of people were born here. It doesn't make them ... ' her voice tailed off. Her mouth was so dry she could hardly speak.

'No, Katherine.' Now he spoke very slowly, separating out the words. 'No. I was born here while the church was being built. Over the old one. Beside the ruined house.' She looked at him with huge eyes. 'Oh, God. I'm trying not to make this frightening. I was born a very long time ago, Katherine.'

She was standing and backing off from him. He took her hand between his familiar rough palms and she dragged it away. The pumping in her chest was unbearable. Incoherent thoughts hovered in her mind. He had the old blue-green shirt on, the exact colour of his eyes, and Bella was running towards them. At last she spoke. 'Seven hundred years?' The pulse in her throat nearly choked her. 'Is that what you're telling me?' He was silent. She looked at him one minute more, and then turned and ran, down the old Ridgeway, slipping and stumbling, until she reached the road.

Bella followed her excitedly, until Richard called her back. He held the dog's collar for a moment, saying nothing. The anger had gone from his face, leaving it sad. With uncharacteristically slow movements, he stamped the fire out methodically, and scattered the ashes. Then he packed the rucksack and heaved it up. 'Come on, Bell', he said. 'That's probably it.'

30

Katherine ran off the Ridgeway onto the road, and almost into the path of a red car, which braked and swerved to avoid her. As it pulled away uphill she stood still at last, shaking.

She would have to walk downhill, she thought, the other way, back to Benson. She set off, half-running, half-walking. In spite of her exertions, she felt cold. After a few minutes, she heard an engine behind her, and looked around to see the red car again. It overtook her, and then stopped. The driver got out. It was Piers Finch.

'Can I give you a ride somewhere?' She gave a heaving kind of sob, and he went on smoothly.

'I've got two passengers who have been at a birthday party.'

As she drew nearer she could see two little girls in the back seat, nearly covered by balloons.

'Yes, please,' she said at last, and got in. He began driving. The landscape looked blurry to her, and passed in slow motion.

'Where to?' She turned and looked at Piers blankly. 'We're going to Wallingford, to take Zoe home', he said, helpfully. 'Is that any good to you?' What on earth was the matter with her, he wondered. Had she been attacked? She looked stunned, the marvellous hair flying in a mess around her. When they passed through Ewelme she seemed to recover, and said,

'Could you go via Benson? I've left my car there, at the top of Tidmarsh Lane.'

Even as she said it, she realised her car keys were inside Richard's house. Only one thing at a time, she thought, and repeated, 'Yes, the top of Tidmarsh Lane. I'll show you.'

At Oak Farm House, she got out and thanked him. 'Good

bye!' She looked properly into the back seat for the first time. 'Thank you both, too.'

'Are you sure you're all right?' Piers said.

'Absolutely.' He looked at her doubtfully, but glanced at the children, and then drove away.

Almost before his car had disappeared, Richard arrived. He pulled up and through the Saab's sloping back window she saw Bella pacing and turning.

Richard got out and released the dog without speaking. He held out his hand to Katherine.

'Your sunglasses.' She took them.

'Could I go inside and get my car keys?'

'Of course.'

He unlocked the front door and held it open for her. She stepped inside and saw her car keys lying on the table, beside her set of his house keys. It was very quiet in the house. She took her keys. Richard was still at the door. When she reached him again, he spoke calmly.

'I know it seems a bad choice. I'm mad, or a freak. I don't like it either, Kathy.'

She went past him and unlocked her car. She threw it into gear, and drove away.

Richard unpacked the rucksack slowly, and threw the meat into a bin. 'Chops, so no, Bella, you would choke', he said, mechanically. He opened his back doors and stepped into his garden. For a while he stood by the log seat, kicking at it lightly while he stared ahead of him. He returned inside and lay on the couch on his back. In a minute he put the palms of both hands over his face, and made a frustrated, groaning noise into them. Then he went into his workshop and selected a piece of wood. He sharpened the chisel carefully against the lathe, and worked concentratedly for several hours, only stopping to reach for his phone.

Katherine lay on her bed until it was dark, and beyond. She felt empty and hungry, but too sick to eat. She had been near to something dangerous. What did he mean, she had known? She forced her mind to places it had avoided, and held it on them. It was like trying to keep a shaky focus still. There were not many books in his house; she had noticed that. Maps, but only those any driver might have. Most people she know were academics; such a small number of books might be quite average for other people. But for someone who knew about Dorchester Abbey owning St Helen's Church for a couple of hundred medieval years? About exchanging knives to register a land purchase? That Henley was once merely the port for Benson manor? Could someone who seemed to spend little time with books know those things? And the Roke Elm roads. Why had she talked pleasantly about those as if they were at a seminar, for God's sake. Never wonder how he knew? Because she hadn't wanted to, of course. It was exciting. Her eyes felt hot and dry. It had been exciting, a fever of exploration that had continued in bed.

The telephone rang and she was as frightened as if someone were battering the door. When it stopped ringing she got up, stiffly, and made a drink of neat gin over ice, and then poured it out and made tea. She thought of the woad plant, and talking about the Abbess of Godstow, and Richard pointing out where the Benson ferry had run. They flew to her mind so fluently she knew they had been uneasily absorbed, all along. She thought of his rough hands building the fire today, and gave a moan. The phone went again, and this time she answered it immediately.

'Are you all right?' he said. 'I just wanted to know you were home. You drove off like a bat out of ... '

He sounded calm and normal, faintly tired.

'I'm all right. But I don't want to see you.'

'Ever?'

'I don't know. Maybe.'

'I love you, Katherine. Think about that and not everything else.'

'Maybe. But I can't now.'

She hung up. I'm too scared just now, she added silently. And why do you talk like that? With that rural accent? Anger swamped her, then misery.

After a few hours sleep, she woke early, with a head-ache. I need to eat, she thought, and mixed a plate of cereal. She swallowed without tasting it. From the jumble of her night's thoughts one idea had floated to the top. He had taken her preoccupations and made them obsessions, yes, obsessions, as Orlando had said. His house, his town, his hills and his river had merged with what she was looking for. Her real life was sliding away under a kind of history, in an old territory, centuries ago. He had pushed it too far.

31

At the Gallery she said to Olivia, 'Did you say Dawn wanted a few days off this week?'

'She wants to go to Wimbledon. Once a year she has a passion for tennis.'

'I don't mind covering for her. I'd like to. I'll work every day, if I can.'

'Sure, that would be good. Lots of tourists, we'll be busy, I hope.' Katherine looked different this morning, intense and tired. 'I want to go and see Sven and Heather, too, this week.

She tells me he has a garage full of pots no one has seen, and a new glaze. She's his great advocate now.'

Katherine made an effort.

'Haven't we been here before?' There had been at least two other women in Sven's past who had advertised his pottery to them.

'Yes, but it's different when it's your sister. Much more worrying. And interesting.'

'It must be.'

A customer came in and after much choosing bought two white crackle-glazed dishes.

'And would you believe it and can you bear it?', Olivia said as the bell clanged when the door closed, 'She's going to use them as ash trays.'

She filed the invoice copy in her desk. Her mermaid earrings dangled, one black, one red. Joe had told her that Orlando was due back soon, but it was not a good time to mention it. Katherine was fiddling with the till, almost but not quite depressing the keys.

'Guess who I saw over the week end?' she said abruptly. 'Piers Finch. He was collecting his daughter and a friend from a birthday party.' Suddenly tears were running down her face.

'Oh, Kathy.' Olivia rushed to put her arm round her. 'I know his hair is terrible and everything, but not that bad? What's the matter?'

Katherine made a noise that was half laugh and half sob. 'Not Piers. Richard.'

'Richard. Something with Richard? But he looks so ... ' Dawn's word, beautiful, seemed inappropriate. 'So kind.'

'Kind!' said Katherine vehemently. 'That's just what he might not be, kind!'

They had had a Sunday outing, Olivia worked out, which had ended badly. Piers had been incidental to the crisis. She possibly wanted to see Richard again, but probably wouldn't.

'And I don't want to do any more work on my book for a while', she said.

'Well, okay,' Olivia said soothingly. 'But be warned. I could offer to whisk you off to Meredith ... '

'To Meredith?'

'Yes, For primal screaming. His upset patients do it. He's had a petition from two lots of neighbours to step up his sound proofing.'

Katherine looked at her in horror. 'But do you?'

'Oh, no. Ours is the opposite. We lie there peacefully.'

'We?'

'He lies beside me. To share my trance and communicate through it.' She laughed so much that Katherine had to join in.

That evening she found the day's mail on the mat inside her door. In a creamy envelope was a letter from Tim Rothwell.

'What timing', she said as she opened it.

'We are all delighted with your draft so far. We particularly like the clarity you have brought to the very complex questions of the early Anglo-Saxon years, and the maps which show how early boundaries may still survive unrecognised, in roads, footpaths, and modern parish outlines. There is increasing depth and warmth, of course, as written documents proliferate, and we look forward to a more people-orientated history as the Middle Ages advance.' Oh, yes? Katherine muttered bitterly. Then came one of Tim's personal asides. 'I must say I had no idea how much info. you could glean from Domesday Book. Fascinating!' It ended with a promise to ring her about the Henley lunch, at which they might wish to consider, *inter alia,* the professional arranging of illustrations - and finally, an expression of the confidence with which they looked forward to the second half of her book.

She put the letter on the table, and spread her hands, palms down, over it. How could she write a book about it?

32

Early on Friday afternoon, Katherine was wrapping one of Dawn's ceramic bottles for a customer, and slipping in a fact sheet about the artist. 'You know Dawn Hammond works in here sometimes?' she said to the woman, who had a pleasant unmade-up face and dull navy blue clothes. 'In fact, you would normally find her on a Friday. Just this week she's not here. So if you would ever like to talk to her about ... ' She tailed off. The door had opened and Richard walked in, with a box under one arm. She swept her eyes over him and away, back to her customer. Her heart pounded.

' ... interesting. I will, thank you.'

With great concentration, she took the woman's credit card, and put it through the machine. It seemed slow. She heard Olivia and Richard talking behind her. 'What is the music you're playing?' the woman said conversationally, as she signed her form.

Katherine clenched both hands. 'Grieg, I think. Yes, probably Grieg.'

'It makes a real difference. In some places it's so loud you have to go straight out again.'

'Yes.'

'And, of course, some awful stuff, too.'

'Yes, sometimes.'

'Anyway, this Grieg is very nice.'

'Good.'

At last, the woman slowly finished replacing her card in her handbag, and left the shop, clanging the bell behind her. With an enormous breath, Katherine turned around.

Richard was smiling.

'I have a feeling she wouldn't like Eric's musical selections.'

Katherine looked at him, shaking her head slightly. She let the deep breath out.

'I think not.'

Richard put his box down on the table in a business-like way, and reached into it.

'These are yours.'

He got out her two beech wood bowls, and stood them beside it. Olivia looked immediately interested.

'Katherine? These are yours?' She handled them, and Katherine showed her how they could be fitted together. 'They are wonderful', Olivia said. 'We could do with more if you ever have a surplus!' She expressed it very charmingly, and then said, 'I'll be here in the catalogues, Katherine', and disappeared down the stairs.

'I miss you,' Richard said immediately. 'I thought you might feel better if I came to say it here, in a public kind of place.' He shrugged his shoulders.

'I was cross. Am cross, but I over-reacted. You frightened me.'

'I'm sorry.'

There was a silence, and then with a laugh he said, 'And our time has come!'

'What do you mean, our time?'

'We are invited for a day on *Halcyon Daze* on Sunday. I was to relay it to you if Zinnia didn't see you between now and then.'

'Oh, Richard!' Irritation and relief mingled in her.

'Nowhere could be safer than aboard with Eric and Zinnia. You'll hardly manoeuvre out of the boat yard before cards and Pimms and minor repairs and back again ... '

Olivia heard them both laugh, and when she ventured upstairs again, Richard had gone.

'He's pretty nice, Kathy. He could sell this stuff, you know.' She picked up the smaller bowl and smoothed it. She glanced furtively at Katherine. 'And we'd want his picture in our catalogue ... '

'Olivia! Let me be confused in peace!'

She picked up her bowls and packed them into their box, careful with their frail wooden curves. She thought of the workshop where they had been made, and imagined Bella bounding in and out of it from the garden. She missed Oak Farm House.

Perhaps to believe him fraudulent or mad was less frightening than the alternative.

33

Zinnia's boating outfit was cut-off jeans corseting her hips and thighs, and a man's denim shirt over it, open low. She wore wobbly high heeled sandals, but stepped around the narrow strips of deck deftly. Eric wore beige shorts and a neat shirt with a quiet check pattern. His baseball cap, with yacht club motif, was very large, and covered most of his tidy hair.

Katherine watched Richard most of all, in old shorts and one of his darker blue shirts, sleeves rolled up. It was the first time she had seen him since his visit to the Gallery, and she had driven straight to the boatyard. He and Eric already had a glass of beer to hand, and were coiling ropes, very nautically.

Richard stood up and came over to Katherine.

'Hallo,' He took a basket from her and then took her hand. He was as warm as ever.

'Hallo.'

'I brought this,' she said to Zinnia, passing her a foil-wrapped ginger cake.

'Come on board, Katherine,' Zinnia said warmly. She proudly showed her the saloon cabin and all its fittings, and beyond it a hatchway down to their bedroom, where a neat double bed was made up, closely surrounded by cupboards, lockers, and a dressing table, incongruous with make up and little bottles displayed on it. 'I could move tomorrow,' Zinnia said. 'But actually,' she looked in Eric's direction and lowered her voice theatrically, 'Actually, I don't know how long I'll last without some land life. You know, shopping, getting your hair done. Although you do meet other people along the river, more than you'd think.'

'I expect you do.'

'Richard'll be pleased you're here,' Zinnia said as they went out on deck again. 'Everyone needs someone behind them, don't they? The less they look as though they need it the more they do, I often think.'

It was a very hot day, without a breath of wind, and the river was crowded. Richard glanced ashore as Eric cast off, fumbling with the rope and kneeling to reach it in the water while Zinnia steered for a moment, and Katherine looked discreetly away. They passed successfully between two long boats, where families were being inducted into boating skills before a canal boat holiday, and made for the centre of the river. As they chugged slowly upstream, Zinnia began to unpack Pimms and lemonade and cucumber, and Eric called out from his place at the rudder, 'Get us some music, would you, Zin. Break out and play Shania Twain. Show Katherine it's not just the oldies we go for ... '

'Oh but I like the oldies,' Katherine said, and realised it

was quite true. Cline and Kristofferson and Jim Reeves and Billie Jo Spears had seamlessly merged with other passions this season. For some reason she thought of the dried woad leaves in her kitchen, and resolved to start fermenting and boiling them tonight, squeezing out some colour.

'Pimms, Katherine?'

'Please, Zinnia.'

'And take this one to Richard up the front, would you?'

She sat beside him in the sun, not quite touching, and he watched her as though they had been apart a long time. They talked about the boat and the music and the school teacher Katherine had met in the King's Head, who now wanted to bring an A-level Art group in to the Gallery. But when Eric called out that their view of Benson was surprisingly different, even this little distance away, and that now you could really see how it lay on a curve of the Thames, they both only nodded and agreed. Their old topics were not safe ground any more. Nothing must provoke another strange outburst from him, Katherine knew. She could not bear it, and in the same way, she was afraid of him touching her. When she left the boat she would go home to Wolvercote again. For a while, everything needed to be kept on the surface only. Richard and the history of Benson had got themselves in a muddled knot.

34

After several more days when Benson work lay untouched, Katherine was galvanised by Tim Rothwell's phone call.

'This putative lunch,' he said. 'I fancy a Friday afternoon by the river. How about tomorrow?' They arranged to meet in Henley the next day. 'I'll make the booking,' he said, 'I look forward to it.'

Katherine looked on her watch. Ten in the morning. I should go in and do some work, she told herself, or I will have nothing new to speak to him about at all.

In the library, the readers had changed. In place of the tired-looking students of a month ago, now departed for post-exam frivolities, were older men and women, sometimes working in couples. Many were Americans, cramming research into their summer vacations, and next to Katherine sat an immaculate looking grey-haired woman looking through a German-English dictionary, resting it on a pile of photocopied documents. She smiled politely, and pulled some of her papers aside to make space as Katherine hauled the big Hundred Roll volumes from shelf to table.

Despite herself, the familiar surroundings had lifted her heart. Perhaps one wild event, one man turning bizarre, shouldn't stop this, after all.

'The manor of Bensinton', she found, running her finger through the Latin and translating in her head. Here it was, all the things she had made a start on, and abandoned a few weeks ago.

In 1279 the manor belonged to Edmund, Earl of Cornwall, cousin of the King, and included eight subsidiary hamlets ... religious houses like Dorchester and Godstow and Oseney were major landholders, and the tenants fell into three groups, freemen, sokemen, and the unfree. Here were their rents and duties and rights, and here their ...

The name hit her with such a blow she gasped. Here was the Cotel family. Cottell, Cotel, the erratic spelling varied over the pages. Robert Cotel, tenant of half a virgate of land, Hugh Cotel, with rights to pasture on the hill, Thomas Cotell, with a messuage and a croft, Robert again, working iron ploughs, Walter Cottel, granter of three acres to, and special intermediary of, the Abbess of Godstow. Godstow! I've never been here, he had said, surprised. Imagine the clerk getting on his horse and riding down to talk to them in Benson.

Imagine, she had answered, in the hot sun among the ruins.

She felt faint, and lay her forehead on the book. The German woman glanced at her, and then looked away. She made herself read it again. Then she left the library, making an effort to walk steadily, and crossed the road to buy some coffee. She looked straight in front of her as she drank it, and forced herself to be calm. There is no need for exotic explanation at all. She had found it in a library, and so could he. The Hundred Rolls are rare and obscure and in Latin, but - he could have. It is more likely than ... Or, it could be pure coincidence, similar names.

She went back into the library, and worked intensely the whole day, without stopping further. She searched documents and files, and searched again. By evening she had found twelve Cottells in Benson, scattered through different medieval records, from a Hugh and a Robert in 1257, to William and Benet and Clara, William's wife, in 1381.

Just before the library closed, she placed the books and records she had consulted on the issuing desk.

'Will you be wanting them again?' the assistant asked.

'I don't know.'

The young man looked impatient.

'All right, no. I won't.'

Out in Broad Street, a few tourists were still catching the last sun on the old stone buildings. Their voices seemed loud, and Katherine took a minute to orientate herself. She felt elated, on the edge of laughing. She was very tired, she thought, and also had eaten nothing all day. She passed the locked windows of the Gallery, and rested her eyes on the smooth ceramic curves and colours of the pots on display. She would go home and try to think of nothing at all.

35

Tim Rothwell was very pleased with the place he had chosen for their lunch, a riverside pub with a post card view of water, boats, and town centre flats. 'Henley is a desert in Food Guide terms,' he said to Katherine when she arrived. 'Hardly an entry, so this is a gamble; complete, high-risk gamble.' She guessed he was a year or two younger than her, but with a contrived, middle aged manner. The danger of unpleasant surroundings averted, he was now waiting more confidently for their food. They ordered asparagus, taking the risk, he said, that it might be just a shade too late in the season. The waiter assured him that, on the contrary, they picked their own at a nearby farm, and quality was certain.

Katherine leaned back, a glass of wine in her hand. She had dressed carefully, in a black linen dress and high-heeled shoes. She noticed him looking at her bare arms. She told him about the new rowing museum, just out of sight along the river and that her brother and various friends were keen rowers. 'We've just missed the regatta of course. Last week.' She seemed to him excited, or excitable; slightly brittle.

'I'm sorry,' she said, after she had paused in the middle of a sentence. 'I'm a bit tired, I think.'

'How is the work going? Hard to maintain, at this time of year, with distractions?'

'I'm not a student. Summer doesn't make so much difference.'

'Beg your pardon!' He raised his hands, palms forward.

'I have got going again, now. I'm thinking, actually, about what you wrote about 'people-orientated.''

'Well, yes. You mentioned six slaves, I think, in about the eighth century ... '

'Ninth.'

'Ninth. I thought that was such a nice touch, reminding us how anonymous history is for centuries, just a few national figures flitting through ... '

'I think that's how people, historians, come to choose their period, finally. How many people they want in it. From no individuals at all in prehistory, to every last letter and diary and bus ticket of twentieth century stuff.'

'You choose the degree of intimacy you feel comfortable with? Is that what you're saying?'

'I mightn't have chosen those words, but, yes.'

'The eighteenth century was my favourite ... '

'Early medieval is great.' She interrupted again, looking at him with dark eyes. Fine lines were beginning at the corners and under them, he noticed, emphasising her smooth cheeks and forehead. 'You can begin to find people, but they are still distant enough to feel you see their patterns ... you're not overwhelmed by their personalities, but you love it when you guess anything at all. You long to ask them questions, but actually you're safe because they can't answer ... '

'Surely you'd love them to be able to answer?'

'But then you might have too much information ... then it would be just like the present.'

'You need it to be different from the present?'

'I suppose so. Secrets, that you're cracking.'

'But people go to any lengths to look for the past. Dendrochronology, Rosetta stones, computer counts of baptism certificates, you name it ... '

'But', she said, quite loudly, 'You have to stop while there are still some unknowns! Or you'd be a scientist.'

'Oh, bad news,' he agreed politely, and was glad that the waiter arrived. He did not remember her being so intense, on their only previous meeting.

Once they were eating the large dish of asparagus which lay between them, and dipping ciabatta bread in the olive oil and sea salt he asked for, Tim was about to start on a different tack, but she spoke again.

'I've found an eighteenth-century map - coloured and detailed. They're photographing it for me. I think it might make a good illustration, or at least part of it.'

'Oh, excellent', he answered. 'We'd like to see that. And I'm thinking of a possible cover picture.'

'Oh?'

'You will know that Paul Nash painted Wittenham Clumps scores of times?' Katherine seemed quite silent now, picking at the asparagus slowly.

'One, in particular, is a beautiful autumn coloured scene', he went on. 'Now, I know that the Clumps is actually in Berkshire now, but what do you think? Near enough?'

'Oh, yes.' Katherine looked calmer. 'Wittenham Clumps was significant all right. But in the earliest Celtic, Roman days, maybe even earlier. We could make a map, and I could show you how the road system took its bearings from it, all over the territory ... but I'm afraid ... ' She suddenly looked sparkly again, 'No people-orientation at all. Completely safe!' She laughed at this, and Tim joined in courteously.

'Now, what about something really solid after that light start?' He reached for the menu.

'Cheesecake? Rhubarb crumble?'

To his surprise, she said instantly, 'I'd love rhubarb crumble. I hope they put orange in it, too.' Now she was radiant, almost flirtatious. Perhaps the lunch was going better then he thought, Tim hoped.

Still in the black linen and high heels she had worn to Henley, Katherine arrived at the King's Head just before closing time. Richard's face lit up, and he came out from behind the bar. He held her arm. Bella gave her such a greeting she was touched.

'I haven't keys any more. Shall I come home with you?'

'I would like that,' he said, and pushed the dog down. 'Go away. Can't you see she hasn't got Bella-proof clothes on?' He spoke so gently that Katherine's throat tightened.

'You look amazing. This wasn't just for me, was it?'

'I'm afraid not. I had lunch in Henley with my editor.' He raised his eyebrows. 'He's quite boring. A fuddy-duddy.'

'Not at all like anyone here, then.'

'Absolutely not. Young, though.'

'Mmmh.'

She had meant to confront him, and confront herself, with all the questions that her discoveries of the Cotels had raised. But now that she was with him it was more urgent to blot out all the thinking with sensation first.

Outside beside his car he kissed her and ran his hands over the black dress and her arms until she said, 'I mightn't be able to drive, now.'

'Don't.' he said. 'Get in this car. We'll get yours tomorrow.'

At Oak Farm House they did not even get to the bedroom, but to the couch, and held each other as though the most intimate and passionate love-making they could devise could seal up the fine fault lines. He got up to open the garden doors, and a light wind blew on them, and on the clucking of disturbed birds.

36

In the morning, as soon as they awoke, she began talking.

'Do you know what the Hundred Rolls are?'

'Hundred rolls? Very large ... '

'Richard! Do you?'

'No. Tell me.'

'It's a massive document, from 1279. It tells about Benson in great detail.'

She felt the quality of his attention change, although he hardly moved.

'In it I found lots of references to a family - well, presumably they were related to each other - called Cotel.'

There was a tense silence.

'And?'

'And I thought ... of course I thought ... Richard, were you joking, or why did you say that thing on Swyncombe Down?'

'Will you run away again?'

'No. But ... don't touch me.'

'Don't touch you? All right.'

'Tell me again.' This time she was ready for it.

He moved slightly away from her, and looked ahead of him.

'When everyone else got older, the ones who were left, and started to die, I didn't. That's all.'

There was a deep silence. Katherine heard them both breathing.

'What do you mean, the ones who were left?'

'After the plague. Ellen and our three children died, and most - lots of the others. I stayed around here for some more years, and then I could see, everyone could see, that something ... odd was going on. So I moved away.'

Controlling her voice carefully, Katherine said. 'Then what?'

'Then the same. After some years in a place, when ... nothing happens, I move away.'

Katherine sat up abruptly and got out of bed. He turned to look at her.

'I'm not going anywhere. Well, downstairs. Let's have some coffee and go outside.'

He heard her in the bathroom, and a tap slamming on and off.

With the table between them, in the sunlight, she spoke again. 'So when you said you had come here from Chichester, and Dorset before that ... ?'

'Part of the moving.'

They both had cups in their hands, but drank little. In the bright light Katherine noticed how the cut above his eye had healed without a mark, and a moment of insight, or panic, swept her. Only the heavily calloused hands and feet were flawed. She chose her words slowly, selecting from a flood of questions.

'Why did you come here?'

'Here? This is where I was a child, where ... everything happened. It's where I lived like an ordinary person, before I knew.'

'Is it the first time you've been back in Benson?'

'Yes, it is.'

Katherine stood up and walked around and stood and looked out of the window. Her head was full of confusion. 'You're talking to me like an animal that might bolt!' she said over her shoulder. 'Speaking carefully.'

'True.' The slight humour in his voice, even in this tense moment, warmed her.

She came back to the table. He reached out and covered her hand with his, and she left it there.

'Do you know any of the people I saw in the Hundred Roll?'

'Is this a test?' He spoke quite mildly.

'Yes.'

He looked at her thoughtfully. 'Hugh and Robert', he said. 'I don't know your exact dates, but there was usually a Hugh and a Robert.' She pulled her hand away and jumped to her feet again. The careful calm was slipping. She nodded wordlessly. They were common enough thirteenth century names. 'Any others?'

'Katherine, I don't know the date of your, your papers or whatever they are ... ' his voice was rising, too. 'But what about Walter? He was important, or certainly thought ... '

'Yes, there was a Walter.'

And there were Hughs and Roberts in all the records, over many generations. She looked at his face, his light eyes and his curly hair, his wide shoulders and the competent hands she liked so much. She felt sick with what she was asked to believe. Half of her did. Half of her thought that records could be found, with the same sort of effort she had made, and that he had a very good memory.

'So have I passed? Do you believe me?'

Believe me. It was a common phrase of his.

'I don't know', she said, honestly.

He stood up, with one of his brisk movements. 'This is probably enough for anyone right now. Why don't we walk in to town, for this impatient dog, and pick up your car?'

She had entirely forgotten her car.

'Yes', she said, with relief. 'I couldn't have run far, could I?'

It was already hot by mid-morning. The summer trees were at their heaviest and fullest, in dark green leaf, and a dusty smell floated from the hedges as Bella brushed against them. For the first ten minutes they walked almost in silence. When a car passed, driving slowly and towing a horse trailer, they had to flatten themselves into the hedge, and when it had gone they stayed there for a moment, with their arms and shoulders touching.

'I've got one more question,' Katherine said, 'And then I don't want to talk about this for a while.'

He looked at her and waited. He was brown from the sun, and his light eyes looked green and clear.

'When exactly do you ... when were you born?'

'I knew then that it was the year the old King Edward died, and I know now that that was 1307.'

'1307.' Despite her best intentions she felt panic rising, and consciously steadied her breathing.

'Did you have any brothers or sisters?'

'Two older brothers. Robert was dead before the plague; John died in it, but he had several children who survived. That's more than one question.'

Her legs felt shaky. They continued walking. In a minute she almost shouted at him.

'Can you imagine what this is like for me!'

'Can you imagine what it is like for me?' She looked at him.

'Well, no. Because ... ' Because to do that she would have to believe him. Believe that he had a secret that separated him from everybody else. Her mind struggled with it.

'Secret is not the right word,' she said aloud.

'No, maybe not. A fact. But it usually also is a secret.'

'Have you had this sort of conversation before?' She stopped walking.

'Yes, I suppose so. Not for a very long time. But a few times, yes. It ended badly. So you give up, for years.'

Now she did glimpse a life where patterns repeated, and he lost things again and again.

'Come on.' He took her hand and they began walking again. 'I haven't told you this morning's dream yet. I was in some very huge room, a hall, or a barn. I was painting the walls. Some other people were helping, standing around on ladders. We were in a hurry because a judge was coming, or there was going to be a court case of some kind. It was shadowy, and I wondered if we could see well enough for what we were doing. I knew the other people were more worried than me, although we didn't talk to each other.'

'Why weren't you as worried as the other people?'

'Don't know. Typically cheerful and unimaginative, I presume ... Anyway, the judge arrived, and I was surprised but quite pleased that it was a woman. I'd seen her photo in the paper, and knew that it was her, the judge. And no, it wasn't you! Although I did wake up and find you were asking me about your Hundred Rolls ... '

'I don't think that was a subtle enough dream, Richard!'

'Subtle enough for what?'

'Painting over things, and judges. Subtle enough to disguise things the way dreams are supposed to.'

'But I am uncovering.'

Katherine's car came in sight, parked somewhat crookedly outside the King's Head.

'What we're talking about is outrageous.'

'Perhaps. But we've got time.'

'So you say', she said sharply, and they were surprised to find themselves laughing.

'Where exactly did Walter live?' she asked suddenly.

'Warborough', he answered unhesitatingly.

'Hell, you're right.'

A look of great happiness came to his face. 'Get in the car,' he said. 'Drive me somewhere.'

She chose Wittenham Clumps, with Tim Rothwell's book cover suggestion in mind.

'This is where I had been the day I first saw you,' she said as they arrived. 'A freezing winter day, Christmas Eve. I walked to the top, so pleased with myself. And later on came back and unwrapped my watch in the pub.' She rubbed her cheek against his shoulder. By unspoken consent, neither mentioned his time-bubble remark. Near the top of the hill she showed him the Poem Tree.

'A man called Joseph Tubb carved it on last century.' The inscription was almost impossible to read, but they ran their fingers along it, and made out the word 'Thames.'

'It was portentous,' Katherine said. 'About Mercia, and Romans, and Fate. Nice, though.'

Bella ran wildly about at the top, kicking back grass with all four feet. Richard dived on her and tussled with her, and they sat in the hot air, mildly breathless. The sun lit the river, and glass houses and the occasional window reflected it back in glinting flickers.

'I knew it was a significant day,' Katherine said, referring again to Christmas Eve. 'And it was, but not for the reason I thought it would be. If you follow.'

'No,' Richard said. 'Explain to me in more detail.' He leaned over and kissed her for a long time. Katherine lay still, and let ideas seep through the cracks of least resistance in her mind.

37

On Sunday evening, with books on the great monetary inflation of the early middle ages neglected on her desk, Katherine was scrolling through her computer screen on quite different territory. Life span, she was looking up, life span and ageing. In the Hunza region of the Karakoram Mountains, and in certain villages in the Caucasus and Andean mountains, too, astonishing claims of longevity have been made. On careful investigation, though, these claims evaporate; what these three regions really have in common is poor or non-existent record-keeping. The great ages claimed for three famous individuals, Thomas Parr, buried in Westminster Abbey, Charlie Smith in America, and Shirali Muslimov in Georgia, have all been disproved.

Katherine dropped her arms from the keyboard. This is ridiculous, she thought. There were many other things she should be reading. Even a walk on the Meadow might be more useful. When the telephone rang she answered it willingly.

'Kathy?' Olivia's voice was cautious.

'Hallo.'

'Are you ... ? No. Would you like to drop round for a last-minute sort of dinner?'

'Yes, very much.'

'But the thing is, Orlando is here.'

'Orlando?'

'He came straight here from Heathrow.'

Katherine digested this. She was shocked to realise how little she had thought about Orlando recently, and how far in her past he seemed.

'Katherine?'

'I don't know what to do, Livvy. You know about ... other things.'

'Yes, I do. But you'll have to work it out some time. He came here to talk to Joe. He says it needs to get sorted before he can pick up his Oxford life.'

There was another silence.

Then Katherine said, 'Of course I have to come and talk to him.'

'Do you want us to be out when you arrive? Go and buy some wine, or something?'

'No.'

'What are you going to say?'

'That I've ... changed. That's all.'

'That's true.'

Joe and Orlando were in the tiny walled garden behind the Beckley cottage. Joe greeted her affectionately, and disappeared straight inside.

'Did you have a good flight?' Katherine said.

'Painless.' Orlando looked tired, with dark rings around his eyes. There was a medical journal on the table, open to a page he had been showing Joe, and the sports section of the Sunday paper.

'I'm sorry,' Katherine began on the words she had planned as she drove from Wolvercote, but he soon interrupted her. If it was no better than before he left, he said, it was clearly over?

'Yes,' Katherine said. 'No. It isn't better.' Her eyes filled with tears.

'Is there someone else?'

'I don't know.'

'Strange answer.'

'I would have known, a few days ago, but now I don't.'

He looked impatient.

To her surprise, the evening ended quite tolerably. Joe was at his best, with sparkling stories for both his friends, and Sven and Heather arrived from a weekend in London, on their way home to Winchcombe. Heather spooned pasta on to Sven's plate, while he talked, and poured wine for Orlando.

'I'm falling asleep,' he announced suddenly, and after an awkward moment, Joe offered to drive him home. He kissed everyone good bye, on both cheeks in Brazilian style, including Katherine.

Her eyes filled with tears again, but when the two men had left, Olivia said, 'Burning boats! Who needs them?' and put her arm around Katherine.

'What do you mean?' Heather asked, and Sven said, 'Should be obvious, sweetie. The man's in grief, but not terminal. Isn't she nice and innocent?'

38

At home in Wolvercote Katherine sat in front of her computer for a while, but decided against switching it on. She lifted the telephone to dial Richard's number, and hung it up again. After a while she got out some music, selecting her disc carefully, for something with no associations at all. In the end she played George Gershwin.

The next day, when the library was open, instead of walking confidently through the rooms to the history shelves and catalogues, she stopped at the desk.

'Where would I look up ageing?' she asked.

'Do you mean geriatric medicine, or life-extending sort of things? Like in Florida clinics?'

'Nothing like that, I don't think,' Katherine said, surprised. 'I mean, how we get old? Why we do.'

The librarian skimmed through the on-screen catalogue. She had rings on every finger, and long silvered nails.

'The science of ageing: chromosomes and immortality', she read. 'That sort of thing?'

'Yes, more like it.'

'There you go, then,' the woman said, cheerfully. 'Plenty of it.' She stood up, and Katherine took her seat at the screen.

'Thank you very much. I can see what I want, now, and I'll make some notes.'

An hour later she was surrounded by books and journals, discovering a frontier science world of cells, genes and chromosomes. She read and reread the pages, trying to take in the new terminology. Ageing is not biologically inevitable, and the organism is not a machine which need wear out. Most cells repair and replicate themselves, and in the early years of our life we actually grow stronger and bigger, not weaker and more faulty. Why the change? The germ line is immortal, through sperm and egg cells. No matter how old its parents, each new-born starts with its age clock set at zero. Some mechanism in the germ cells overrides ageing. But all the other cells of the body, the hundred thousand billion, gradually accumulate deficits, and stop maintaining the system. There is a limit to the number of times cells will copy themselves. After that the telomeres, protecting the ends of the chromosomes like plastic tags on shoelaces, will have shortened to a point where the chromosomes themselves will fray. Only the germ cells have the enzyme telomerase, to add back the shortened ends of the telomere after each cell division. And if the telomerase could be switched on in other cells as well, would that give us immortality? No, because it happens by chance, in rogue cells. It is cancer.

Katherine leant back in her chair and looked unseeingly out at the Radcliffe dome, her mind running with ideas. The silver-nailed librarian was returning journals to a shelf nearby, and stopped beside her.

'You found enough, then?'

'I'm beginning to know the questions, at least. None of the answers, though.' The librarian nodded encouragingly, and went behind the desk again. Katherine turned her eyes from the window ahead back to the books. The genes were her real quarry, the orchestrators of the cells. How much power did single genes have, and could they ever mutate? It dawned on her that several of the most helpful looking references were to work by Professor Moira Johnson. Moira Johnson, she recalled, was the Oxford scientist she had briefly heard on a radio discussion a few months ago, and switched promptly off as a distraction from writing about Benson. They had been talking about Darwin, she remembered vaguely, and the occasion came back to her complete with its aura of associations - the first mild evening of spring, and being in love with Richard still an overwhelmingly new sensation. She had met Moira Johnson once with Orlando, whose work, occasionally, overlapped. She checked the departmental address, and wrote down a number, and left the library.

Later in the day, she phoned from the Gallery.

'Yes, I think you could speak to her', said the voice, sounding surprised itself at the Professor's availability. 'Just a minute, and I'll put you through.'

In a minute the breezy Scottish voice came on, familiar from radio and television. 'Hallo. Moira Johnson here.'

Katherine introduced herself, and reminded her where they had met. 'Would there possibly be a time I could come and ask you some questions?' she asked. 'I would really appreciate it.'

'Sure,' Moira said lightly. 'It'll be a couple of weeks, because I'm just off to America. Holiday, would you believe? But what about lunch soon after that?'

They arranged a date and a place, and she rang off, feeling as relieved as if Moira Johnson's answers would make everything clear.

39

'The fourteenth century was a period of dramatic transition, in the Chiltern Hundreds as everywhere else in England. It was the period when population numbers climbed to a level they would not reach again for centuries, and the pressure on land extended settlement to areas uncultivated before or since. Without time for fallow years, and with shrinking pasture areas for stock, which in turn could fertilise the arable land, yields per acre fell at the same time as population levels grew. Growing towns, in particular London, needed feeding from the same countryside. The years 1315-1317 were famine years of disastrous harvests, followed by seasons of sheep murrain and then cattle disease ... When the Black Death of 1348-49 arrived it found a population and an economy already stretched and weakened to breaking point.'

Katherine threw down her pen. She was writing erratically, distracted and tempted by Richard's fantasy, or illusion, or truth. Here is a typical place, she thought, with the now familiar mix of fear and excitement in her mind. We know almost nothing about the plague in Benson. She could concoct the best possible account, drawing sober, limited inferences from later records, and analogies from nearby villages, or - she stood up and walked around - or she could ask Richard about it.

On the next day, sitting with him at Oak Farm House, she tried.

'You said that Ellen - your wife, and your children died, together?'

'Yes,' he answered matter of factly. 'And most other people. Maybe a quarter of us were left. None, in a few places.'

He put down the book he was thumbing through, a glossy book on hardwoods recently bought by David Freeman.

'But you didn't get it?'

'Oh, yes, I did. After the little ones were gone. But I got better. I thought for a while Ellen would make it, too. But she didn't.' He spoke quietly. He sounded sad but not angry. Katherine thought of a concentration camp survivor she had seen interviewed on television, and she had known that his eyes had seen sights of horror beyond her imagination, and yet he could still talk about it. Now she looked at Richard's serious eyes and calm expression.

'You had it? Bubonic plague? But ... you have no scars, or ... ' She thought of the clear skin of his arms and chest.

'Well, no.' He gestured towards the fine scar on his brow, and shrugged, resignedly. 'I heal quickly.'

'What happened?'

'How did it start, do you mean? Two men from London, up to collect wheat. They walked over from Henley, and the next day died on us, both of them.'

They talked on for an hour, and stopped for a lunch neither was specially hungry for, and talked again. They were called Hugh and Alicia and Thomas, his children, he told her. And Alicia was after his first wife, another Alicia who had died in childbirth.

'What was her name, Alicia?' Katherine asked, hating her own suspicion.

'Restwald,' he answered. 'Ellen, too. They were cousins.'

It was such a prominent medieval name in Benson Katherine had no need even to check it. She looked at him in deep bewilderment.

'I'm sorry,' she said eventually. 'That's all I can take, now.'

'I'll show you something. Something ordinary but nice.' He jumped to his feet. 'First look at this.' He flicked through the pages of David Freeman's book, and showed her a page headed 'Boxwood.' 'This pale yellow wood,' she read, 'is remarkably dense and heavy. Once well dried it is fine for engraving, and has been used for decorative items since Biblical days.'

He disappeared into his workshop beyond the kitchen, and she heard a drawer opening, and the click of Bella's claws as she crossed the kitchen to follow him.

'Look,' he said, holding out his hand. 'No engraving at all, but it is boxwood.' He passed her a small bowl, dull brown, and with an imperfectly round rim. Rough blade marks were rubbed smooth all over it, and it had a thick uneven base.

'Heavy, as the book promises,' Katherine said, uncertainly. It was coarse, compared to his usual tactile pieces.

'This was Ellen's.'

'Ellen's!'

'Yes. Such an ordinary little bit I didn't sell it or have it stolen, and for some reason I haven't lost it ... so here it still is.'

She almost dropped the little bowl, and then held it with both hands. 'This was ... ?'

'Yes, it was.' He glanced at the bowl but was looking at her, enjoying her surprise.

Katherine was silent for several moments, overwhelmed by questions. She turned the bowl in her hands, and then brought it to her nose and smelled it. It was scentless, warm against her face. We could have it carbon-dated, one part of her mind said. But no, it is his precious possession. Neither a museum piece, nor evidence for or against ... her mind skipped away from that thought.

'It never occurred to me you might have ... is this the only thing?'

'More or less.' He took the bowl back again, and turned it over to tap the base. 'This isn't one I made, I'll have you know. I think even my early efforts were better than this. But it is interesting to remember how they were. This would have been just scraped and carved out with a knife, of course, and it is very hard wood.' He spoke in his usual brisk voice, and seemed to have pressed the plague stories back into a remote compartment of his mind. As ever, he had a plan for the next few hours.

'Let's go back to the pub at Britwell Salome,' he said. 'Do you remember, the one we ran away from once? You do? I'm so pleased ... it was you who wanted to leave on that occasion, I think. Anyway. We'll do clever things with cars first, leaving one outside the King's Head and then walking. We'll have a late afternoon drink, or whatever. Then I must go back to the King's Head for the evening, and you can stay or not - as you want, by then.' She felt a rush of warmth for him allowing for her uncertainty.

'Do you also have a military history I don't know about? You're so bossy.'

'Commanding, we call it. Kathy ... ', He put his arms around her when she stood up. 'Darling Kathy. I hated it when you ran away from me.' He spoke against her mouth, quietly, and she breathed in his air as he breathed it out. 'And you can't imagine - can't possibly, how it feels to refer to other parts of my life in a nearly normal way. But you must stop me the slightest moment I frighten you.'

'I will. I think I will. I might come to the King's Head with you. Eric's music would be very good for me.'

40

Eric's music was a live trio, three women who were witty and funny about their country music and the distance between Nashville, Tennessee, and Reading, where they actually came from. Zinnia introduced them to Katherine. 'They are wonderful' Zinnia said. 'The more mournful they are the better it gets.' One of them had been an archaeology student 'In another life.' she told Katherine, and she looked back on it with horror and boredom. 'I always got the middens. That's what you had to call rubbish dumps - middens. But history might be better', she said politely. The other two women were older. Richard smiled at her over their elaborate curly heads, as they sat with their guitars in front of the bar. He looked full of happiness, and she heard him laugh at something Eric said. She would accept the impossible thing, she knew, as long as she could possibly make suspended judgement last. When Richard teased her later about kissing him violently, she said, 'I'm so relieved. I love you very much.'

'Relieved?' he said. 'Well, if that's what it takes ... I love you, too, as it happens.'

Their lives took up a kind of rhythm. Katherine worked her Gallery half-days, and once he visited her there and Olivia made him promise to collect up the next few bowls he made and bring them to her for approval. Occasionally he came to Katherine's Wolvercote flat, but more often, several times a week, she drove down to Benson. The house and the garden, with Bella padding around like a benign partner in the arrangement, became a framework for the high summer evenings and weekends, and their constant conversations. Katherine was full of questions.

'How come you can do that?' she asked, when he read her a local news item from the paper.

'What, bear to think about our council inflicting worse traffic mess?' he said, deliberately misunderstanding.

'No, reading. And writing. Only churchmen were supposed to do much of it.'

'And my writing isn't very good, you will have noticed. I was taught by the Abbess's clerk. So it was near enough to the church.'

'The Abbess's clerk?'

'The Abbess of Godstow's clerk spent a lot of time in Benson, or Shillingford, to be precise. His right hand man there was my grandfather's brother, Walter. I used to hang around Walter, who also permitted fishing, and the clerk, not really busy enough, took pity.'

Sometimes the images were so bright and clear Katherine needed minutes to digest them. In the Hundred Roll there had indeed been a Walter Cotel, mediator to the Abbess; she remembered making the notes.

'But you hadn't been to Godstow yourself?' She thought of him wandering the nunnery ruins during their picnic.

'Never. It was somewhere he came from and went off to, with several spare horses each time, I remember. That impressed me.'

Katherine looked at him in silence, and then reached out and touched his hair, letting the crisp strands push lightly on her palm.

Later the same day she said 'Do you think the Abbess's man thought you might become a monk, too?'

'Possibly. But they liked to have people who could read properly, scattered around. They could send lists of taxes required much more easily.'

In a minute he said, 'He was quite nice to me. Extraordinarily fat. I think he eventually he had to get himself transported by cart, on the journey. Yes, he did!' He was amused at the memory.

On another occasion she asked, 'Was this where the Hundred meeting place was? Roke Elm?' Richard was in the kitchen, shaking dirt off lettuces and carrots he had picked.

'Of course it was,' he called back. 'Out in the open, every

month or so. Lots of arguments, committees and pledges on everything under the sun. The bailiff with his trestle table. You know how it worked, you've read about it. Permitted to use the church if it was really freezing, and more often if the steward was doing his rounds.'

'The steward? The King's steward?' She stood at the bench beside him.

'Sure. Or other visiting bigwigs showed themselves here, too.'

'Who? Tell me some.'

'Kathy, I can't remember every … Well, John of Gaunt stood about there once. Lancaster.' He pointed beyond the front door. 'He gave a talk, or at least a sort of viewing of himself. There was some political situation, and he wanted to garner a good following. Store it up for a future occasion. I think his mistress came from somewhere round here, and her sister.'

'Yes, Catherine Swynford.'

When she felt moments of sceptical panic and worry, she repressed them. In the same way, she wrote little down. Now research occupied a strange new place between solid work on the random documents which existed, and conversation with Richard.

'It amuses me to live here, on top of it.' he was saying. 'Same horizon, same hills … but everything else different.'

'And some of the same boundaries.'

'Yes, some of the same roads and paths and field names. Hollandtide and Rumbolds and Shimming, which you don't believe.'

He turned around and leaned back on the bench and pulled her to him with his wrists, holding his wet hands off her back.

'It was already quite fun for me being back here. I had put it off … for ever. But the timber job materialised, and David Freeman is good. It was better than I expected. Then you arrived in the pub with your lovely hair ... ' he stroked it, 'And big eyes, and legs in those boots ... and with all those names in your mouth. Names I thought no one knew any more. Mmmh!' He made a triumphant noise, and squeezed her. 'I thought about it, and waited for you to come back. Then you did, and it was Christmas and I couldn't interrupt you with your present - and thought it was probably from a man, anyway. Then when I found myself thinking that, I had to admit it wasn't only maps I was thinking about with you ... So I went home and began training Bella to attack rhubarb on sight.'

Katherine giggled at the vision of Bella the rhubarb warrior.

'And it paid off' he went on. 'I hung around anywhere there was rhubarb, and it all happened. You appeared in the High Street, looking a bit pale.'

'I had flu.'

'Looking lovely', he said, soberly, and kissed her.

When she was almost drifting off to sleep that night, she said to him drowsily, 'I liked your story about us in Benson.'

'That's good,' he said, and moved his leg against hers. 'Bella likes it, too. And it's true.'

41

The next day she sat at the desk in the Gallery. It was a quiet morning, and Olivia was about to leave for an appointment with Dr Baker-Lynn.

'I'm going to give it till the end of the year,' she said. 'It's very good for me whether or not anything, you know, anything happens. He says we are achieving an unconscious rapport. And dream work would be useful, if only I could remember any. I can see how people might end up inventing things to please a therapist. Ciao!' She drifted out of the shop, with sun glasses perched high on top of her short hair. The bell rang almost instantly again, and she was back.

'I forgot to tell you, Dawn is delighted because all her own bottles and those tall candle-holders have sold, and guess who the last one was to?'

'Who?'

'Orlando!' Katherine thought she should have guessed, as Olivia had said 'Ciao' for farewell. 'He was in on Saturday, and said they had caught his eye long ago.'

'Is he all right, Livvy?' Orlando was a slightly awkward subject between them.

'Pretty well, yes. Well, I think so. For a Brazilian, he always seems unpassionate, doesn't he? Could be English. Yes, he's okay. You had to do it, Kathy. It was obvious!'

What was obvious, she wanted to say, but the door clanged again, and Olivia was gone.

She stood and walked around the shop. The stock was slightly low, in advance of the autumn exhibition planned for August. She rearranged a shelf of ceramic cats, spreading them out to take up more space, and returned to the desk. She took a folder out of her bag, and found the last Benson paragraphs she had written. She had neglected them and they seemed distant. She read the page again, and then began adding to it.

'Contemporary chroniclers called it the Black Death.' she wrote. *'Let us take an imaginary family in Benson ... '*

42

When Richard next came to Wolvercote, she showed him an egg cup with a splash of pale pink water over a few grains of sediment at the bottom. 'Isn't this a flop? This is my woad leaf brew, after weeks of attention.'

'You certainly wouldn't be in business with this. You didn't make it smell enough, clearly.'

'I like it,' she said. 'We collected those leaves on such a cold, wintry day.'

They were going to the cinema, to see *Shakespeare in Love*. 'Will you mind, seeing people dressed up and cavorting around in historic costumes?' she asked. He looked surprised.

'No, because that's all they'll be, people pretending. Would you mind seeing people pretending to be, say, Oxford academics?'

'No, I suppose not.' She could never believe it could seem so straightforward, so matter of fact. It was unusual to be out with him, away from Benson, and surrounded by other people. She held his hand in the cinema and pressed against it. 'Mmmh. Do you remember levitation?', she said, repeating their old code word, and he leaned against her, and laughed at the swaggering Elizabethans on the screen.

'Realistic?' she whispered, and he laughed more.

'What do you think? But wonderful!'

As they were leaving, Katherine was greeted by two people who looked vaguely familiar. 'The Bartholomew dinner', the man said, helpfully, in an American voice, and Katherine recognised the Rabbi and his wife.

'This is Richard Cottell', she said. 'Mark and Shelley Morris.' They shook hands.

'Richard is from Benson,' she said, remembering her conversation with Mark, and he nodded significantly.

'How is that book?'

'Going pretty well, mostly, thank you.'

'Wasn't that great?' Shelley said, about the film.

'No,' Richard said. 'I thought it was too sad that he couldn't have her in the end, and she sails off to the other life.'

'What a romantic,' Shelley answered approvingly. 'But I had to love the photography, though.'

'Shelley is a photographer', Katherine told Richard.

'You're from Benson,' Mark said. 'You could almost be American by your voice. I'll never get used to English accents.' He told Richard about his father being based there during the war.

'I wasn't there then,' Richard said.

'I guess not! Well, we look forward to this book.'

They had walked a little distance up St Giles as they talked. All of them glanced at a restaurant door as they passed it, and Katherine was glad no-one suggested stopping. She suddenly longed to be alone with Richard.

'When are you off home to Boston?'

'Too soon, I'm afraid,' Mark said. 'Our year here finishes in another month.'

'Time to get back to our children,' Shelley added. 'Much though we love it here.'

When they said goodbye, Mark shook both their hands very warmly, and Shelley touched their shoulders and glanced from one to another before she said, 'Now, you have a good time, you two.'

'Have you been to America?' Katherine said afterwards.

'Of course not.'

'I've been only once, and then not to Boston.' Putative Boston life with Orlando passed through her mind.

'Would I have a passport? Ponder that.'

'Oh God!' She stopped walking and stood still. 'All your documents. Where are they, certificates and licences and stuff? I never thought of that.'

He laughed at her shocked expression. 'Don't worry. There must be hundreds, probably thousands of people in England without birth certificates. They're probably only a problem if you ask for them, and I don't. I have a driving licence, which covers all sorts of requirements. I got it long ago, and its dates are beginning to look a bit old, I agree.'

'But what will you do when ... ' She tailed off. She had struggled over the past few weeks to accept the huge impossibility of historical associations and they had become like a wonderful story she listened to. Now the mundane details of accepting the idea in present reality struck her.

'I'm going to take Bella out on the Meadow,' he said. They had arrived in Wolvercote and the dog was waiting patiently in his car. 'Are you coming?' Katherine nodded, still silent.

Bella's happiness was infectious. She ran in huge circles on the darkening fields, and they sat on the dry grass to watch her. Richard threw her a stick and she returned it instantly, prodding at him for a repeat. 'Stupid dog,' he said gently. 'You are one of life's time-wasters.' The dog held her head on one side, with sparkling eyes. 'But time is just what we have!' Richard turned to Katherine exuberantly, lying down and pulling her on top of him in one movement.

'How old did you say you are? Seventeen? Twenty-two? Oh, all of thirty-two ... Honestly, Katherine, darling. Compared to some of the things about my ... my quirk, documents and papers are nothing. Easy, small, solvable or neglectable things.'

'Quirk!' She pulled herself up from him and looked down at his familiar face. His teeth were white in the dim light. 'What are the harder things?'

He rubbed her back, and played with the dangling plait of hair. 'There are hard things. And yes, I will spell them out for you. But not tonight. Tonight is too mild, and lovely, and our minds are full of that gorgeous place, Elizabethan England, where most people wrote plays or were actors.' He sat up and looked out for Bella. 'No one had a nuisance dog', he said loudly, and she appeared beside him immediately. He threw a stick in a huge arc, and she raced after it, out of sight. 'She'll never find it now; it's far too dark', he said contentedly.

43

Katherine exchanged some Gallery hours with Dawn, and went to see her mother and Diane in London for two days in the middle of the week. It was the first time she had visited them since telling them that her engagement to Orlando was over. After a few hours with them, Elizabeth said, 'But, darling, you look wonderful, just like when we saw you last time. It must have been getting this terrible decision over.'

'We even had sad music ready on the tapes,' Diane said, laconically. 'Don't think we'll need it.'

'We were never very clear what happened?'

'Nothing, really. I'm afraid I changed. I got heavily involved with my book, and maybe, neglectful. It was more me than him. But ... ' she suddenly realised, 'but he accepted it pretty easily. Maybe it wasn't right for him, either.' A memory of Richard jumped into her mind, in bed only one night ago, dragging his hand quite hard along the length of her spine. 'We didn't know enough about each other, I don't think, even after all that time.'

She didn't offer them any more, and the two women glanced at each other.

'Is there, um, someone else? For you? For him?'

'Sort of.' They looked alert. For a moment she thought of saying that James had met him, in May, but decided against it. 'But I don't know if it will come to anything. It might be just an interlude. It's impossible to tell, yet.'

'Shall we do some shopping?' Elizabeth suggested, and was happily surprised when Katherine said 'A great idea. Yes, I could do with some clothes that are really fun! Come and help me. You know I'm helplessly unskilled.'

'Hair-cut?' tried Elizabeth, hopefully, and they all laughed when Katherine said,

'No. That is going too far.'

She and Elizabeth walked out and made their way along Kensington High Street. The day was hot and sunny, and the shops were crowded with tourists and barely dressed girls with tattooed shoulders and high strappy sandals. A pair of mounted police rode towards them in the road, and a kindergarten class was being marched along the footpath in a double line, holding a long rope between them, reaching from one adult in the front to another at the rear end. Most of the children had yellow sunhats, and they made an erratic, winding caterpillar among the shoppers. Elizabeth noticed her daughter's bright smile as she watched the infants, pushing the hair out of her face, and showing the round watch on her thin wrist. She had been braced for a sad or a nostalgic visit, and was realigning her picture of Katherine's social life.

'This is another world', Katherine said, looking at her. 'I completely forget it when I'm buried away in Oxford.' She had also looked visibly happy on the day of the birthday lunch, Elizabeth recalled. Whatever it was that was happening had clearly already started by then. 'Here we are,' she called, and turned them into a shop with only one or two subtly draped garments in the window. 'Shoes too, perhaps?'

By the end of the afternoon they had several large bags

to carry home, and a smaller box with a wide green *art nouveau* design bracelet. 'I want to give you that, for your other arm,' Elizabeth had said. Before turning the last corner Katherine said, 'Let's get something for Diane', and darted into a wine shop. 'The d'Arenberg Shiraz she likes,' she said when she came out. 'Even in summer.'

The three women cooked together, stuffing bright red peppers with couscous, and spreading cheeses and meats and salad on a large plate Katherine had admired since childhood. She felt a pang for her father as she arranged it, remembering very clearly his hands washing and drying it after many meals. But he was always talking to her mother as he did so, she thought, hardly ever to her. It was only now her mother was available to her, just as she herself was moving irrevocably elsewhere. Then they ate the meal with the door open to the small, civilised urban garden.

'Do we wish James were here?' they discussed, and decided that it was very pleasant as it was.

'He has a new girlfriend,' Elizabeth told her. 'But is also in line for a transfer to Los Angeles. It's a tight call, we gather.'

'Now,' Diane said as they finished, and were sitting with the last of the wine. 'It's time for you to show me the day's work. Model it please, Katherine!'

Claiming very unconvincing reluctance, Katherine came and went and swirled in front of them, first in a blue, skimming dress with wide low shoulders, and then in black trousers, and lastly a creamy, crinkly skirt and tight top. 'And a jacket, and shoes', she said, laying them out.

'I thought mothers were supposed to restrain daughters. She didn't.'

'You don't do it very often,' Elizabeth restricted herself to saying. Actually, never before, she was thinking. She watched Katherine run her hands sensuously over the cream skirt. It was remarkable.

44

Katherine drove straight to Benson when she left London.

'I missed you.'

'I missed you. It was much too peaceful, no-one asking questions.'

'Do you want to see my new clothes?'

'Not yet.'

His hair and shirt smelled of bark and wood. She clasped his hands and held them still on her collar bone. 'I've brought things to cook for dinner. As well as the new clothes and lots of questions in my mind. Shall I make us something?'

'Yes, that too,' he said.

In a few minutes they were in the early evening light of his bedroom, and she tried to keep her eyes open to watch his face above her as they moved together, now familiar with each other. But she shut them, and spoke incoherently, and pressed her nose to his wood-smelling chest.

After a long time, when his own breathing had slowed, Richard said in a matter of fact voice,

'What was that you were saying a little earlier?'

She matched his voice and said formally, 'I think, Richard, it was that you make me very happy.'

'Oh, good. I hoped it was something like that.'

In a minute he said, 'I love this summer,' and she knew he meant not the weather or the light still in the sky at ten o'clock, but the last few weeks when they had been uncomplicated with each other. She thought he sounded faintly sad.

'Hey, Rich!' she said, copying what Eric called him. 'Guess what I read in the paper yesterday in London?'

'What?'

'In Australia this has been declared the Year of the Older Person.'

He tilted his head back on the pillow and laughed. 'My time has come! But wrong country.'

'You could emigrate. People would respect you properly. Slow down when you cross the road, that sort of thing.'

'But they're fussy about dogs. No, I don't think I could take Bella.'

If they were joking about it, she thought, did that mean that for a moment it was true? After lying over his shoulder a little longer, she moved to the edge of the bed, and said, 'Dinner!' and swung her legs out.

45

Two days later, on the first weekend in August, Zinnia organised a party aboard the boat. Richard and Katherine arrived at the river by mid-morning. Bella had been left at home, with regrets and reminders about how untrustworthy she was near water, and how liable to jump overboard and cause a disturbance. Katherine was surprised to see a very similar black retriever running among the parked cars at the boatyard, and pointed it out to Richard.

'Sam!' he said, looking around. 'Bella's brother. Somewhere nearby must be - yes. It's David.' A tall man with well-cut fair hair, slightly long, was already approaching them. Richard introduced them.

'This is David Freeman. David - Katherine Laidlaw.'

'How do you do?' David said, and they shook hands. He had a deep, pleasant voice.

'We're about to go off on that - ' Richard pointed to *Halcyon Daze*. 'An all day cruise up river, I'm told.'

'Oh, yes? Lucky you.' He had such a charming manner

Katherine couldn't tell if he meant it or not. They discussed the weather. It was warm and still, but cloudy. David looked at her with obvious interest. 'Do you live here, then?'

'No, in Oxford. I'm a visitor.'

'It's Katherine I've been convincing about the footpath from the Yard up to Rokemarsh,' Richard said. 'But actually she knows more about it than I do.'

'He does have ideas about things like that', David said. 'But all harmless, I think. Well, nice to meet you. You'd better think about boarding!' As he went, Katherine noticed his dog was heavier than Bella, with a square, wide head.

'Is that the brother who is handsome but dull?' she asked as she watched them get into a Land Rover.

'Right. That's Sam.'

'Now he,' she said, 'David, I mean, as opposed to Eric and Zinnia, perfectly matches his wife.' She thought of the blonde woman in the antique shop on the day of the thunderstorm. 'They are pretty well identical, except for gender.'

'Your thought processes are unusual, but yes, I see what you mean. He will know all about you from the grapevine, of course, but is far too discreet to let on.'

Zinnia welcomed her visitors onto the boat. A striped tablecloth flapped on the galley table, held down nautically by metal clips at the edges. Bottles lay in ice in a vacuum bin, and wrapped sandwiches and a cake were neatly covered. Katherine placed her offering of a cheese and poppy seed tart among them. The other guests were the large school teacher and his wife, Martin and Carolyn, familiar from the King's Head, and Eric's sister and her husband and teenaged son. He already wore headphones and a blank expression as he listened to his own Walkman. 'This is Anthony,' Zinnia said, and he took the earphones off to smile quite graciously, and replaced them.

'Come on, Eric, cast off!' Zinnia instructed. 'No drinks till after that.' Today she had knee-length tight white Capri pants and a white collarless shirt, open enough to show the guitar pendant on its gold chain. Eric and his brother-in-law untied the boat, and reversed out into mid-stream, before turning up river to Shillingford. 'Forward now, Stuart. Right hand down a bit.' Eric instructed, and Katherine observed that Stuart had usually carried out the action just before Eric spoke.

'Stuart and Marion used to have a boat', Zinnia confided to Katherine while including Marion in the conversation. 'But we love them coming with us, now. Pimms, or is it a bit early? Oh, good for you.' She passed drinks around, fluttering her blackened eyelashes. Katherine took one down to Richard at the front of the boat.

'Zinnia has a great knack of making you feel approved of,' she said to him. 'It's very relaxing.'

He nodded. 'Come and sit here. I'm working on relaxing.' She sat close beside him, feeling his arm warm against her side. 'Did you see where the old ferry landing was?'

'No. I was helping make Pimms.'

'Have you lost all sense of responsibility and toil?' As he looked at her the sun pierced a break in the clouds and made the water sparkle in front of them, and she squinted into it.

'In fact I haven't written much lately. I wish you wouldn't remind me. Things are very ... distracting.'

'I know,' he said, and held her bent bare knee for a moment.

Martin clambered forward and joined them, his fat frame rocking the boat as he lowered himself. 'Where exactly are we going? Do we know?' Before Richard could answer a blast of 'King of the Road' hit their ears.

'Sorry, sorry, sorry', they heard Eric shout above it, and it faded to a pleasant background strum.

'Oh, what a pity,' said Martin, the music teacher.

'We're going almost to Dorchester, I believe.' Richard tried again. 'A scenic, historic run,' he mouthed 'historic' sternly at Katherine, 'And no locks.'

The clouds broke up and drifted apart until the sky was clear blue, and the overhanging trees at the river's edge cast black, rippling shadows. Katherine drifted between conversations with Carolyn about local artists, and the bringing of her students into the Gallery during the autumn show, and listening to Martin and Anthony, occasionally without his earphones, argue about their music. They chugged slowly up the river, steadily nearing Wittenham Clumps ahead, and turned into the quiet mouth of the Thame without mishap.

'Eric and Stuart make a great team,' Zinnia said happily. 'Lunch now?'

They tied up near the footbridge across the meeting place of the two rivers and Martin pointed out dragonflies, skimming over the water around them, iridescent blue. 'Do you know this will be their only day of life above water? After years underneath?' he informed the party as they set out their food.

'Ever the school teacher,' his wife said, rolling her eyes. Anthony chewed steadily, with the wires of his headphone moving up and down on his ears, and his feet dangling into the water, white and magnified beneath the surface. Behind them the footpath to Dorchester crossed the flat meadows, and on the opposite bank of the Thames the forest sloped thickly down to the opaque green water. Further up the river a cluster of young men were fishing, and as Katherine watched them a girl separated herself from the group and wobbled off on a bicycle towards the tower of Dorchester Abbey beyond the meadow, pedalling hard through the silky grass. The smell of earth and hay and grass was heavy and close around her, and she felt peaceful and slightly light-headed from eating and drinking in the hot sun. It was very quiet. Through half closed eyes she saw the name of the boat hovering beside her, *Halcyon Daze*. This is one, she thought sleepily, a halcyon day. In a minute she said to Richard,

'Lie with your arms wide out and keep very still and concentrate, and you can feel the world turning. I could when I was a child, anyway.'

'No, I can't feel it,' he said. 'I haven't been helping Zinnia as thoroughly with the Pimms. Anyway, when I was a child I didn't know the world was supposed to turn.'

She stiffened for a moment, and then relaxed again. This was what she had committed herself to, for a while at least.

'Who did you play with when you were a child? Your brothers?'

'No, they seemed much older. Various untidy little ... ' He thought for a minute, and mentioned several names, family names known to her, and a few new ones. 'A lot of them were cousins of one kind and another, anyway.' He rolled over with one of his sudden energetic movements, and pulled at pieces of grass. 'There were lots of deaths, second marriages, illegitimates ... looser and yet tighter, in the villages. My parents, for example, were cousins, very common.'

'First cousins?'

'I believe so.'

She deliberately kept her eyes closed, not looking at him. First cousins, small gene pool; did that mean anything? Did he tell her these things by chance?

After a long silence she said, 'Did you ever think of having more children? After ... '

'I did. Twice.'

She sat upright. 'More children?' She lowered her voice. 'You didn't tell me!'

'Kathy - how could I have told you everything? Much,

much later, in Southampton, during a war, there were two more boys. I hardly knew them, I wasn't married to their mother, she eventually took them away. I was very sad. End of story.'

She was aware again of selecting from a maze of questions.

'What war?' she said, eventually. He gave a short laugh.

'Your chronologies, darling. Always consistent. Against Spain, in Holland, I think, then. I went to it.'

'You went to it?'

'Fussiness about passports is quite a new idea. People rounded up in ports weren't asked for papers, funnily.'

'Oh, God.' She lay down heavily, almost winded. 'I've reached saturation point again,' she said, dangerously.

'You asked.'

She pushed her head hard back into the grass, and tried to blank her mind out, squeezing her eyes shut against the bright sun. For a few minutes she almost slept. Then like someone coming round to consciousness, she began to hear Carolyn and Zinnia laughing, and saw that Martin had lumbered ashore near her and was erecting a deck chair very fast. He threw himself into it, making the striped canvas almost hit the grass, and shouted triumphantly 'How long?'

'Sixty-seven seconds!' Anthony and Eric shouted together, and began to drag more folded chairs from the cabin.

'We can't have this,' said Richard, and jumped to his feet.

All three men held the chairs and when Zinnia shouted 'Go!' began a whirlwind of unfolding canvas and slamming wooden arms and slats.

'Forty-four!' Zinnia shouted, when Richard easily won, and then 'Sixty-five!' to Anthony.

'This one is a menace,' said Eric about his own chair a

second later, and Zinnia said, 'You're right, the blue one is always tricky.'

Stuart was prone on the deck, clearing weed from the propeller.

'Competitiveness is so sad,' said Marion, looking admiringly at Richard.

In the evening, home at Oak Farm House, when Richard was kissing her and Katherine felt herself begin to melt, she said, 'Shall we do this outside? Everything outside has been so good, today ... '

'Rustic, do you want?' He teased her. He was breathing heavily, but held her face between both hands, very gently. She didn't answer, but pressed against him.

'I want to hold you like this forever,' she said soon, with all her limbs around him.

'You can't,' he said 'Not practical', and instantly arched into her and groaned.

Afterwards when they lay there, he said, 'What was your favourite part of the day? Apart from this. Deckchairs? Dorchester from the river? Martin's figure in shorts?'

'Oh, no' she said, thinking. 'It was the dragonflies, I think. Yes, definitely, the dragonflies.'

46

Moira Johnson was a distinguished academic, but also a popular scientist. She was a frequent voice on radio, instantly recognisable, with swift, lucid flights of conversation only interrupted by laughs. Answers to questions often began with 'Firstly ... ' and the fluid paragraphs flowed out without hesitation, and reached a neat conclusion. She gave Reith lectures, and Christmas lectures at the Royal Institute, and spoke to sixth form groups uncertain of career direction, and looking for role models. She was about forty, and dazzlingly, eccentrically elegant, with tiger-skin leggings and skimpy jackets and two-tone blonde hair. She had a childless marriage, famously happy, to an actor called Rupert Leeson.

Katherine was due to meet her on the great day of the total eclipse of the sun, with newspapers full of timetables and astronomical charts. They were meeting in the restaurant in the Ashmolean Museum. 'If we sit in the college dining room people interrupt,' Moira had said. 'It's sometimes more efficient to talk elsewhere.'

Katherine reflected on that phrase as she made her way there. The backward shadow of this appointment had given her permission not to think efficiently, and had allowed her wonderful weeks of entering Richard's world, weeks of a great secret. Not yet, she had thought, over days of talking, and nights of physical pleasure. It can wait. But today she was thinking carefully.

Moira was approaching the museum steps when they met, slender in black jeans and a very low and tight lime green T-shirt. Hanging from one shoulder, she had a black, beaded textile satchel, and pulled it off to shake hands.

'How was it for you?' she said.

Katherine looked blankly at her for a second before responding. Her mind was entirely elsewhere, Moira thought, and she seemed taller and more beautiful than she remembered.

'Oh, the eclipse! There wasn't too much to see, from here, was there? The clouds blurred what we might have noticed. More like a dark thunderstorm that never developed.'

'We all stood in our quad', Moira said, as they made their way downstairs. 'Personal astrophysicist laid on, but also couldn't see much. Exciting, though. I wish we could have got away to Cornwall, but - just back from America and all that.'

They settled at a table, moving their chairs cautiously on the noisy stone floor. Moira sat with her back to the light, flattering the blonde hair. She looks so familiar, thought Katherine, from television viewings, it feels as if I know her when I don't. Closer up, there were faint diagonal lines below the high cheek bones, and above the strongly-outlined lips. They ordered sandwiches on walnut bread, and sparkling mineral water. 'Bit limp,' Moira said cheerfully, 'But I have to keep going this afternoon.'

'Is this an occupational hazard for you? People coming to ask questions.'

'Only a good one. I'm insufferably curious about other people's activities. How is Orlando?'

'He's fine, I think. We're not ... together, anymore ... '

'Oh, I'm sorry. If that's the right thing to be. He has a big statistical survey up and running - in Boston and Brazil, is that right?'

'I believe so.'

The waiter brought the water, and when he had gone, Moira said, 'I covet that jacket you have.'

'It's new, or fairly new.' Katherine said with pleasure. 'I bought it in London under my mother's close supervision. She doesn't think I have the hang of clothes.'

'Mothers never do.' They smiled at each other. Moira was curious. 'Okay,' she said. 'Fire away.'

Katherine fingered the tablecloth. 'I'm working on a history of the Oxfordshire Chiltern Hundreds', she began. 'Mainly Benson, which had a specially unusual pre-Conquest history. Do you know Benson?' Moira nodded, but was silent. 'But now I'm thinking about the early medieval population, before and after the plague, particularly. Trying to work out inheritance patterns for local landholdings, that sort of thing. I thought I should incorporate some medieval death rates into it.'

'And, what you want to know is ... ?' Moira sipped the water. Her blue eyes were outlined in smudgy dark grey liner.

'When medieval people died younger than us, were they actually ageing differently? Could there be genetic reasons why most of us live longer now?' To her great relief, Moira picked up the vague question and set fluently off.

'Absolutely not. Genetic differences between human populations anywhere and at any time in history have never been proven. That's not to say longevity doesn't run in some families, it clearly does. But as far as we know the pace of ageing hasn't slowed or changed since ... well, ever. All that has changed since medieval times in Benson, say, is the hostility of the environment. By that I mean diet, accident, medical treatment, whatever. Improve the handling of those, and the average age of death rises, wherever you are.'

Their food arrived, thick nut bread with cheese and chutney piled on to it.

'So any time, if you survived external pressures, you might live to ... ?'

'About eighty or ninety. About like today. Actually, all things being exactly equal - and we can't make them exactly equal in human life; that's why proving something about the life span of a single-cell thing in a test tube in a lab, or even fruit flies or mice isn't necessarily significant - that is where a genetic difference comes in. Your genetic inheritance might decide whether, under perfect circumstances, you might live to eighty or even to a hundred. But not much more than that.'

'So if we could look at the genes of all these medieval populations who died often in their forties and fifties, we would find things working about like they do today?'

'Yes, that's about right. In terms of cell replication,

telomere shortening, damage from free radicals, all those technical things, the accumulation of all those random bits of cell damage - things would be the same. So what is actually measured in all population studies is the hostility of the environment, nothing else.' She described it a little further and then said. 'Oh, God, was that far more than you wanted?' Moira bit into a large mouthful of cheese. 'Now this,' she said through crumbs. 'This is probably environmental hostility.' She watched Katherine re-arranging the generous quantity of bread and cheese on her plate, but eating little. She refrained from interrupting obvious concentration by admiring the green bracelet around her right wrist.

'No, it couldn't be more interesting. So what are the genes that affect ageing then, that might be different in some families, as you say?'

'A mass of genes, maybe thousands. Everything controlling the repair system. To repair themselves from injury, or wear, or illness, cells have to recreate themselves. They only seem to be able to do this a certain number of times. They want to be able to pass on the germ line, the reproductive cells, in the best possible condition. Once that's done, the other cells needn't keep on working - it's an evolutionary trade-off. Most species begin declining at the end of their reproductive age. That's why there are such differences between species, but not much within a species. Yes, I know there are unanswered questions there, like, why live after the menopause? But that's where we are at the moment!'

She paused and looked around the large, light basement. When Katherine still said nothing, she added. 'So these families where people seem to live longer, may have genes which allow more replication of cells. Why, have you go some anomalous statistics in Chiltern graveyards?'

Katherine looked startled. 'No, I was just thinking of the

generalised statements that are always made, about how each generation lives longer. It seems that we do, up to a certain point, but they could have?'

'Yes, very good summary.'

Katherine took a long drink of the water. Moira was bright and stimulating, and she didn't want only to interrogate her. 'I hope you forgot about all this sort of thing in America?' she said. 'Was it pure holiday?' She talked entertainingly about her own few trips to America, and made Moira laugh with her description of vast American meals which had surprised her.

'Are you a cook?' Moira asked.

'Moderately good. In my next life I will run an amazing restaurant.'

'I can't cook at all. Thank God for the college dining room. And Rupert.'

'But I have to conquer medieval history yet, in this life.'

Just before they finished, over coffee, she returned to her preoccupation.

'So if there were just one gene, which could control life span, what would it be?'

Moira looked at her speculatively. 'It would have to do two things, simultaneously. It would have to stop telomeres shrinking, so they never wore out, but make sure the cells also didn't become cancerous. And the enzyme telomerase has already made some simple cells apparently immortal, in labs at least. So that's one. And the other is, it would have to inhibit the production of free radicals, the oxidation and rusting we talked about. And that happens in most metabolic processes, so it's tricky.'

'Rather a tall order.'

'Rather. But mutations happen. Wouldn't it be exciting, if you could get your head around the philosophy of it all? The end of evolution, the annihilation of death, but would we still be human?' She gestured dramatically, and stood up, laughing. 'I have to go. I'm afraid we wandered a bit from mediaeval ageing patterns.'

Katherine stood up too, looking strikingly flushed and animated. 'Thank you very much for talking to me about ... everything.' She looked at her watch.

'It was a pleasure. And it probably will all have changed if you ask me again in a few months!'

At the corner of the Banbury Road they stopped again.

'I always feel a philistine coming here just to eat and not to look.' Moira looked towards the Museum. 'Good bye, Katherine.'

'Good bye, and thank you very much, again.'

They turned in different directions and Katherine hurried off towards the Gallery. Moira walked thoughtfully towards the science park. What had all that been about? Not quite what Katherine said it was, for sure.

47

Katherine arrived at the Gallery, slightly late, to find Olivia sitting with a pile of attractive post-card style invitations in front of her. The picture was of a cluster of Sven Hansen pots against a background of hazy autumn colours. On the other side, the Gallery invited its guests for a preview and drinks to celebrate their September exhibition of ceramics and small sculptures.

'And maybe a few wooden bowls,' Olivia said, pointedly, 'But I'm not sure enough to put that.'

Katherine shrugged, and went to stand beside her. One customer stood in the shop, peering at the cabinet of jewellery. Olivia had just shown her own ear-rings, a different shell, cast in gold, in each ear, and pointed out more work of the same designer.

'You know,' said Olivia. 'This doesn't sound very professional, but you and Dawn and I are all trouble for the guest list. I want to ask Meredith, but of course Joe will be here. Sven will have to be invited, without question, and Dawn might suffer a bit. And I hope you'll ask Richard, but Orlando is on the list, as a recent customer.'

'Not very professional at all. Ask everyone. They mightn't come.'

'You sound crotchety. Have you been at the library?'

'No, I had lunch with a woman ... '

She was rarely at the library now, Katherine realised. Her steady progress through Chiltern history, from Ceawlin and Cutha, through charter boundaries and land grants and Domesday Book, was changing. Her absorption in the past had gone off at a different angle, and she was not so certain how to write it out for public viewing. She thought of Tim Rothwell confidently waiting for the next set of chapters, and unease filled her.

'A historian, or a friend?' Olivia was asking.

Katherine let out a laugh. 'Only you could put it like that! No, not a historian. A friend, I think. Yes, a friend.'

Richard arrived home late that afternoon, throwing off boots and a dusty shirt at his door. Bella hurried through the house and out to the garden, to lap noisily at her water. He followed her and walked among his fruit trees, checking on green apples turning pink, and scattering the hens as he collected eggs. He put them carefully on the ground and stopped to tie a bean plant more securely. He smiled internally at the patch of ground where Katherine had insisted they lie last Sunday, and kicked at scraps of twig that had poked into backs and legs. Bella bounded round him, and he scooped the eggs out of her reach and retreated inside. He put the television on, and watched with interest the replays of the black shadow of the eclipse racing over the world, and the crowds gathered underneath it in France, in Germany, in Hungary, in Turkey, in Iran, in India. The last total eclipse of the sun visible in Britain was in 1927, in the north of the country, the commentator told him. Before that, we have to go back as far as 1715, when a great eclipse caused consternation in southern England, and put London itself into total darkness for more than three minutes. Richard snapped the television off, and went to the phone.

'Hallo, Kathy,' he said. 'Did you see it?'

'I saw it get very dark, but it was too cloudy to catch more than that. Good and atmospheric, though.'

'Same here. How are you? It's a long time since Sunday. What about meeting tonight? Come over and make sure our garden is all right, post-eclipse.'

'I don't think I will, if you don't mind. I need to think about things, and do some chores ... '

'Okay ... '

'Olivia asks if you are making some bowls for her?'

'I'll think about it right now, to occupy myself.'

But he went into his green bathroom and slowly bathed before going into his workshop, and then he reached into the drawer behind Ellen's boxwood bowl. He pulled out a small object and turned it over in his hands a few times, and took it to the window to hold it in the light. 'As if I don't know what's on it, Bell,' he said to the dog. 'If you show it to someone, is that as good as handing it over?' He blew on it and rubbed it on his shirt, and returned it to the drawer. Next he set out several blocks of wood he had, and one small log, and pondered over them for a time. He picked up an old block of elm, and weighed it thoughtfully. But then he put it down and turned vigorously. 'Come on, Bella', he said. 'We need some food and some drink and not to think too much. Let's walk to the King's Head and hear all about the eclipse.'

Katherine spent a restless evening, sitting with her neglected books and Benson papers in front of her, but replaying her talk with Moira in her mind. She undid her long plait, and pulled the strands between her fingers, and then felt irritated by it and tied it as far back as she could.

Moira had told her the scientific things, and spelt out the near impossibility of what she was thinking. But what about all the details Moira didn't know, those of which she, Katherine might in fact be the only person to recognise? She walked around the small room, prodding at curtains and cushions. With tight fingers, she moved her two beechwood bowls a fraction to one side. She threw herself on her chair, and lay her head on her last written pages. In a minute she picked it up, and began reading. It was about the Black Death. 'That's not quite right,' she moaned, and stood up again.

She went into the kitchen and looked out at Port Meadow. It seemed lighter and pinker than Wolvercote on the other side. The sun was setting beyond the hills. She thought about Richard himself; his buoyant spirits, his endless practicality, his grace and kindness when Eric muddled things or Martin's fatness got him stuck behind a railing, or Zinnia's clothes peaked in ridiculousness. She thought of him concentrating on his lathe, and standing her carefully behind him when chips flew, and she had a vision of him on the exact bit of meadow she was looking at now, hurling a stick for Bella. He was calm, he made her feel safe. She banged her hands on the window sill, feeling desperate. The bitter choice of what to believe he had given her after Swyncombe Down was quite, quite impossible.

She went to bed, and slept poorly.

In the morning the phone rang, early.

'Hallo, darling', he said. 'I've got a plan. Let's go away

for the weekend. I've told Eric I mightn't be free on Friday or Saturday. What do you think?'

'Oh, Rich!' she felt uplifted. 'That's a great idea. I would love to.'

To get away from Oxford and Benson seemed wonderful. She made coffee and sat at her desk, stacking papers in order, and managing, at last, a few written pages.

48

'We're going to drop her off at the Freemans,'' Richard told her, just before they set off. Bella was pacing round the Saab as Katherine transferred her bags to it early on Friday evening. 'She's going away for the weekend, too. It makes us much more flexible about where we can stay.'

'Poor Bella.' Katherine sat on the doorstep, fondling the dog's ears. Richard leaned beside the bonnet of the car with a map spread over it. It was the first time she had seen him since her lunch with Moira, and she felt a passing streak of detachment, as though since they had talked about him she looked at him with Moira's lens as well as her own. Then the thought was gone.

'Ready? Shall we take some apples?'

The little apples were barely ripe, but they picked a few of the reddest. There was an early evening hush in the garden. The trees were in their heaviest leaf, and the birds quiet and invisible. The air was still and almost palpable, held enclosed inside the fence.

'Do you notice it?' she asked Richard.

'You're only feeling it because we're leaving it. And I've mowed some of it for once.'

'You are not sensitive enough.'

'This was a hard bit to mow; the grass was all flattened.' He walked across the patch where they had lain last Sunday night. She frowned at him, showing mock sympathy, and liking him for remembering it aloud.

He was as brisk as usual. 'Let's go, let's see how far we get before it's dark.'

David and Prue Freeman lived in a rambling house of many harmonious additions and renovations, just outside Dorchester. It was out of sight from the road, up a long curving drive lined with shrubs and trees. Prue came out of the front door as they arrived, a man's shirt swinging crisply over putty-coloured jeans. She was carrying a dog's leash, but put it down as Richard opened the car door for Bella to jump out.

'This isn't for her, naturally. My four year olds don't need those any more! Yes, of course I remember Katherine.' She gave her a pleasant, business-like smile. She had little make-up, but the smooth hair seemed perfect. 'I think I'll get her round the back straight away,' she said to Richard, reaching for Bella's collar. 'She won't even notice you've gone.'

She and Richard spoke for a moment more, and Katherine stepped inside the car again. After watching them disappear through a side gate, Richard started the car, and turned it crunchingly in the gravel, and they left. 'She'll be fine,' he repeated. 'She'll find Sam around there.'

'It feels odd without her in the back. Empty'

'Think of it as light, or spacious.'

'I'm working on it,' she said, using one of his phrases.

They decided to follow the river west, and Richard found roads where they had an orgy of place-name games, laughing and thinking of more unlikely origins as the journey progressed. 'You should be much better at this than me,' Katherine said.

'I am. They are just not very complicated at the moment. Lower Village and Newlands, and that sign to Seven Bridges is actively unimaginative.'

'Seven Bridges? I think that's on the Roman road. Ermine Street.' She looked at the map more carefully. 'Just across Ermin Street is Cricklade. Shall we stop there?'

'You read my mind,' he said, cheerfully. 'Don't ever stop doing that, will you?'

She glanced at him in surprise and he glanced back, not smiling, but looking happy.

'That's as far as the Thames goes, more or less. We could explore it tomorrow. Tonight let's see where we can sleep.' They looked at each other and she felt the familiar rush of sensation.

In the wide high street of Cricklade, sloping down to the river, they stopped at the White Hart.

'I doubt they'll have a room free', Katherine said.

'I think they might.' Richard took their bags from the car.

'You've booked one!'

'Actually, yes.'

She hung onto his hand for a minute.

'The man at the next table is watching you,' Richard said conversationally, half way through their meal. They had found a table by the window, lit at first superfluously by candle-light, and now, later, somewhat dark. 'So he should be. You look ... beautiful.'

Katherine noticed his accent as he spoke, which she now rarely did. The streak of uncomfortable objectivity came briefly back to her. She had also observed a woman watching him, as he lounged near a map at the reception desk. 'You look pretty nice yourself', she said, honestly. Their legs touched.

'I told someone this week that I'm going to run a restaurant in my next life,' she said, idly, and immediately regretted the wording. Before he could respond, she asked, 'Have you been here before?'

'Right here, in this hotel? No, I don't think so. Around Lechlade, and Cricklade, and hereabouts, yes, I suppose so.'

When she was quiet he leaned forward and spoke more intensely. 'Are you surprised? If you believe I've had a long time, and ... moved every now and then, it must be very likely, surely? I avoided cities, don't like them, can't work in them. So, yes. I did live here once. A long time ago.'

'But what does that mean?'

'A long time ago for me. I would have to make a long list, and I don't even know if I could. I only thought about it as we were driving here, in fact. While we were playing games with place-names, I realised some of them were familiar. Hannington, and Hannington Wick, we drove past them. And Highworth.'

She looked at him with stony eyes. 'I don't like thinking about the details of it. The whole ... general idea is hard enough.'

'You will notice that I try only to answer what you ask.'

'Yes, that's true.' But did that make it more or less convincing?

He put his hand over hers, and she felt how warm it was, and looked at it in the candlelight. The skin was smooth and brown, the knuckles unwrinkled. From the back, her own looked little different, merely smaller.

'I'm going to have a huge pudding,' he said. 'This walnut, treacle, caramel, ice cream thing ... You?'

She shook her head, but smiled again. 'No. Some of yours.'

'Don't you believe it. I'll be guarding it from you.' He gestured to the waitress, and ordered it with a last quizzical look at Katherine.

When he finished, they enjoyably delayed going to bed

with a walk to see their river in the dark. 'This water's on its way to Benson', Katherine called on the bridge, invigorated by the midnight air.

'And points further east,' he agreed. 'London, lesser places like that.' St Samson's tower loomed over them as they returned, already close in step. The strange bedroom was exciting, and during the night they awoke from deep sleep and made love a second time, but as he held her and muttered something, Katherine felt disorientated, as though she neither quite understood him or knew where she was.

49

The next day was sunny and mild.

'Now, I really haven't made a booking for anywhere tonight,' Richard said, as he devoured what the hotel called The Very Full English Breakfast. Katherine was eating a dish of stewed figs, guavas, tamarillos, and mangoes. 'I suppose it's from some exotic fruit packet blend', she said, critically. 'But it's very nice.'

'Shall we proceed further west?'

'Sounds fine.' She looked at him and felt filled with affection. Yesterday's inarticulate doubts had faded with the night.

'A brief non-guided tour of Cricklade first.'

Outside they wandered the Saturday morning streets, and watched shoppers at a few market stalls. Just to the north of the town cows were rambling in a meadow of high grass, still colourfully strewn with wild flowers. 'That must be a Lammas meadow,' Richard said. 'The cows will have been put here last week.' He calculated in his mind for a minute. 'Last Thursday. Horses soon, and last of all sheep will get a go, if they have any. Then all off in February, at

Candlemas. Fancy them still doing it here.' He looked at the meadow with interest.

'Can you imagine, Richard, how the media would love to get hold of you? Tell us, if you would, Mr Cottell - oh, no, they'd be chummier. Tell us, if you would, Richard, are we doing it right with this meadow? What about this building restoration work, does the National Trust always get it right? You say you saw John of Gaunt in South Oxfordshire, Richard. Was he an impressive man? How does the traffic seem ... '

For a moment a look of absolute horror crossed his face. Then he joined in cheerfully. 'Could I get traffic re-routed, do you think? I'm afraid you're crossing a sacred well here, and over there the M25 is obliterating five undiscovered villages and the foundations of a forgotten monastery? We were glad when the monastery went, mind you, but laying six lanes over it seems a bit extreme.'

'Tell us more about the press-gang in Southampton, could you, Richard? Rough lot, were they?'

'Compared with you lot? Not bad. The sea-crossing was poor, though, and the naval issue amateurish. You worry about guns jamming today? I could tell you ... '

When they stopped laughing he said, soberly. 'It would be horrific. I only discuss it with historians I love, called Katherine, with wonderful hair, who know about Roke Elm, and can cook. That narrows the field.'

She nudged him with her shoulder and only said, 'We have to find the source of the Thames. It's our real mission for the day.'

In the end they stopped beside a small brook, running like a wide natural ditch beside a winding lane. 'This is not where the river authority has put its plaque,' Katherine said, doubtfully.

'No, but it's actually a shade above, it,' Richard was looking at the map. 'Who can say, with several tributaries and changes in wet and dry years?' He sat down on the lane's edge, near a clump of beech trees, untidy with undergrowth. The little stream ran below his feet, just audible in the silence. In a minute she sat beside him.

'I would have liked a spring, gushing magically out from a bank.'

'There probably was one, once. Here, or hereabouts. No, that is nothing but a guess!' He raised his hands defensively. She stretched her legs and felt the sun warm on them. It was very peaceful. As they sat quietly, a blue shape flashed over her shoulder, almost too fast to see. It touched a tree on the other side of the stream, and swooped back.

'Kingfisher', she breathed.

They watched and waited, and saw two of the birds, diving and flickering over the water, and finally posing as if to display their iridescent blue bodies on the tree opposite. After a moment's pause, they darted away downstream, out of sight.

'Does that convince you?'

'Absolutely. Would the water be clean enough to drink?'

She bent over and splashed a handful over her face, allowing one cautious drop into her mouth.

'You're the superstitious one,' he said. 'Wells and springs, for goodness sake.' But he bent down and did the same.

Slowly during the afternoon, they idled their way west. Katherine pulled on her sunglasses, and lost their place on the map as they wound on the smallest possible roads. Finally, she said, in a reporter's voice, 'Tell me, Richard. Where do you think we might be?'

'What a navigator,' he said, peacefully, and stopped the car.

After solemn study of the map, he said 'I don't know. But over the Cotswolds. We're on our way, gradually, down to the Severn. It doesn't matter, that's the pleasure of it.'

Within a few moments he stopped the car again at a crossroad. 'A sign,' he said, teasing her about the kingfishers earlier. He was looking at a black retriever, very like Bella, tossing a rubber ball on the scrap of lawn in front of a small pub set back on the curve of the road. 'It calls itself an inn, so let's see.'

Inside the pub an old-fashioned decoration of hop flowers circled the bar, and tables were spread with knives and forks as well as beer mats.

'Yes, you can stay the night,' said the man behind the bar. 'We have only one bedroom, but it's free. Would you like to see it?' Richard looked at Katherine.

'No,' she said. 'It's okay, we'll take it.'

'Dinner, too?'

'Yes, please.'

The bedroom was tiny, with not much room for more than a large bed beneath the eaves and a deep windowsill with another arrangement of hops on it. The bathroom was up and down steps, across a passage.

'I love it,' Katherine said, throwing herself back on the bed.

'You may not like it so much tonight during drinking hours. We're above the bar.'

'I'll love it again after that.'

He looked at her suggestively, and she laughed and closed her eyes. 'Don't spoil aesthetic moments.'

Outside near their car the young retriever approached them at a run. He offered them his rubber toy, shiny and unappetising with saliva, and crouched beside it, front paws down. His eyes sparkled.

'We're supposed to be on holiday from all this,' Richard said, and picked up the ball gingerly. He threw it high into the air and the dog watched its arc, quivering with excitement, and caught it on the first bounce.

'Absolutely no more,' Richard said. 'Just one more, that means.' He threw it once more and then turned towards Katherine.

'Come on, gullible person,' she said, careful to choose his other hand to hold. 'Exercise for us, too.' They walked for an hour from their own village to the next, and back along a hillside bridle path with views of long wide valleys, golden and ripe. When they arrived back the little pub was surrounded by cars, and filled with noise and people, spilling out to the lawn.

'I warned you,' Richard said, glancing up at their window above it.

'It'll be fine after dinner,' Katherine said, and surprised him by kissing him passionately, amidst the drinkers.

'What was that for?' he said, inside.

'We've had such a ... such an all right day. You make me happy, as I think I have told you.'

He grunted non-committally, and ordered drinks. 'How nice not to serve them myself.' His face looked changed, heavier and resigned.

During their meal, erratically served by rushed bar staff, he was almost silent. Katherine was surprised and uneasy. She was aware of creating conversation, and his replies were brief. 'Rich,' she said, and put her hand over his. 'Are you all right?'

'Sure.'

In a minute he said. 'Shall we have another bottle?'

She nodded. 'We don't have to drive anywhere.'

When the second bottle came, she talked carefully about the Gallery and its autumn exhibition, and described how Olivia's sister, Heather, was forcing their most famous potter, Sven Hansen, to the grindstone. 'To the wheel, is a better way to put it. He promised us four pieces, and we have nine already. Heather has found her role in life, a sort of cross between muse and agent. It's very productive. You wouldn't think so, to look at her.'

'How are people supposed to look?'

She looked startled at his sharp tone, and he immediately said, 'Sorry, Kathy. I'm crabby tonight.'

'Yes, you are ... '

He took her hand briefly, and drank the last of his glass. 'Shall we go?'

50

In the large bed under the eaves she lay in silence beside him. Doors were slamming outside, as the last customers left, and she heard their cars wind the hilly roads into the distance. There was a muffled clatter of glasses as the barmen cleared the tables. They had left a crack of the deep-set window open, and the curtain moved against the dried hops, rattling them slightly. She rolled on to her side and moved against him, putting an arm across his chest.

His eyes were open and he looked up at the eaves and the low beams. After several minutes he turned and lay facing her, shoulders pulled back so he could look at her eyes. One hand played with her long, unplaited hair. For once, unlike after his evenings of work at the King's Head, the smell of alcohol was in his mouth, not on his clothes alone.

'You see, it is nice in here.' She said, eventually.

'Katherine,' he said with anguish, 'The whole day was very nice, as you pointed out. Cricklade was *nice*. The driving was *nice*, the source of the river was *nice* ... They were all ... ' He swore and muffled it, pushing his head painfully against her neck.

'Richard!' She pulled away from him. 'Richard, what is the matter?'

She reached out to put on the light, but he stopped her hand from reaching it. She put her arm back around him and felt his next breath almost like a sob.

'What is the matter?' she repeated, with a reminiscent

flash of the fear of him she had felt on midsummer day on Swyncombe Down.

He sat up and leaned against the bedhead. She could see his face now, in the shifting light from the window, and his wide smooth shoulders. Her heart was beating fast.

'Lovely Kathy. Lovely, passionate Kathy.' His voice was slow and unlike itself. He reached out his arm and touched her face. 'No, don't flinch.'

Her mind raced in the silence. The dark roof beams seem to crowd over them in the little room. One of them should say something, but she couldn't. Then he was speaking again, in a more normal voice, but intensely.

'Katherine,' he said, 'Have you ever thought what this is really like for me? Not the technical bits, the birth certificates and so on. Not the freaky, science fiction bits' She had never heard him use the term before, and a wave of embarrassment washed over her. 'Not the bits that are fun, for you especially. Goodness, can you remember the Abbess of Godstow, how was the tower of Dorchester Abbey built, how do you get colour from woad, how did Benson really work? No, not those bits. I mean actually, daily, what it is like.'

She was silent, her eyes fixed on him. 'What it is like,' he said, 'Is always, slowly, losing anyone you love. They grow old, they die. You start again, you lose them, children too. You start again again -' he waved his arms to acknowledge the eccentric wording - 'And they get old and you look after them and they die. And you don't. I don't.' His language was jumbled. 'There are the more minor things of not actually ever having a family to refer to, or a childhood, or a place, and thinking carefully before you answer almost anything. But those can become habits. They're nothing compared to ... to those other things.'

Katherine was wordless.

He looked at her and tried to soften what he was saying

with a half smile. 'Today was so ... *nice* ... as you said,' He pressed the top of her thigh. 'That I looked ahead.' He stopped.

'No,' she said, finding her voice at last, and clearing her throat. 'No. I hadn't thought it through ... quite like that. Although now it seems so obvious, I can't think why.' Like a transferred thought now, she felt his loneliness. Zinnia had sensed it, she thought, even Zinnia.

'I was too much in love to think about it,' she said, following the idea slowly along.

They lay down and embraced with such desperation that she breathed, 'Hey! You'll break my ribs! Let go,' and at last he gave a laugh.

They talked on, in whispers which kept them close to-gether. Eventually Richard fell asleep, but Katherine was awake much longer, lying with one arm under him until it prickled with pain, and she eased it carefully out. She had been too much in love to think about his solitude; that was true. But there had been other ways to protect herself from thinking of it. She need not quite believe him. She could take the extra stimulation - what he had called the fun - of believing enough to ask the questions she loved to hear the answers to, but not enough to go inside his mind. When she enjoyed the game, she believed it. When it frightened her, she stopped. Those were the rules, and tonight he had broken them. She shifted restlessly. Could they go on playing the game, then? Moira Johnson came into her mind, hypothesising the immortality gene. 'Wouldn't it be exciting?' she had said, blue-eyed and bright. In theory, Katherine thought, confusedly - in theory, yes. She would go and see her again. As her mind began to swing, Moira's image was followed by Richard tussling with Bella on Wittenham Clumps, and then Richard sitting in the wrong pub, the Lamb, in Benson. Ploughman's bread would have been very heavy, he was saying, heavy and porridgy, not properly, risen like this bread. For some reason this made her smile, and then she slept.

51

She was awoken by Richard pulling back the curtain of the small window, and letting sun stream in.

'Wake up,' he said, superfluously, and lay himself on top of her, above the duvet.

'People will see you,' she muttered, with her eyes closed again. 'At the window.'

'There's nobody outside, and we're miles from anywhere. We don't know where we are,' he said, cheerfully.

She reached up and hugged him to her. 'I can see you.'

'Katherine,' he said, and kissed her. He looked at her soberly for a moment, and it was the nearest they came to acknowledging his distress the previous night. He seemed relaxed and happy, full of energy.

They had coffee and toast on one of the two outside tables, with the dog in attendance.

'What is the name of this place?' he asked, spreading a map on the table. 'We saw it last night when we were out walking.'

'I've forgotten. We'll have to find the sign again.'

The publican gestured toward the map when he returned with more coffee.

'Are you going to see the tree?'

'What tree?'

'The chestnut. The Tortworth Chestnut, about two miles away.' He put down the coffee and pointed on the map. The tree was even marked itself, they found when they looked.

'What is it?' Katherine asked.

'It's hundreds of years old. Maybe a thousand. It's a great sight.'

Katherine went tense, as though he had said something very tactless, but Richard looked amused and interested.

'Really? A thousand?'

'Well, it's certainly supposed to be the oldest chestnut tree in England.'

Richard raised his eyebrows in a question to Katherine. She nodded.

'I'd like to see it. Very much.'

An hour later, checked out of the small attic bedroom, they found the tree. Its vast hollow bole, contorted and wrinkled, stood in the centre of a grove of growing side shoots, gnarled old trees themselves. The whole little forest, all one tree, was like a mass of misshapen wooden caves, linked by hollow corridors and steps of trunks, and crowned by branch after branch of dense, flourishing greenery. Katherine walked and climbed among it, lost in admiration. Richard stood for a moment at the low iron fence surrounding it, where they had read the inscription on the iron gate.

'At least six hundred years old in 1800,' he repeated to her.

'I was sceptical till we got here,' she started saying, and then thought how surreal this was, here with him. 'But now I believe it. It looks every bit of its age.'

He laughed his unconcerned laugh. 'Yes, it shows it.' He felt the bark in its low, innermost trunk, damp and ridged and mottled brown and red. 'It stayed in one place', he said, as he walked among the sunken side branches, rooted and shooting up anew, 'And did very well.'

Katherine was poking around on the ground, looking for chestnuts. 'Pretty puny ones,' she said, holding up a few small, dry nuts to show him. 'I'm going to take them home and try them in pots. Wouldn't it be amazing if they sprouted?'

'Amazing,' he said, and she suddenly knew they were having an indirect, proxy conversation.

'Why this tree, this one?' she said. 'Why do you think?'

'Who knows? It's not the only one.' He glanced around the field beside them, where several more big old chestnuts stood above little clusters of staring sheep. 'So it started in a good but ordinary place. There was some nurturing.' Now he waved towards the ruins of the manor house behind them, in whose vanished garden the tree had stood. 'But not for long. No one attacked it directly, or if they did, not successfully.' They looked at a huge fallen, separated limb of the tree, lying dead among the healthy body parts. 'So it just kept going,'

'Does it make you feel ... anything? she said cautiously.

'Interested,' he said, cheerfully. 'Less surprised than you. Maybe there are dozens of old trees like this?'

'But you haven't come across any this old before?'

'No, I haven't.'

'Do you think they should do tests ... and investigate it more?'

'I presume they already do. And it doesn't make any difference at all to the tree, does it?'

'I guess not ... '

'So, no! Absolutely not.' He put his arm round her.

She nodded and leaned against him. 'But I'm going to plant these chestnuts, anyway.' she said. 'We could transfer them to your garden if they sprout. It's a wonderful, beautiful tree.'

52

On a Tuesday soon afterwards, Katherine decided to drive to Benson and take some photos. The cruck cottage is an obvious one, she thought, and put her maps and some notes in the back of the car. She drove slowly through the familiar roads. The browning flowers and lank greenness around her signalled that the season was on the brink of turning. Harvesters rumbled across fields, spraying fine yellow dust in the air. A cluster of tents lined the river bank at Chislehampton, front flaps all firmly closed on sleeping inhabitants.

She parked at the boatyard. It was a long time since she had walked in Benson alone, she realised, and counted back the months. Since February, deep in the winter. She lingered on the river bank, watching the water, and noticing *Halcyon Daze* neatly moored further up. Her recent sunny trips on it had relegated her first glimpse of it, but now she remembered Richard pointing it out on their cold first walk, and making her smile with his doubts about whether his friends Eric and Zinnia would ever actually take the plunge and live on it. They had talked about Ceawlin and Cutha, and Richard's open, attractive face had momentarily imposed itself over these unknown personalities. A faint blurring had begun, between facts and emotions. And down here too, on a starry night, an unknown man had cut Richard's forehead, and afterwards they had spent their first whole night in bed. She walked in from the river, and up the high street, and carefully photographed the cruck cottage. This is not historic, she thought, but photographed the florist's tables. A group of school children, on holiday, were sitting at them, talking loudly. She walked along Mill Street and looked into the weir, and photographed it with care from several angles.

Here had been the pond for which Ralph Restwald paid his rent in sticks of eels in 1279. The man Richard said had been his father-in-law. The ludicrous monstrosity of it hit her as if for the first time, and she breathed heavily and turned away from the water. She began to walk slowly back to the car. She paused in the churchyard. A workman's wheel-barrow was disrespectfully tipped against a gravestone beside her. She looked towards the squat tower without seeing it while the summer replayed in her mind, infused with sensation and happiness. She was, almost physically, a different person. The feeling of levitation still caught her. She thought of how quickly Orlando had drifted from her mind, and how little guilt she had felt, as though he had belonged to someone else. The canyon of worry which had cut open the middle of the season, she could somehow now cross. But when she crossed it, she realised, she came to Richard in bed a few nights ago, filled with an unreachable grief. She crossed the road to the riverside, and got into her car. After sitting in it for a few minutes, she turned the engine on, and drove to the King's Head.

'Hallo! Is this research, or thirst, or to see me?' Richard looked delighted, and reached up to lower the volume on the music.

'All three, I suppose. Hallo, Bella.' The dog appeared at the sound of her voice, and waved her tail. Richard looked at Katherine, loving the contrast between her intense eyes and vague, untidy movements. She looked full of some unspoken idea.

'I've been taking photos - the cruck cottage and so on. If they're not good enough, at least they will give the publisher's photographer an idea of what I want.'

He nodded. 'Do you want a drink?'

'Yes, please. Shall we have dinner tonight? Shall I go

back to the house and wait for you there? I'll make something.'

'Of course. Have you got a scheme up your sleeve?'

'Not really. I missed you.' They touched each other. 'What is this music, exactly?'

'Exactly, it is - ' He picked up the disc cover and read it. 'Patsy Cline in the Big Country.'

She rolled her eyes at it and at him. 'Quite good, actually, isn't she?'

After a few minutes she left, and soon let herself in to Oak Farm House. It was quiet and orderly, and the garden was welcoming. In the workshop, she noticed, Richard had started work on a bowl. Its thick shape was completed, and hours of careful turning would make its form as thin as glass. She picked it up and smelled it, drawing in the fresh sweet wood fragrance. All her senses felt alive.

When he arrived a few hours later he found her sitting at the table, adding to a page of notes headed '*The Decline of the Medieval Village: the Fifteenth Century.*'

'That looks serious.'

'It's not going very well. I keep making more and more notes, instead of writing the thing. Nearly there, though. Hallo, Rich, darling.'

He kissed her and said, 'That's what I wanted to do in the pub today. Thank goodness you are here, so I can make up.'

He threw his beer-smelling shirt off, and disappeared to the bathroom and came back with clean clothes and wet hair. They sat and drank beer and eventually ate her chicken casserole, packed with vegetables she had picked in the afternoon. Bella lay looking away, but wrinkling her nose at the smell.

'Did you feel guilty looking at my hens through the window while you made this?' he asked, remembering a complaint of hers.

'Yes, I did a bit. I didn't look them in the eye. You don't feel guilty, do you?'

'Never. Not about my hens at least. They love living here.' He dished himself more as he spoke, brown forearms moving neatly.

She told him about the photos she had taken, and reminded him about the first time he had pointed out *Halcyon Daze* to her. She came and stood behind him and put her arms around him and his chair. She stroked him.

'Are you doing that deliberately?' he said in a minute.

'Yes.'

'What shall I do with you?'

'Guess?' She lay her head on his crisp, curling hair, and pressed against him.

Later she lay beside him with her eyes open, and still holding him and said, 'Rich, you know I'm on the pill.'

'Mmmh.'

'I want to stop. Come off it.'

'What?' He sat up in one movement, and looked down at her. 'Kathy! Why? Aren't you well?'

'Of course I'm well!'

He lay down again and cradled her in his arms. 'Darling, after all I've said about children ... and ... '

'I know,' she interrupted urgently. 'That's just why. Ever since we talked about it, you talked about it, when we were away, I couldn't think of anything else.' She sounded tearful. 'I don't want you to be lonely; I don't want to leave you! Our children could stay with you more ... Oh, God, I know that's not logical.' She cried and he held her, stricken.

'Darling, darling. Think about it.'

'That's all I do!'

'No, I've thrown you off balance. That stupid outburst.' He groaned. 'I was drunk.'

'You weren't.'

'I was!' They both laughed at the ridiculousness of the disagreement.

'Kathy,' he said more calmly, resting her on his shoulder. 'Darling. It doesn't work.'

'Don't you dare say 'I've been here before'!'

'Well ... for whatever reasons, do you think I should be fathering children?'

'Clearly, yes!'

'I used to ... try not to ... because it was sad, and now I know more, it's also because ... it shouldn't happen.'

'But you don't know more! You never investigate it!'

He looked at her. 'Shall we just do one thing at a time?'

'Yes, you're right.' She subsided.

'But Richard,' she said in a minute, almost crying again. 'What about me? How am I ever going to have children?'

He pushed away and turned over. 'With someone else, of course!' he said into the pillow.

'I don't want someone else!' she shouted. 'I want you!'

'Darling.' He turned over and took her in his arms again, and stroked her hair.

'Will you wait a few months? Promise me you'll wait a few months. It is unforgivable of me to have got us into this situation; it is completely my fault.'

She said nothing, and in a minute he continued. 'When you believed me, about ... '

'I mightn't believe you', she said, still almost shouting. 'I haven't decided yet.'

A smile crossed his face. 'My Katherine. Well, if it's not true, of course there's no problem.'

She lifted her head, but he put his hand over her mouth.

'But there is a problem.'

'So will you wait a month or two?' he said, after a silence. 'Promise.'

'What will be different then?'

'We will have thought about it. I will have thought about it.'

53

A few days later, she had a few more chapters completed. She got her film printed, and added the Benson photos to the pages, and they lay wrapped on her desk now, ready for the post. She included a letter promising more to follow soon. She had no idea what would be in it, and she thought about it for a while, drumming her fingers absently on the desk. It would have to be about the fading of community living, she decided, and the dawning of the age and identity of the individual, and the break up of old power structures like the church. But physically, on the ground, how much of this would show? In Benson the strips and furlongs of the open fields would continue to lie in place for five more centuries. Until then, anyone returning would find the landscape unchanged. Except that no one could return, of course.

She stood from her desk and walked to look out at Port Meadow, and came back to her desk and looked for a long time at the last few photos, which she had taken at Oak Farm House. In her favourite, Richard sat on the grass outside, squinting slightly into the sun, smiling, impatient for her to finish the task. One side of him was shadowed, and in the background Bella was passing by, turning to look at them both. She stood the pictures of Richard and his house along the window sill, and then looked up a telephone number and dialled it. Once again, she got through unexpectedly easily.

'Moira,' she said. 'It's Katherine Laidlaw here. Do you think we could meet again?'

Moira answered without surprise. 'Sure,' she said. 'Why don't you suggest a place this time?'

54

Katherine was responsible for ordering food and drink at the Gallery party for the opening of its autumn exhibition. 'Get anything non-staining and unmessy.' Olivia had said. 'If it looks pretty and tastes edible, that's a bonus.' Olivia herself was setting up the display, and printing and reprinting the catalogue list. Even at a late moment, she had hoped for wooden bowls from Richard, but he had demurred. 'They're only fun, Kathy,' he had said, the last time she mentioned it. 'I don't want to turn them into serious work', and Katherine had been obscurely pleased. Her own bowls seemed more precious.

'I'm very fidgety about Meredith,' Olivia said, half an hour before the guests were due. 'Joe still doesn't know.'

'For goodness sake,' Katherine said, more calmly than she felt. 'There'll be a crush of people. He's hardly going to say, 'Hi, Dr Ash! By the way, your wife and I meet twice a week.' He'll be professional.'

'I suppose so.' Olivia's hair was newly-shaped again, and she wore her star and moon ear-rings. She had a plain white dress on, sleek and smooth. She looked at Katherine's concerned eyes, and burst out. 'Guess what? I think it might be happening! I might be ... '

'Livvy!' Katherine's face flickered through several expressions before it registered pure pleasure. 'Are you sure? Since when?'

'No evidence at all, yet. But I feel different, I'm sure.'

When Katherine looked doubtful, she said, 'Ask me next week.'

'You should know', said Katherine, with surprising emotion.

Meredith Baker-Lynn was the soul of discretion. He arrived with his wife, a groomed, fit looking woman who reminded Katherine of Prue Freeman, and was introduced to Joe with formal politeness. He had straggling, gingery hair, and smiled showing his insecure looking teeth. His voice was deep and pleasant. Surely not, Katherine thought, looking at him speaking to the Ashes and other early arrivals, surely not? Olivia looked radiant but business-like, and muttered, 'One tricky moment over', as she passed Katherine to greet more visitors and pass out the catalogues. Dawn was handing drinks around, the white wine only, which Katherine had stipulated, or watery-coloured non-alcoholic mixes. Penguin Cafe Orchestra discs played in the background, and outside in the High Street people trailed past on their way home from work, or to early evening appointments. Katherine noticed them peering in at the growing crowd in the Gallery, and as she looked, Richard arrived. He wore one of his usual blue-green shirts, and light coloured trousers with very polished tan shoes. He met her eyes immediately, and steered through the visitors to reach her.

'Surviving?' he said, holding her arm for a moment.

She nodded, and returned his look, with a slight movement of her lips, as if to say she would like to kiss him, but couldn't, and he squeezed her arm and let it go. Dawn brought him a glass of wine, with her prancing walk. She had a short black dress on, and black, strappy sandals.

Katherine took him to see a few favourite objects. A little court of admirers was gathering around Sven Hansen, and Heather was eating canapés steadily, looking proud and flushed, dressed in yellow.

'Look,' Katherine said to Richard. 'Red dots like that

could have been yours.' A few of the pieces of pottery and pictures already had red 'sold' stickers on them.

'I don't regret it. These are ones I like.' He returned to look at Alun Palmer's white, shell-like pots, and in a minute she saw him exchanging words with Meredith and Mrs Baker-Lynn.

'Weird eyes that man has', he said to Katherine later. 'As if he is working on making them piercing.'

'That's Olivia's therapist', she whispered, and giggled. 'You know, the visualisation?'

'Oh, him,' he said, and turned happily to glance at him again. 'His wife seemed quite normal.'

She thought about what Olivia had told her earlier. 'Rich,' she muttered again, following his glance towards Meredith. 'You don't think ... do you?' She looked from Olivia to Meredith.

He laughed his unrestrained laugh, and said, 'No, honestly. Impossible. Absolutely not.'

As if summoned by worrying association, Joe appeared, and she introduced them. Joe was at his most charming and outspoken, and put his arm around her while he said, 'Katherine is responsible for more sales in my wife's shop than you could imagine. And I have known her since she couldn't have sold anything.'

'What nonsense, Joe,' she said fondly, and left them talking. A minute later she noticed a very fat figure approach them, and recognised Martin and then Carolyn. Carolyn was studying her catalogue and locating objects carefully, while the men talked. She was about to wave at her when the door to the footpath swung open force= fully, and a man entered unsteadily, and gave a single shout. She couldn't understand what it was, except something like 'Heavy!', but he made straight for her, and she smelled alcoholic fumes wafting ahead of him. 'Heavy!' he tried to shout again, but Richard had detached himself from his group and was already there. 'No, you don't', he said calmly, and in one movement caught the waving arms and wrenched them behind the man's back and turned him round. 'Outside, I think', he said, and the other visitors came to life. Someone in a dark suit held the door open and stood back politely, and Richard walked the man out onto the footpath and disappeared with him down the High. In a minute he returned, shrugging, and a hum of conversation closed smoothly over.

'Have you done that before, Richard?' Martin called, and he and Carolyn laughed. Katherine touched Richard's hand briefly, and turned to talk to a woman she realised after a few sentences was Mrs Piers Finch.

'Is your husband here?' she said, her last encounter with Piers rushing back to her, and remembering how she had jumped out of his car and left the little girls wide-eyed in the back seat.

'Of course.' They were turning to look for Piers when there was a commotion in the doorway again. The man was back, swaying and shouting violently. As Richard reached him the man took a swing at him, and their fists met in the air, thudding. Richard grabbed the hand and wrenched it hard downwards and the man almost fell. This time Richard walked him out of the door and was gone for a longer time. The Penguin Cafe Orchestra sounded louder. Katherine talked uneasily to the Finches, and Olivia and Dawn circulated with drinks and food. When Richard came back he crossed to Olivia and said to her, 'Delivered him to a policeman this time. They seemed to know each other,' and laughed.

'Please, please have a drink,' Olivia said, and kissed him on the cheek.

'Are you all right?' Katherine asked. 'I hated it when he came back.'

'Well, yes,' he said, and rubbed his wrist. 'It's not so different from the King's Head here, is it?'

'It's added a frisson, I think.'

'He could have smashed some of Sven's pots,' Heather told them.

After another hour, the Gallery rapidly emptied, and finally Olivia stood behind her desk, counting off the red sold marks, and commenting on the purchases. 'I'm tired,' she said. 'All that talking and still trying to tick things off.'

'Very tired?' Katherine said significantly, and Olivia nodded with pleasure.

'I don't think I'm imagining it.' Heather and Sven were still there, and Joe and Richard.

'Dawn's gone,' Katherine remarked, and Olivia said cautiously,

'Yes, do you know who she's gone to meet?'

Katherine shook her head.

'Orlando. In great excitement.'

'Oh, my word ... he wasn't here.'

'Yes he was, just briefly. Long enough to buy this ... ,' she pointed to a Dawn Hammond ceramic vase on her catalogue list.

Katherine felt a passing pang, and knew that Olivia was watching her. 'It's quite a good idea,' she said, and discovered she meant it. 'Dawn would fit in brilliantly in Rio, if she ever gets there. An Ipanema girl if ever there was.'

Olivia looked relieved. She glanced at Joe and Richard, helping themselves to the last canapés. Heather was making a list of her own, of the purchasers of Sven's pots. 'Shall we go and eat?' Olivia said, 'The six of us.'

In the restaurant, at the end of the narrow lane opposite, they ate mussels and garlic bread, and Sven ordered the most expensive wine he could see. 'This is the only thing to do with profits,' he said, and Heather looked flushed with pleasure.

Late in the night, Richard and Katherine took Bella for a walk on Port Meadow. 'This was a very public night for us,' she said, thinking of Orlando and Dawn, and Richard marching the drunk man away while another guest held the door for them.

'It was.' He sounded as relaxed as ever, looking out for Bella's dark arrivals and departures around their feet.

'I mean, it seemed very far from your house. From Roke Elm, when we found it.' She laughed at her own sentimentality, but Richard agreed.

'Oh yes', he said. 'We're far from Roke Elm.'

55

Moira and Katherine met for lunch again, this time at Gee's, in the converted greenhouse further up the Banbury Road. Katherine had chosen the venue with care. It was an easy walk from the science park for Moira, and offered tables far enough apart for carefully pitched conversations not to be overheard. She had also dressed with care, trying to look sane yet academic, and with no streak of eccentricity. She wore the jacket again, over a long clinging skirt, and her crinkly hair was smoother than usual in its plait, and hung neatly over one shoulder. She smiled at her efforts as Moira came in sight, very short skirt over wine-coloured tights and high-heeled boots.

'Hallo!' Her bright face broke into a smile as she found Katherine's table. 'Sorry I'm late. Pre-term chaos. The new year's admissions into my department are still all up in the air ... '

She banged the beaded satchel on to the empty chair

beside her, and sat down. Today Katherine looked extraordinarily pale, she thought. She had a most changeable face. Her dark eyes looked tense. They ordered lunch, and talked about Moira's department and her teaching load. 'I love it, of course. It's what we all should be doing. But once you're Head of Department, inevitably, you do less and less. It goes with the territory; you spend all your time raising money. Extraordinary long meetings, full of very intelligent questions, but no answers!' Even feeling slightly sick, Katherine laughed. 'This morning, for example, while running in and out discussing things with the admissions people in the intervals, I sat in a meeting where we did have something to decide, something really quite major, affecting university policy as a whole. So what did we do? Decided to go away and write reports on it and come back in eighteen months ... Eighteen months!'

'The art of decision-avoidance,'

'You sound quite envious.' Moira said instantly.

Katherine was saved by the arrival of their lunch, plates of mixed fish, sea bass pieces delicately separated from tuna, and crusted cod beside shrimps sprinkled with olives. The waitress stood a bowl of green salad between them.

'Wine?' she asked, and they shook their heads. Moira waited.

Katherine ate one mouthful, and put down her fork.

'You know when we met last time, and I asked you about ageing and genes and ... '

'Yes.'

'Well. In the course of the history I'm working on ... ' She picked her glass up and put it down.

'Take a run at it,' Moira said, lightly.

'I've met someone who says he is seven hundred years old, and I think he might be.'

Moira's head and shoulders flinched back as though she

had been struck. She looked at Katherine's set face and open lips.

'Why?'

'Why does he say it, or why do I believe it?' They were speaking very slowly, with several beats between responses.

'Why ... either?'

'I haven't thought about why he says it.' Katherine thought about it now. 'I think he just ... wants to talk about it. He needs to.'

'He talks about it?'

'Oh, yes. When I ask him.'

After a minute Moira said, 'Where do you see him?'

'Where do I see him? Everywhere. But mostly there, in Benson. He comes from Benson.'

She gave a huge sigh, as though she were short of breath.

'Katherine, what sort of man is he? Is he, say ... ' Moira fluttered her hand. 'A mystical sort of person?'

'Mystical?' She alarmed Moira by laughing before replying. 'No one, but absolutely no one, could be less mystical. He works in a timber yard and a pub. He makes wonderful wooden things. He has a garden and a dog.'

Moira was so distracted by Katherine laughing again, that she said, 'Well, how old is he?' and then covered her face with her hands. 'I mean ... '

Then they both laughed, and Katherine spoke more normally. 'No, it's a sort of sensible question. He's about forty two. That's what he seems, that's what I guessed, and that's what I suppose most people think.'

'Why on earth do you believe any different?'

Katherine prodded the fish with her fork, and then took a breath and began talking as though a dam had broken. She told Moira every historical detail she and Richard had talked about, and about all the people in Richard's stories. She described the Cottell family and the Restwalds and all the records in which they appeared, over several centuries, and their lands and taxes and marriages and court appearances. She spoke with intensity, thoughts rehearsed over and over in her mind. The waitress reappeared, but when Katherine glanced at her without a break in the flow of a sentence, she retreated again. Moira listened in bewilderment, and then consternation.

'But is he actually in these records?' she interrupted at last.

Katherine was hardly stopped. 'No, and that's correct. These records are far from continuous, and none dates from exactly the time he was around, or around as an adult with a family. Moira, what you have to know is that this is a pretty specialised patch of history.'

When Moira only looked at her with concerned eyes, but said nothing, she carried on. 'I started out, of course, thinking just what you must be thinking now. I was scared, and thought he was mad. But he so clearly isn't mad, that I began thinking about the facts he knew. There were some that I was pretty well sure I was the only person who knew them. They would have been meaningless to anyone but me.' She gave some examples, like Walter Cotel having given the Abbess of Godstow three acres of land before 1279. 'Who else could know or want to know such a detail?'

Moira, also not hungry any more, drank water. Katherine rushed on. 'Then there were other things he told me I didn't happen to know, but could check. Like the name of William Cotel's wife. Clara, as he said. And William and Clara survived the Black Death, also as he said. Their names reappear in taxation lists.'

'But he must have seen these records too? Must have!'

'In theory, yes. I've thought of that so often,' Katherine said miserably. 'But it's taken me several years to track them down. They are in Latin, they're only in rare, specialised libraries, and not all in one place. Some are only in the Public

Record Office in London. This is a man who works full time, in a very unacademic job, in Benson.' She spread her hands, palms upward.

'Why are you telling me?' Moira asked gently. She knew what the answer would be.

Katherine's eyes were large. 'I suppose I want you to tell me, scientifically, yes it's possible, or no, it's not. I feel a bit desperate.' She tried to laugh, to lighten her phrase, but felt as though she might choke.

Moira was silent for a minute. Her mind was running, but she spoke calmly. 'Can we go back to the history bits first? I haven't quite grasped everything. How did you meet this man ... '

'Richard.'

'Richard. Where did you meet?'

'In a coffee place in Benson, when it was raining. He spoke to me.' She could see Moira look doubtful. 'But he had heard me talking to someone else before that, it turned out. I was asking about footpaths, and used some obsolete old names for them, so he was interested.'

'Was he targeting you, then, would you say?'

'Targeting me?' She sounded horrified. 'Of course not. Well ... yes. But not ... not in a strange way.'

The four people at the table next to them stood up to leave, and there was a moment of moving chairs, and nods and smiles. Then Moira said, 'Look, I have to ask you this. Are you and he ... um?'

'Yes, we are.'

'Okay,' Moira said, cautiously. 'Okay.'

She thought a little longer and said, 'Has he ever produced historical facts that are wrong, or impossible?'

'No,' Katherine answered immediately. 'Some that I can't check, nobody could. Personal details, visitors to Benson, the place where outdoor meetings were held - that sort of thing. But all plausible, never an anachronism.'

They sat looking at each other. A new group arrived at the neighbouring table. Moira was bewildered by Katherine's conviction.

'What does he look like?'

Katherine described him. 'Completely physically normal,' she finished, blushing, which Moira noticed. 'Except awful old palms and the soles of his feet. They really could be ... And I've noticed that any scar heals abnormally well and quickly. And his parents were first cousins.' She shook her head. 'I can't tell you more. He is, apart from this bizarre thing, just ... ' Her voice tailed off, and she picked up her fork again as though she had newly discovered they were at a table. She held it above the food and looked at Moira.

'His parents were first cousins?'

'Yes, and maybe their parents, too, for all I know. Who knows, in those little Chiltern communities ... '

Moira sighed. 'You know this is unlikely beyond ... well, beyond statistics?'

'Of course. But, 'unlikely', you say?'

'Impossible is a risky thing to say in genetics. The more we know, the more we know we don't know. We could look at DNA, and cell structure, and few other things. But what would we use for comparative matter? We would notice any startling anomaly, for sure.' She raised her eyebrows and looked at Katherine questioningly. 'Is that really what you want?'

Katherine silently tidied the food on her plate. 'Perhaps.'

'Does your relationship depend on this? I mean, it's hard to imagine ... do you talk about it all the time?'

'Certainly not!' Katherine smiled and then looked sad. 'But the longer it goes on, the more difficult it is. I think about it more, and I think he does ... I know he does.'

'Are there other avenues you could explore?' Moira asked carefully. 'For instance, some medical ... '

'Are you thinking of a psychologist?' Before Moira could

reply Katherine said 'And a linguist, to analyse his speech patterns, and an etymologist, to think about his vocabulary, and an analyst, because he dreams a lot, or maybe I could get him to list every place he's lived for seven hundred years, and go over all the historical records of each place to see if he appears there, too! And what about the police, with a lie detector?' Moira sat back in her chair with her hands in the air in submission, and Katherine flopped back, too, and they both laughed, weakly. Moira signalled to the waitress, and when she arrived at their table, said 'We've changed our minds. Could we have a bottle of your house white?' The girl glanced at their uneaten meals, and nodded in surprise.

'Good idea,' Katherine said, and took several quick mouthfuls when the wine arrived. 'You could make a lifetime career of it, doubting him all the time. Trying to catch him out.'

'You couldn't,' Moira said. 'Nothing could last like that. It would be awful.'

After another few mouthfuls Katherine said, 'It was very good of you not to get up and run away when I told you. I did, when he first said it to me, and I stayed away for several weeks.'

'But you missed him?'

'Terribly.'

Moira rubbed with her fingers on the lipstick mark she had put on her wine glass. 'What a revolting side effect of make-up,' she said cheerfully. 'I'm going to go away and think about every kind of test we could run, Katherine. You think about it, and if you're sure you really want to try some, ring me and we could get started.'

'And he has to agree, of course.'

'Of course.' She started to gather up her bag, and look for her purse inside it. 'Most of me feels utterly sceptical and rather worried', she said, looking straight into Katherine's eyes. 'But a bit of me feels incredibly excited.'

'That's how I've been for months,' Katherine said, and felt a tearful surge of relief.

56

The evening before she went to Oak Farm House on the following weekend, Katherine made an elaborate cake. A layer of walnuts and jam and burnt brown sugar nested inside a coffee cake, moist with a liberal amount of sour cream in the mix. She listened to the radio as she worked, and commented aloud on the speakers' opinions, and then tiring of them, changed programme. A television personality was choosing his favourite discs. 'I'd have to have something very sad, for that half of my psyche,' he said, importantly, and chose Beethoven's Kreutzer Sonata.

'That's not sad,' Katherine said to him. 'It's wonderful.' She listened to the two instruments sighing and chasing each other, only to be curtailed when the interviewer thought enough time had passed.

'And for the optimistic half of me,' the man said, 'Well, even the optimistic half of me needs something a bit sad. But with a humorous bite. Some country and western, and preferably Patsy Cline. What about 'Missin' kissin'?''

'I don't believe it,' Katherine said.

'Oh, yes, joyous,' said the interviewer earnestly. 'Joyous.'

The chords streamed out, and she slid the cake into the oven, and closed the door slowly to avoid a rush of air. Just as she did so, the telephone rang.

'Hallo?'

'It's me here,' her brother said. 'What's that racket?'

'Patsy Cline. I'm cooking. Just a minute, I will subdue her.' She reached out and turned the sound down.

'Hallo, James. How are you?'

'I'm okay. I'm just back from California ... no, not at all glamorous. Airport hotels and boring meetings.' He sounded very flat.

Katherine commiserated.

'Could I stay with you tomorrow night? I have to come up to Oxford.'

She thought for a moment. 'I'm sorry James, I won't be here. But you are very welcome to use the flat, of course. What are you coming for?'

'A funeral, actually. A guy in the office topped himself.'

'What? What a horrible phrase.'

'He was called Toby Bernschmidt. He had the desk next to mine. Did it while I was away.'

'That's terrible! I'm so sorry. Why?'

They talked about the suicide for few more minutes. The man had been a heavy drinker, he told her, but there had seemed to be no other distress signals. It was the most common cause of death for young men after traffic accidents, it seemed. His parents lived in Oxford.

'Of course you can use the flat,' she finished. 'Will you be all right?'

'Oh, fine. He wasn't a very close friend. But it won't be fun. Are you going to be with Richard?' he asked, surprising her by remembering his name.

'I liked him', he said magisterially, before he rang off.

Bella ran out to meet her when she arrived.

'She's endlessly flattering,' she said to Richard. 'She makes me think my arrival is so wonderful. I think you should get a cat to cut us down to size.' They embraced and she held him tight.

'You're quite flattering yourself,' he said.

'Look what I've brought us.' She extracted herself and reached into the car seat. 'One cake.'

'It's a beautiful cake,' he said, carrying it inside. 'Why?'

'It's my birthday. Well, on Monday. Near enough.'

'Kathy! Couldn't you have warned me?' He looked genuinely concerned. 'Monday?'

'Yes, just on the cusp of Libra.'

'Darling,' He kissed her again, ignoring the astrology. 'I owe you lots of presents, then.'

Later she asked him cautiously, 'When is your birthday? We haven't neglected that, have we?'

He waved his hands in a hopeless way, but laughed. 'Approximately December. I call it December the sixth, when necessary. It's about right.'

'Could you bear it if I spent the afternoon in the garden?' Richard asked her. 'It's a mess, and I want to clean it up and plant some bulbs. And I might remove the ducks' residence if they've abandoned us for good.' Katherine watched him as he worked, and made some desultory efforts at helping, dragging away sacks of fallen leaves. Bella jumped around him, pleased with the outdoor activity, until she suddenly lost interest, and retreated inside, to lie near the step. 'Fair-weather friend,' Katherine heard Richard call her. He had undone his shirt and rolled the sleeves above his elbows, and smelled faintly of sweat and damp earth when he came and sat beside her.

She told him about James's office friend, and that James would be in Wolvercote that night.

'It's hard to imagine, isn't it?' she concluded. 'Suicide?'

'Not hard to imagine, no. But hard to do.'

She pressed her lips together in concern. 'Of course I've thought of it occasionally,' he went on, answering her unspoken question. 'This year, once.'

'When?'

'After midsummer's day. When you had gone. We'd had such a good few months, and I had talked about very old memories, things no one else knew about, for years and years. It seemed as good a time as any.'

'But ... ?'

'Not my style, is it?' He spoke almost humorously, and nodded towards Bella. 'Who else would want that?'

'Don't,' she said, inadequately, and pressed her hand on his thigh until he complained it hurt.

'Rich,' she asked later. 'Can you read Latin?'

'I shouldn't think so. Why, on earth?'

'But when you learned,' she persisted, 'It must have been in Latin. Weren't things only written in Latin, then?'

He pulled a face of ostentatious concentration, with his hands between his legs, rubbing Bella's head. 'I suppose so,' he said after a long pause. 'You're right. But repetitive things, like rents, and tenancy rules, you always were translating in your mind into English anyway. It was like a code in which things had to be put. And the church things, who minded whether you understood it, anyway?'

She nodded, looking at his clear eyes and relaxed hands. She moved closer and sat against him. He felt hot through her own shirt and jumper.

'Then I suppose it must have gradually just become English.' He frowned. 'Same principles, but it wasn't in code any more. No,' he turned to look at her, and pushed Bella gently aside. 'In answer to your question, I'm sure I can't, now, read Latin.'

'I suppose not,' she said, and sighed.

'Sorry!' he said, sharply.

'Richard.' She rested her head guiltily on his shoulder for a moment, and then jumped up. 'Let's cut this cake now. I have to wish, of course. Without benefit of candles, though.'

'All of twenty-nine,' he said teasingly as they drank coffee and ate the cake. 'Did you wish?'

'I can't tell you.'

He disappeared across the kitchen and into his workroom and came back with one fist clenched. 'Hold your hand out.'

She held her palm under his and he silently placed a small silver object in it. She looked at it wordlessly for a minute, and then turned it over and picked it up. In a second the ordinary afternoon vanished. 'What is this ... Richard, is this a seal?' She looked at him in disbelief.

'It's a seal,' he agreed.

Her heart was beating with excitement and worry. She was holding, she knew, something rare and precious. The thick round disc had a perforated lug at one end. 'For suspending it?' she queried, fingering the little hole.

'From his belt, usually.'

'Whose belt?'

'Walter's. It's his seal from the Abbess of Godstow. Nothing counted without Walter's seal slapped on.' He spoke lightly, but she could see he was moved, and looking at it intently.

'I don't know what to say.' She sounded dazed. She squeezed her hand shut over the little object and then opened it again. 'What's on it?' She leaned over it, and he waited, watching.

'Godstowe' she spelt out the letters around the edge. 'Godstowe 1204.' Below the letters, in the centre of the disc, was a cross. She turned it over, breathing unevenly. On the reverse were the letters 'Wa C', and beneath them an image like a pictogram, a house with a triangular roof, made with six engraved cuts. The engraved lines were black with age, and the remainder of the little disc glowed a dull, clean silver.

'The house is a cot, of course, a cottage. A play on his name.'

'They did that,' she said with a dry mouth.

'Would you like it?'

She let out her breath. 'Oh, no, Richard. I can't keep this. It's too ... it's yours.' She handed it back to him, keeping her eyes fixed on it. Where could you get such an object?

He was looking at her with his tender, intent expression. 'I was the one who could read, remember? We just discussed it? So I got it, after him.'

She still said nothing, and he bounced the little object in his hand, and said, 'I'll keep it for you, shall I? When you're ready for it I'll hand it over.'

'If I'm ready.'

He came closer to her and put his arms around her and repeated, 'If you're ready.'

Then he moved towards his workshop and called to her, 'Come and see where I'm putting it. Just in case.'

She followed him into the room and watched as he pulled the drawer out. 'Here it is,' he said cheerfully. 'Behind Ellen's bowl.' He put it carefully in, and closed the drawer.

'Now,' he turned around. 'I have to get ready for the King's Head. It's Saturday. Are you coming?'

She was just behind him. 'What would you say about having some blood tests?'

'Blood tests?'

'Yes, or cell samples, or whatever they need to take?'

'Katherine.' His expression changed. 'I'm not a guinea pig. What good would that do anyone?'

She put her hands on his chest, but looked down. She heard Bella's claws clicking across the floor towards them.

'I don't know. It might be ... interesting.'

'Interesting!' He took her hands off him and dropped them. 'It's not actually my great wish to be interesting like that.' He walked past her and ran up the stairs. 'I know it's alarming for you, I know you want proof', he called as he went. 'But no. Absolutely no, Katherine, and please don't mention it again.' She heard bath water running. She thought he had finished talking, but then he shouted, over the noise of the water. He sounded enraged. 'Do I seem like a person who wants to be a research project, or entertainment? Some big newspaper articles about me, or what about a sighting place and a plaque, perhaps, like the tree?'

Tree, she wondered wildly? Oh, the Tortworth chestnut. Then she was running up the stairs after him. He was flinging his clothes into a corner and she ran and tried to embrace him. To her surprise he took her in his arms, and stroked her hair, breathing heavily. 'Okay, Kathy, darling, darling. I'm sorry I shouted. I know it's hard.' She clung to him until he suddenly said. 'This bloody thing will overflow.' He turned the taps off, and put his arms around her again.

'No, you don't seem that sort of person,' Katherine said, sadly. 'Not in the slightest.'

'Well, good,' he said. 'Will you come to the pub with me, then? Imagine how mortified Eric and Zinnia will be if they can't offer birthday drinks.'

When they got home from the King's Head they went straight to bed, almost without conversation.

'I want you so much,' he said very soon. 'Don't ever attack me in the bathroom like that just before we go out somewhere. Did you know it, all evening, while we talked to everyone else ... ?' He held her left breast and pulled her hair back with his left hand, moving above her. 'That I was only waiting, waiting for this.'

'Yes, I knew. This?'

'Kathy?' He moved faster.

The room swung around her eyes, and she shut them.

'Hold me, hold me!'

He gave the groan she loved and she made a choking noise, and then fell as limp under him as if she had fainted.

He lifted his head up to look at her, and she raised her

arm with an effort, and lay it on his back. 'I love you,' she said, so quietly he could hardly hear.

57

Richard was soon asleep, but Katherine lay awake, lying with her eyes closed but very aware of the familiar room around her. The occasional car passed, and she knew exactly when they would change gear to turn the corner to Roke. If she opened her eyes the Breughel picture would be intermittently visible on the wall as the curtain fluttered, letting in the moonlight.

Wooden bowls stood on the shelf, and their clothes were strewn on the chair. Downstairs Bella would be lying in her permitted place by the back door. Katherine turned her head restlessly from side to side. She wanted air.

Very quietly, she took Richard's shirt from the chair, and went cautiously downstairs. Bella looked up, surprised and blinking. 'Yes, I know. I've woken you up but you're prepared to be polite,' Katherine whispered to her. 'Let's go outside.'

She unlocked the door and stepped out into the garden. It was cool but without wind. She held the shirt around her and walked to the end, stumbling over some gathered piles of cuttings still not stacked away. Clouds came and went across the moon. Ripe apples glinted in the occasional light. Going inside for a minute, she took the rug from the small old couch, and went out again. She wrapped it around herself and sat on the wooden trunk seat. Now she was used to the dark she could see the garden as clearly as a black and white film. 'Come and sit here!' she called to Bella in a low tone, and the dog came obediently out, settling at her feet. Katherine could just reach her soft, warm ears. She fondled them, and looked ahead, her eyes blank. She thought about the seal. If you obtained it by ... stealing, how could you obtain a seal so specifically Walter Cotel's? Walter's and the Abbess's, whose connection she knew of quite independently. Museums would compete at auction for it, but Richard kept it in a drawer ... Her mind wandered quickly away, and came to James's visit to Oxford. Suicide could save you from a long future you didn't want ... but Richard said it wasn't his style. An idea flooded into her mind and made the blood beat in her ears. But how would you do it, killing? Had no one ever loved him enough before? The pulse in her throat was so violent she put her hand up to it, and as she did so, Richard appeared in the doorway.

'Kathy, what are you doing?'

'I couldn't sleep.'

He crossed the grass to her. He had pulled on trousers and they looked ghostly and pale in the dark.

'Come inside, it's not warm enough. You're trembling.'

He ushered her inside and put on the light. Bella ran in after them and stood near the door, glancing from them to her bed of rugs.

'You are cold,' he said, hugging Katherine. 'Why didn't you wake me up?'

'I didn't mean to stay so long. It was nice out there.'

'No it wasn't. Not warm enough. Come back to bed and stop shaking.'

He held her against him until he felt her relax. 'You looked like a fairy woman out there, from this window,' he said. 'Hair streaming every where.' He stroked it.

'Or a witch. I was having three-o'clock-in-the-morning thoughts. Have you had a dream tonight yet? Tell me it.'

'Yes, I think I have,' he said, reliably. 'Wait a minute. They try to escape the minute you catch at them ... Oh, yes, I was at the coast somewhere. In Dorset, probably. There were cliffs. I was on the beach, and looking up at someone on the cliff's edge. I was worried he would fall over. Then he moved away and I couldn't see him anymore, and was pleased. Then I had somehow got up above the cliff, too, and there was a town in sight. I knew you were in the town, and I didn't have to do anything else. I wanted to get back down to the beach then, and was about to do so when I woke up. You weren't here.'

'I was still in that town, of course,' she said, dreamily. 'You would be an analyst's delight.'

'Go to sleep, witch.'

58

The next day was fine and mild, a last retrieval of summer. Katherine decided they should have a picnic lunch, somewhere high up on the old Roman road across the Chilterns.

'I won't abandon this one,' she promised him, 'It'll be much better than our effort a few months ago.'

They parked Richard's car near Nettlebed, and walked in to the edge of the woodland. 'We don't come in this direction often enough,' she said. 'Look at this view.' To the east the old hundreds lay spread out, and behind them the woods rustled, gold and yellow. 'Do you think Roman engineers stood here, shouting at soldiers to get that agger out and laid!'

'Hhhmm, hhmm,' Richard cleared his throat pointedly. He was holding the bag of food and rugs towards her at full arm's stretch.

'Okay,' she laughed. 'Picnic! Food! But other people pay good money for my historical ruminations. Well, not good money actually, but money.' She felt light and happy, and the dark complications of the night had vanished. Bella was circling around them, tail flying.

When she took the bag from Richard he unrolled the map he was never without, and looked at it for a minute. 'Wait', he said triumphantly. 'We need to walk a little further. 'Kate's Copse', look.' He showed her the scrap of green on his map. They found the clump of trees, and spread the rug and the food. 'For Kate on or near her birthday, this must be place,' he intoned solemnly. 'No', he added without a break, 'It must not be. Deadly nightshade.' He moved the rug and showed her the black, poisonous berries.

'I'm not sure I would have recognised them,' Katherine said, peering closely at them. 'You're good at plants and trees.'

'Not specially,' he said cheerfully. 'Not compared to many. I know about wood, I suppose.'

After they shifted their rug to the other side of Kate's Copse he looked around them. 'That,' for instance, he said, pointing to the left, 'Is ash. Very curative, supposedly. And protective. I have some ash logs at home. Shall I make you something from it? I would like you to be protected at all times.' He poured two glasses of cider carefully.

'Yes, please.' She leaned against him.

'Specially from warts, I'm afraid ... '

'Richard!' she pushed at him and he pushed back.

'Don't spill things!'

They smiled at each other. She lay down on her back and reached a hand back over her head to where it could just touch his ankle. As the comfortable silence extended, she found herself thinking of the deadly nightshade he had shown her. What abysmal, frightening thoughts had invaded her last night! Today, in the sun, she was thinking longingly about a baby again. He was right; she was off balance.

At home in Wolvercote, several hours later, she found a note from James. 'Thanks. I've only just noticed the date,' she read. 'Happy Birthday tomorrow!'

59

'Da-dah!' Olivia arrived triumphant at the Gallery. 'It's yes! Had the tests and it's all official!'

'I am very, very pleased, Livvy. Congratulations. What about Joe?'

'What about him? He's so pleased you would think he'd done it all by himself. Well, he did, but you know what I mean.'

Katherine gave her a kiss. 'All that Gallery minding and discretion ... it was worth it!'

'I haven't rung him yet', Olivia said, referring to Meredith. 'It feels a bit odd. I'll suddenly say to him, thanks, but I don't need to come any more. And I don't know whether to tell Joe about the therapy, either.'

'You might need Meredith again.'

'Sceptic. I should write to Shelley Morris and thank her for the idea.' Olivia was unpacking her bag and wafting around her Gallery, looking at the display like a visitor.

'Do. She'll be delighted. And so am I, Livvy, really.'

'I can't wait to come out of the closet, as it were. So we're having a few people to dinner pretty soon. Will you come? And Richard, of course.'

'I would love to come, thank you. But ... ' she paused. 'Could I think about the invitation for Richard?'

'Well, of course. But I'll miss him if he doesn't come,' Olivia said, robustly. 'He's lovely, Kathy.'

'I know, I know.'

'As was Orlando, I may say.'

'True.' They laughed, and then Olivia said. 'If I ask Orlando and Dawn, would that be all right for you?'

'Of course, Livvy. It's nothing like that.'

'Okay,' said Olivia doubtfully.

60

Richard was placing a sawn-off square of ash wood in his lathe when Katherine arrived the following Saturday. She slipped into the house and found him in the workshop. It was violently windy, and the trees in his garden were being stripped of their leaves as she looked. The branches rose and fell, framed in the window behind him. Several other ash logs lay around him. He had obviously been choosing the one which pleased him most.

'Hallo.' He held the square balanced on the fingers and thumb of one hand while he kissed her. She looked at his palm and remembered she had wondered if he were a rower when first she saw the calluses.

'How was last night', he said companionably, as he tightened the lathe. He could smell the faint, leafy perfume she wore. She looked tense, and moved away to the other side of the room.

'It was fun. Olivia and Joe are pleased with themselves.' She sat on the chair in the corner and looked through the window. Bella was out in the windy garden. She described the party to him, and volunteered, 'No, Meredith Baker-Lynn was certainly not there.'

He smiled and went on working. 'This is your birthday present, of course', he said. 'This shape that I'm using will make a wider, flatter bowl, almost a plate. Now's the time to speak if you prefer a deeper one.' He looked at her and gestured towards the other pieces of wood. She was watching him, taking in his easy movements and light, warm eyes. His expression was hard to read.

'You could have come, but I thought it would be bit heavy-handed to have you sit through a celebration of pregnancy. We're not talking about it yet, are we?'

He put down the goggles he had been about to put on, and walked over to her. 'Not yet. Would you rather get outside, move about?' he said, perceptively.

'Rich, I'm being irritable with you.' she said, and stood up. 'Yes, I would.'

In the garden she felt energised and collected windfall apples while she spoke. 'We've got so many; shall we try and make cider?'

'I'd want your rustic brewing to be more successful than your dye-making,' Richard said. For once he was watching her work, lolling on the step near Bella, and offering collection bags for the apples. Her plait was unwinding, and more and more hair straggled over her green jacket. As he looked she pushed it back, and then threw the jacket off. She had a low-necked white shirt underneath, sharp and startling against her untidy hair. Her slim legs in tight corduroy bent and straightened as she picked up the apples, inspecting each one before putting it in his bag.

'Stop staring.' she said. 'I think you just leave them with boiling water for a few days, and then add sugar and yeast and it ferments, for quite a long time. Honey might be nicer than sugar.' She carried him over an armful of apples. 'I think it must be more complicated, but we could look it up.'

'Phases of the moon, stirring with hazel wands?'

'Really?' She looked interested.

'I think very clean jars might be a more basic thing.'

'You are so disappointing. I want folk lore.'

'Believe me, folk lore doesn't always produce very nice cider or beer.'

'Believe me!' She hurled a bag of apples to the ground. 'Believe me! Why do you always say that?' Bella came running to investigate the apples, and Richard sat immobile, looking at her.

'It's a phrase, it's ... '

'I've spent months trying to believe you! Sometimes I do, sometimes it's misery. I don't know what I believe! I do nothing but try to believe you. Stop saying it!'

Richard looked icy. He reached out for her hand but she pulled away, still near to shouting. 'And you won't have any tests!'

'You're right, I won't. What have your tests got to do with anything?'

'Because then I would know,' she said passionately. 'Then I could stop thinking about whether I believe you and get on with it!'

'Get on with what?' Richard stood up and walked away from her and then came a few steps back. 'What if your tests say no? He's not how he says he is; he's an ordinary liar. What would happen then?' Katherine shook her head, breathing deeply. She could see him flush under his tan. 'That would be the end, then, would it? It's just the freak you're interested in, an interesting ... ' He cast around for a word, 'A resource?'

'No! It's you ... '

'Yes?'

She collapsed on to the step he had got up from, and sat with her pulse pounding. Richard picked up several of the apples and threw them as hard as he could. They hit the back fence with a splat, one by one. 'Latin last week. Blood and cells. What about Olivia's man, Meredith with the eyes? He might speak to my unconscious? Had you thought of that?' She didn't answer. 'If it depends on other people's tests how good can it be?' he said, much more quietly.

'The tests are for you, not me. I don't need them.'

He stepped past her, inside, and soon she heard the lathe humming. Bella stood by Katherine, but looked in the direction Richard had gone, deeply uneasy. In a minute she walked away from them both, and lay down beside the pond, almost out of sight beyond the trees. Katherine began to carry the apples inside, bag by bag. When Richard still didn't reappear, she selected a few of the best ones and began peeling and slicing, unsure what she would cook with them. When they were all in a bowl, she picked it up and carried it into the workshop. Richard turned from the lathe and then switched it off.

'What shall I make with these?' she began.

'Put the damn things down,' he said, and took the bowl from her. He placed it on the bench and turned back and took her in his arms. 'I tried to explain to you once what the really miserable things are. No amount of investigating can change those or help them. So I'm not interested, and I also would hate the circus-performer part of it. If you don't think you can bear it as it we are ... ' They looked at each other. Then Katherine pulled away from his chest and picked up the bowl of apples. Her hands were shaking.

When David Freeman arrived some time later he found them sitting at the table.

'What meal is this?' he asked, glancing at his watch.

'I don't know,' Richard said. 'Katherine made apple shortcake with some windfalls, so we're eating it hot. Have some?'

'Yes, I will, thank you. I might let Sam out of the car in that case.' He retreated through the door for his dog, and in a minute Sam and Bella shot past the window together.

'It's business, I'm sorry,' he said to Katherine when he returned, and began talking to Richard. She poured him coffee and cut him cake while he said they were suddenly leaving for Scotland, to see Prue's father who had had a stroke. They discussed a timber yard task for some minutes, before he stood up to go.

'That was excellent shortcake.'

They made polite and optimistic remarks about his father-in-law, and Richard walked with him to the car. They stood talking as Sam was rounded up and jumped in, and then David drove away.

'The Lord of the Manor', Katherine said.

'That's an inflammatory thing to say.' Richard stared at her. 'What is the matter with you today?' When she said nothing he stayed standing by the door. 'I won't have any of those tests, Katherine.'

'I'm not coping with it very well this weekend.' She stood up and walked around, collecting her jacket and bag. He grasped her quite roughly as she went toward the door, and held her for a moment. She gave him a dry-mouthed kiss. 'I will sort it out,' she whispered against his throat.

'Yes, but what about the cider?' he answered, and she gave a brief laugh. He ran his hands through the untidy plait, and then she left. He walked slowly to the end of the garden and looked back at the house, like an agent valuing it, or a photographer planning the best view possible. Bella nudged an apple along the ground, and he looked down and pushed it further for her, with the toe of his shoe.

61

Katherine tried to work on her book during the next week. It went slowly. She paced Port Meadow, hoping for inspiration and distraction, both at once. Late in the week she was pleased to see a letter from Tim Rothwell arrive, instantly recognisable in its large brown business envelope, addressed by hand in his attractive, mannered italic script. She opened it, and sat at her desk, reading slowly.

'Thank you for the chapters you sent us recently - although we could wish for the completed work by now! However, and despite a surprising change in perspective - much more personalised than your earlier chapters - we all still have great hopes for it. The difference is, I presume, because written documents are at last more readily available. As long as you can maintain the tricky balance between history and imagination as well as you do, so far, it should be good. We still need to touch on the bigger picture, of-course. I know local history does not exist to illuminate national history but this was, after all, a time of economic transformation in rural England, and we get little inkling of where Benson fits in the general scene ... '

She clasped the page but began skipping sentences.' ... Were enough unfree workers left for the manorial system to function at all ... did land fall into disuse, or did surviving villeins buy it up and accumulate substantial independent holdings of their own ... where do you place your hypothetical free tenant in all this? ... And on a different tack, what evidence do you have for your statement about the whereabouts of the Hundredal meeting place, at Roke Elm? I had understood this was one of the unknowns about medieval Benson topography. Time is now short ... our millennium deadline ... Yours in hope, Tim'

Katherine held her hand above her desk and let the letter drop from it. She sat still for a moment, and then walked into her kitchen. Port Meadow still lay beyond the window. She returned to the desk briefly, and then went into the bedroom. She lay on her back, her eyes fixed on the wall. Did you stop writing history if you wrote someone's story? But if that person ... Was history not an accumulation of stories? Where was the alchemy that turned past events into history? How far away did the alchemist have to stand?

She got up and was leaning on the window-sill, lined with Oak Farm House photos, when the phone rang.

'Katherine? Is that you?'
She didn't recognise the voice at first.
'This is Eric here.'
'Hallo, Eric.'
'Katherine, is Richard with you?'
'Here, in Oxford? No, Eric, I haven't seen him since ... since Saturday.' Her throat closed over. 'Why?' She couldn't swallow.

'He didn't come here on Tuesday, which was odd, but we thought ... And then Zinnia's been trying to get him on the phone since, and there's no answer. We don't know where he is.'

'Have you tried the timber-yard?' As she spoke she knew what the answer would be.

'Yes, I did, but David Freeman is away in Scotland, and the only person I could get there has no idea where Richard is, either.'

There was a silence in which she suddenly moved the receiver away from her head, not wanting Eric to hear her violent breathing. When she put it back he was saying, ' ... some explanation, but Zinnia is worried.'

'Shall I come over?'
'Could you? David Freeman would have keys to his house, but ... '
'Of course I've got keys.' Katherine cut through his hesitations. 'I'll come now, Eric.'

She hung up and then dialled Richard's number herself. There was no answer. She scrabbled her own keys and his into her bag, and ran down the stairs. As soon as she was outside she realised it was cold, and she had no coat, but after a second's pause on the footpath she opened her car door and got in.

At the King's Head it was the quiet mid-afternoon period. Eric and Zinnia were talking to a solitary customer at the bar. Zinnia's red lipstick was startling on her pale face. 'Can you hold the fort?' Eric called into the kitchen, and the Australian cook put her head out of the door.

'We'll be fine. Go on.' She smiled in a friendly way to Katherine, nodding reassuringly.

62

Outside Oak Farm House Katherine pulled up her car, making an effort to move slowly, and appear calm to Eric and Zinnia. For a brief minute she knocked on the door, and then turned her key and opened it.

'Do you want me to go first?' Eric said, touching her arm. She was puzzled.

'No.' She shook his hand off her, and they went in. The large room was tidy and silent.

'Richard?' she called. 'Rich, are you here?' Her voice hung in the air. She took a few steps towards the large glass doors into the garden at the back. They were closed and locked. Leaves were scattered over the grass, and more apples.

'Richard?' Eric called, and Zinnia looked at them both.

'Let's go upstairs.'

'Here first,' Katherine said, and walked through the kitchen into his workshop. The mild smell of wood enveloped her, and she swallowed noisily. Half prepared logs lay on the floor, neatly against one wall. Alone on the bench stood a wide, flat dish of creamy wood. 'That's ash,' she said. 'It protects you ... '

She went to the drawer and fumbled with it, her hand shaking. She pulled it out and it was empty. Ellen's old bowl had gone, and she felt further back. Walter Cotell's seal had gone. She took a deep breath and turned to Eric and Zinnia.

'We can go upstairs now.'

Eric pushed himself in front of her, and almost ran up the stairs. He looked in the bathroom and in the bedroom.

'He's not here,' he said, sounding weak with relief.

'Of course he isn't!' said Katherine. Zinnia saw her cheeks change colour from white to red and her eyes glitter.

'We'll just be downstairs for a minute, Kathy. Won't we, Eric?'

Zinnia shut the door behind them, and Katherine stood frozen for a minute. Then she flung herself face down on the bed and cried. Her voice came out in a howl, and then broke into sobs.

'I hate you so much,' she sobbed, and banged her fists on the bed. 'Why did you make me believe it?' She clawed the blanket and squeezed it until her nails cut into her palms. She turned on her back and made herself look around the room. The contorted Breughel figures looked back at her from the wall, and the lead tokens lay in their dish. The curtain hung limp against the closed window. Soon she heard Zinnia's footsteps approaching ponderously up the stairs, and she sat up and smoothed her hair.

'I'm all right, Zinnia,' she called. 'Just a bad moment.'

She locked the house again, and they stood outside. It was cold.

'We are still a bit worried,' Zinnia said, gently. 'Do you think we should tell the police?'

Katherine looked at her blankly. 'The police? Why?'

'In case ... Richard was often rather sad, Katherine. Much, much better after he met you, and we were so pleased for him ... for you. He was lonely.'

'Was he depressed at all when you last saw him?' Eric intervened, sounding more business like.

'Depressed?' Katherine went on repeating their words. 'Oh, no,' she said firmly. 'He wasn't depressed last week. He was angry with me, actually. We had...something we disagreed over.'

'But surely not this angry?' Eric gestured at the empty house.

'Apparently it was something insoluble. I was quite angry too.'

Eric and Zinnia continued to look concerned. 'For goodness sake,' she said to them in frustration. 'He's got Bella with him!'

Saying the dog's name made her chest heave with grief again, and her eyes fill. She turned away.

'So he has! Of course!' Eric and Zinnia seemed to pick up.

'I think the best thing to do would be to wait till David is back.' She told them where he was. 'And I'll write to him, and send him these.' She dangled Richard's keys, feeling them with her fingers. 'He can decide if he wants to try the police. After all, Richard was his tenant,' she said and her throat ached. 'I'm going to go now,' she said, and rushed to her car.

'No!' Zinnia said, and held on to the door handle. 'You mustn't drive like this!' Her face looked older and flaky, and her eyes quivered with tears.

'Oh Zinnia!' Katherine jumped out of the car again and they hugged each other. Eric looked embarrassed and patted them.

'I'll be careful. Thank you for telling me. I will be so careful, Zinnia. I will ring you when I get home, but I must go, now.'

'She wants to be by herself,' Zinnia said as they watched her car retreat. They got into their own car and drove slowly to the King's Head.

'The man has upset her,' Eric said severely. It was the only sentence they spoke.

In Wolvercote Katherine dialled Moira's number. 'I'm

sorry you can't speak to Professor Johnson now,' the secretary told her. 'You've just missed her. She's in Edinburgh, at a seminar. No, she won't be in Oxford for a week at least. Can I take a message?'

Katherine breathed carefully and changed the receiver from one hand to the other.

'Are you there?' asked the secretary 'Hallo?'

'Hallo!' said Katherine. 'I was thinking. No, no message. I'll try her when she's back. Thank you.'

Moira was the only person she needed to explain anything to. She lay on her bed, and then got up and dialled again. 'Zinnia? It's me. I'm back at home.'

63

The ten days she set herself to wait before Moira might return, and she could ring her again, became as far as Katherine made herself think ahead. No bigger packet of time was endurable and after it was over she would admit to Moira that she had been deceived. Richard had run away because she was pressing too hard on his story, and their delightful, seductive summer game had run its course. That was why she had loved him surely? For their game, that they could reach back into the past through Richard, that he was a wonderful, warm living conduit? But why then had he loved her? He had loved her, surely? She remembered him loving her, and shook with a fever.

Alone in bed she cried tears that were a mixture of misery and fury. The year replayed like a video in her mind. She should have stayed away after Midsummer Day, she should not have been seduced with medieval stories and walks along forgotten roads. He had targeted her as gullible, just as Moira had said. She writhed at how she had told Moira she believed him. She would tell Moira soon that it had seemed highly implausible, of course, all along. Naturally. If she stood up from bed and held the beech wood bowls to her face the mild wood smell flooded her senses and she thought of Richard's hands making them, and the smell of Richard's own skin and hair. Then she would walk out on Port Meadow, sometimes finding herself running, and sometimes brought to a halt, standing quite still.

But when the ten days were up, she found herself reluctant to ring Moira. To tell her would be finalising her mistakes and confirming her misery. She postponed it. In the Gallery she and Olivia and Dawn dismantled the autumn exhibition, and contacted the last few buyers who had not collected their purchases. They set up a larger jewellery display, with Christmas sales already in mind, and hung a new series of collages around the walls. 'These are rather awful,' Olivia said cheerfully as they arranged them. 'I don't think we'll try this woman again.' The frames had wads of sheep's wool inside, pasted over scraps of glass and triangles of newspaper. Katherine didn't answer. She had lost weight rather dramatically, Olivia observed, and was unsmiling. When Dawn was downstairs, disposing of wrapping paper, Olivia said, 'Kathy, is all okay with you? You're not absolute sunshine, these days ... '

Katherine didn't answer directly, but stepped in between Olivia's swelling shape and the ladder, and said, 'Let me do the climbing around now, for goodness sake. Pass it to me.' She held out her hands for the last collage frame. As Olivia reached up with it, she added, 'It's finished with Richard, and he's gone away. I don't even know where he is.'

'Oh, Kathy!' Olivia lowered the frame again in great surprise, and wanted to offer sympathy, but Katherine interrupted her.

'Nothing was how I thought it was. Pass me that thing,

please. If he hadn't gone I imagine I would have had to, by now.'

Her expression stopped Olivia discussing it any further.

At home that evening she took a teaspoon and dug around in the pot on her kitchen windowsill where she had planted the tiny Tortworth chestnuts. Not one of the damp little objects was showing any sign of sprouting, and she threw them away without even feeling their smooth brown skin. She sat at her desk then, and pulled her Benson notes and papers firmly towards her. But she found that correcting tiny, grammatical slips and typing errors was all she could do, obsessively. She read her pages through and through, and added nothing new at all.

Inevitably, one day she drove to Benson, and went to the King's Head.

The lights were wound around the scruffy trees outside again, and music was playing over the bar. She blocked it out of her ears. A barman unfamiliar to her was preparing to change the disc.

'Is Eric here, or Zinnia?' she asked him. 'I'm Katherine Laidlaw.'

He disappeared out to the back, and both Eric and Zinnia emerged almost instantly.

'Katherine!' Zinnia kissed her, her bare white throat moving up and down as she spoke. She wore her favourite winter scarlet, and black beads. 'I'm so glad you have come! How are you, Kathy?'

She felt warmed by Zinnia's clucky movements, and Eric patted her on the shoulder. He had his National Trust acorn tie and a heavy tweed jacket. 'Drink?' She shook her head.

'We've heard nothing,' Zinnia said, without being asked.

'Nothing at all. His car is nowhere to be seen. But look,' she tried to sound more cheerful. 'Something here.'

Eric produced a large flat parcel, carefully wrapped in brown paper and string, and handed it to her.

'What is this?'

'We told David Freeman you seemed to know about this, so he says it should be yours.'

She opened the parcel, feeling its firm wooden shape. It was the ash dish, curved up at the rim, pale and matt.

'It was going to be a birthday present ... ' she said, despairingly.

Eric cleared his throat. 'Good idea, that,' he said vaguely. 'I was keeping it for you.'

Zinnia chattered on. 'Another thing David Freeman asked us about was those coins, buried treasure they looked like, in the ... in the bedroom.'

'I think Richard probably meant him to have those,' Katherine said with an effort. 'In lieu of rent, or notice ... anything like that.'

'Well, good thing, because they're probably in his shop by now.' Zinnia said, and added. 'Good to clear the decks, though, isn't it? Getting nearer the chink of light at the end of the tunnel, sort of thing?' Only Richard could have appreciated that Zinnia-ism, Katherine thought, and almost laughed, and said goodbye to Zinnia with a hug. In the car she put the ash bowl on the seat beside her, in its wrappings again, and at home in her flat put it in a cupboard.

Eventually she decided to write to Moira, rather than ring. Time had worn off the urgency. 'You were quite right, of course', she wrote. 'It was too unlikely to be true, and I must have been suffering from a summer delusion, or perhaps wishful thinking.' She wrote of being carried away by historical research, and then removed it as only half honest, and simply added a final paragraph. 'It was fun meeting you, even under these (for me) foolish circumstances. With many thanks for all your interesting advice, and our pleasant lunches, Katherine.' She sealed it up and addressed it to Moira at work. After a moment's reflection, she wrote 'Personal' along the top of the envelope, and walked in the rain with it to the Wolvercote post office.

64

On the Monday after this, as she stood at her window watching a neighbour build a bonfire of leaves, her phone rang .

'Katherine Laidlaw?' It was an Australian accent. 'It's Simon here,' it went on cheerfully. 'Simon from the photographic department in the library?'

She began to remember bristly hair and big sausagey fingers.

'We're photographing a map for you.' he reminded her. 'We did promise October, I know, and now we've run into November. I hope it's still some good to you?'

The Davis map, she now remembered. Beautiful, eighteenth century Benson, and seven roads to Roke Elm. She seemed to have ordered it in another life.

'Yes,' she said vaguely. 'I suppose so, yes.'

'Well, I hope so', the voice said, 'Because it's here ready for you, ten slides.'

The next day she made time on her way to the Gallery to visit the library. Up the stairs she went, breathing in the dusty evocative atmosphere. Here she had sat, day after day in tense and happy concentration, and then it had all slipped away from her. While she waited for Simon in the map room, she studied a map on the wall, of safe, distant places. It showed the routes of Arab traders down the monsoon coast of India.

'Here we are then!' Simon arrived beside her, and she instantly remembered his plain large face, and big beefy figure. He had a wedding ring on his left hand, sunk between fleshy bulges.

'You'll remember that we needed ten, to cover your whole map. I've overlapped them very slightly, so when you put it all together, nothing could possibly be missing.' He took the top slide out of the little box, and held it to the light for her to see. It was the bottom left corner of the map, with the curlicued title, describing pieces of land titheable to Berwick, 'intermingled with those of Benson and Ewelme.' She read it aloud, running the familiar names around her mouth. A huge lump swelled from her chest to her throat, and she blinked with tears, turning away.

'You might use it for a book illustration, did you say?'

She cleared her throat, and passed him back the slide. 'Some of it, at least,' she answered. When had she been so confident?

'The easiest thing to do is ... ' Simon leaned his large haunch on a table, and sellotaped up the little box. 'You need your slides transferred to paper. We don't have a machine to do that, but I can tell you two printers who will.' He named two local firms.

'Right then.' He straightened up and passed her the slide box in a labelled brown envelope. 'Sorry we were a bit late.' His cheerful smile was small in the middle of his large face.

'Thank you,' Katherine said, and pressed the envelope hard down inside her bag.

She hesitated with the printing task, afraid to unlock doors she was closing. On several consecutive evenings she held the slides against her brightest kitchen light in

Wolvercote, once getting up in the night to look at them again, peering at the coloured patches of woodland and field, and the small square closes. The Messuages and Crofts, she said, bitterly. The next day she took them in to the first printer Simon had named, in a passage behind a shopping arcade. She arrived before any other customers were there, and the man behind the counter was peacefully setting out a comparative range of wedding invitations, listening to a current affairs programme as he did so.

'Oh, that would be much more interesting!' he said to Katherine, taking her slides and turning the radio off. 'I love maps.'

She watched him put each slide under a focusing lens which threw the picture onto a sheet of paper, and with a click he copied each sheet. In less than five minutes she held a neat folder of pages. Tonight at home she could spread them out, and she would have Davis's map put together like a jigsaw, on her own table.

She anticipated it while she worked in the Gallery, and finally put down the correspondence file Olivia had left her, and got out the printer's envelope again. If they used any of it for illustration, she thought, it would presumably be the corner showing Roke Elm, to support her theory about the hundredal meeting place. Richard's seven roads - the phrase slipped through her mind. She shuffled through the papers, and pulled out the Roke Elm sheet. The roads met almost in the middle of the page. The colours were softly distinct, but had faded and merged in a way that washed the whole map with a dusty pink glow. North of Roke Elm the three great open fields stretched out, Berwick and Roke Hill and Scald Hill, and to the south the fields of Ewelme. West, along Rumbolds Lane, were the small private closes, squares outlined in trees. She returned her attention to Roke Elm itself. No close yet, where Oak Farm House later lay, just the higgledy-piggledy open space where the roads met. Along six of them their names were written, and she turned her head to read the letters. This is smaller than the original, she thought as she peered at the words, dictated by the A4 size page. Perhaps if the printer had made it smaller he could also make it larger? She was impatient to ask him, and when Olivia arrived late in the morning, proudly standing sideways to demonstrate her growing bulge, she ignored it.

'I need to go to a printer, Livvy. It won't take me much more than ten minutes, and I'll be right back.'

'Of course. I'll be here for the rest of the day now. Do you know where I've been? That pottery studio on ... '

'Could I go out first? Tell me when I get back.'

65

She pushed through the pavement crowds, now much denser than at nine o'clock, and reached the print shop almost panting. There were now three people behind its counter, and machines humming and spooling out pages beyond them.

'I'd like to wait for him,' she said when a girl offered to serve her. She pointed at her earlier man. 'He knows about the job I'm on.'

'Sure.' She shrugged.

In a minute the man was with her. 'Hallo,' he said. 'More maps?'

'The same one, and just one of the pictures. She got it out. 'Can you change the size of this? Could it be a little bigger?'

He took the page. 'Certainly. We can wind the size up a good bit more than this. You're restricted in the end by paper size. We can't do more than A3 here.'

Twice as big. 'Yes, that would be plenty, I think.'

She gave him the slide again, and watched him project it onto the bigger paper. He turned a dial until the picture filled the page, and then snapped it. He handed her the warm A3 sheet.

She held it up, looking happy. 'Thank you very much. That's much more like the original size, I think.' She paid him and hurried back to the Gallery, holding the sheet carefully.

It was lunch time and the Gallery was suddenly busy with customers. She put her map on a table in the basement, and ran upstairs again to help Olivia. It was early afternoon before she could get back to it. Olivia had been to the Covered Market and bought them both ciabattas filled with brie and grapes. Katherine took hers downstairs and looked at the Roke Elm page once more. Holding the bread out of the way, she leaned over the picture and peered at the meeting place again. Watlington Road ran east, and through the fields Roke Elm Way ran north. She bent over the road which interested her most, her hypothetical Roman road. It had no name, but was lined with small curly trees on each side. She looked at it and suddenly felt a sweep of excitement. There were not only stylised little trees, but also letters. The curly boughs were half concealing a name. She lifted the page with one hand and held it closer to her eyes. She was holding her breath. She reached out and put the sandwich down with great deliberation, and held the map with both hands. Then she ran upstairs and out through the Gallery, back to the print shop.

'Hallo', said the man in surprise. 'A third go?'

'Yes, please,' Katherine said. 'This time could you just blow up the middle part of this?'

He shone the slide on to paper again, and steadily wound

up the size. The picture filled the A3 page. 'Keep going', Katherine said impatiently.

'You're losing all the edges', he warned. Now the rays passed over the sides of the paper, casting light all around it.

'That's all right,' she said, watching intently. 'Keep going!'

She opened her mouth to call 'Stop!' and at the same moment the man said,

'That's the best I can do.' He snapped the photo and handed it to her. She held it in front of her and let out a cry. 'Oh, no' she said despairingly, 'It is! It is!'

Shymmyng Lane, she read. Shymmyng Lane. Shimming Lane. Shimming Lane.

'A problem?' the man asked, folding the extending lamp across the machine and wheeling it away noisily.

'No, she said. 'Or yes. You can only read this when it's blown up.'

'That's possible,' he said, when he turned from the machine, but she had gone.

66

Katherine was on the footpath hurrying in the other direction, down past the Gallery again towards the library. The A3 sheet of paper was clutched more carelessly against her, and she dodged other pedestrians dangerously, swerving out into the High to avoid them. Down over the cobbles of Radcliffe Square she plunged, and across Broad Street, almost running past Blackwells. 'You have to show me your card!' the security officer shouted, and she waved it back at him. In the map room she stood, breathing heavily and flushed in the face.

'Could I see Simon?' she asked. 'Simon from your

photographic department?' The librarian on duty looked as if she were about to hesitate, but took in Katherine's expression and changed her mind. She lifted the phone on her desk.

This time she looked at the wall as she waited, but saw nothing. Her mind was blinkered, tunnelled to a single point. Simon arrived and greeted her pleasantly.

'That map you photographed for me a few weeks ago,' she said abruptly. 'It hasn't been photographed before, has it?'

'No,' he said in puzzlement. 'Certainly not. Otherwise we wouldn't have had to do it again, and you wouldn't have had to ...'

'Who else has seen the map? Do you keep records like that?'

He lowered himself to a table top. She seemed very worked up today, very intense.

'Fairly careful records, for something like that. It's unique, as you know.'

'Would you be able to tell me, then?'

'Exactly what?'

'Exactly who else has looked at the map since you have had it. How long is that, by the way?'

'I'm not sure. I've only been here five years, after all, and this map is as old as ...'

She was not to be side-tracked and she needed his help. She smiled at him radiantly, and said, 'Do you think you could have a look at this map's whole record since you've had it? Is it on a card, or something?'

He heaved himself up. 'I'll get it. Davis, wasn't it, the cartographer?' She nodded tensely.

In a surprisingly short time he was back, holding two large yellowing filing cards held together untidily with string at their corners. Katherine had sat on a chair at a large map table, and he sat himself opposite her.

'Here we go, then,' he said, reading from the top card. 'The map has been in the hands of the university forever. It was commissioned by one of the colleges.'

'So this is its complete history?' She had to stop herself snatching the cards from his hands.

'Yep. Total. And,' He turned to the second card. 'And it's only been looked at, let's see ... a few times over the one particular year last century, by the Enclosure Commissioners ... '

'And their names were?'

'In this case,' he read, 'A Mr J. Spicer and a Mr F. Baxter.'

'Okay,' she sighed out.

'And then,' he went on, enjoying the story. 'Only once since then, would you believe. A Miss Elaine Ellison, in 1953.'

Katherine was staring. Simon read cheerfully on. 'Purpose of her study: eighteenth century paints and inks. She is, or was, a conservator employed by the National Trust. That's it.' He threw the cards down.

'So otherwise ... ' Katherine said softly.

'Otherwise, it's been safely rolled up in that particularly heavy case in which you know it reposes. Unseen by the human eye.'

He was surprised that she briefly rested her head on her arms, across the desk. Then she looked up, and smiled much more calmly. 'Thank you very much,' she said. 'You've been very helpful. Probably beyond the call of duty.'

'Not something we're usually asked,' he said, and paused, but she added nothing. 'But I don't suppose they're state secrets.'

'I hope not,' Katherine stood up. 'Thank you again.'

Out on the footpath she stood still. Gradually she let the images surface and stay in her conscious, scraping inside her chest and throat. The evening soon after she first found the map, the garden at Oak Farm House, before the midsummer picnic. Richard suggesting Shimming Lane as the path's name - but then wondering if he had perhaps got that from her? No? For herself she would have preferred a significant Roman name, she had said - something important, like a Street. Something important! Her heart fluttered. Then there was a second time, later. He was at the kitchen sink, she thought, washing vegetables. Washing vegetables. She let out a sob or a laugh, and a passing woman looked at her sharply. Shimming Lane, he had said. Shimming Lane, which you don't believe. She sobbed in her throat again, painfully, and mouthed the words. Now I believe you, Richard. Now I believe with utter certainty that you knew something about Roke Elm that no other living person could know. Knew it lightly, easily - because you had been there. Now I believe you. And now it's too late.

67

It was like a second, different loss. Now the year replayed compulsively in her mind again, but with a changed subtext, and new colours, the bitter colours of her own disbelief. Something extraordinary had happened to Richard, generations ago, and he lived it in his own most private way. The same fact which she presumed might electrify scientists now, he had known since the time of faith and alchemy and paintings of hell and heaven on Dorchester Abbey walls. With grace and solitude and endurance, he had survived since then. Now she heard her own voice again, sceptical. Have some tests, she had insisted. Have tests so I can believe you. Tell me some names from the Hundred Rolls. Wouldn't it be interesting to know, interesting to think about DNA and cell swabs and genes and telomeres? After all, this is the white-hot age of genetics ... No, Katherine, he had said, I am not a resource or a circus-performer. The tests would be for you, not for me. The images of him in bed, his face looking down on her, his teeth white, tipped often into the single glimpse of his night of grief about death and lovers leaving him. For you, not for me, the tests. That hotel night had been after a perfect day, she remembered: kingfishers, their river, a new landscape. Since then he had gone. When it gets impossible, he had told her, I move away and start again. Between them, they had made it impossible.

Later she sat at her bare and tidy desk and wondered if she should write to Moira yet again, reversing her last letter, and imparting a remarkable, shattering piece of information. But she shrank from it, protecting Richard - needlessly, now he had gone - and aware that, in his absence, she could produce no scientific evidence - no evidence, except her own. Letting Moira think her a dupe was a mild enough mortification, she thought, and lay her head on the desk and cried properly, spreading splashy tears on the clean surface. Twenty minutes later, and after she had nearly dozed, dull with pain, she stood up and walked to her kitchen. While the kettle boiled, she surveyed her Port Meadow view. The late afternoon shadows threw the grassy bumps on the ground into relief. From the sky, she knew, the bumps resolved themselves into the imprints of stone age huts and settlements. She thought about that as she made the coffee, and found it obscurely comforting that they were still there.

She took the cup back to her desk and switched her computer on. While it warmed up, with familiar whirrings and hums, she quickly got out her neglected Benson file, bulging with notes and rough copies, and looked through her book chapters right from the beginning. There's a lot to do. This is what I can do for him. For us.

For the next few weeks, the work absorbed her. Her year

seemed to have turned full circle, and as at its beginning, she spent hours in the library, underneath Duke Humfrey's painted ceiling, hurrying to it along darkening streets after leaving the gallery. She made several trips to London, checking her sources and amending her pages of notes, and sitting at her computer writing them up long into the night. Sometimes she sat for moments on end, gazing sightlessly ahead, and then she would write again, filled with an inward energy. November passed, and she brushed off a despairing phone call from Tim Rothwell.

'It is coming along, Tim. Yes, I know it's later than we thought, but you will get it. Oh, certainly before the Millennium thing is all over - it has to be!' She laughed more than he thought appropriate, and he hung up his phone feeling confused and irritated.

'Bloody academic prima donnas ... ' he said to his colleagues, and persuaded them to wait.

On a day in late December, she wrote the closing lines.

'By the time Henry VII claimed the crown of England on Bosworth Field, five or six generations had passed since the Black Death in the Chiltern Hundreds. The communities which had survived reshaped their villages, or abandoned them. They still farmed on huge open fields on the lower lands beside the Thames, still grazed stock on the foothills of the Chilterns, and foraged for fuel and timber in the wooded uplands. Farm labourers have become a sought-after economic resource, and they can move around the country to find work, all now free of ownership by the Lord of the Manor of Benson. Even as village boundaries become more solid and the stone churches we recognise today stand above them all, increasing quantities of written records tell us that communities are becoming more fluid, and local family names are changing. National powers in London have claims on them; international wars call on them. Roads and

transport improve; many villagers learn to read. Benson people no longer live lives isolated from the national consciousness - they can be anywhere in England; they can be any one of us.'

In a surge of elation, Katherine printed out the whole book, and then packed it into a new file.

'I can't tell you!' she said aloud, her voice husky after hours of silence. 'I can't tell you, but it's finished!'

She looked at her watch, and was surprised to see it was two in the morning. She stirred herself packet soup and drank a mugful, and then, feeling that was not celebratory enough, opened a bottle of wine as well. Now I'll have a headache, she thought, but she slept immediately, and dreamed of Richard, again and again, as if her unconscious were letting him through at last, and had a lot to catch up. He was swimming with her, oddly enough - something they had never done - at the mouth of the Thame river, where Zinnia had held her boating lunch. They were in the middle of the river, and slowly making towards the wider Thames. He was assuring her they would float even more easily once they turned the corner. Then he was at his lathe, but making a sort of toy, or puppet, not a bowl. He wasn't pleased with it, and threw it down to start with a new log, and make a new shape. At one stage they were both looking at Bella, who seemed to be in the back of someone else's car, asleep. 'Don't worry,' Richard said, as robustly as usual. 'She'll get out when she wants to. But we can't do it for her.' Even in her dream, Katherine clearly thought: How different we are: I anticipate decisions I might never even have to make, and you wait for each moment to come to you and then act on it.

68

In the Gallery the next day, she had a crisis of confidence.

'I've finished it,' she told Livvy tentatively, but then added. 'And now I can't bear to think of reading it all through before I send it off. What if it is terrible?'

'You know it isn't. Of-course you know! You're tired. Why don't you either post it instantly, or wait till after Christmas? They're not going to look at it now, anyway. They're probably on holiday already.'

'You're right.'

But she was quiet, and then said again. 'But it might be no good.'

'For goodness sake!' Said Olivia. 'Give it up then! Take a job with Piers Finch! You know he always wants you. Do his sort of history.' She watched Katherine grimace and then shrug.

'A spell back at teaching might be very undemanding, actually. Someone else's syllabus, pre-set. Limited targets, all defined.'

'Well?'

'I couldn't bear it!'

They both laughed.

'Well then,' Olivia said. 'You've done it. Good for you.'

Katherine drove into London on Christmas Eve, avoiding the old roads, sticking to the crowded motorway, and resolutely avoiding the Chilterns. James brought a girlfriend to Kensington for Christmas Day, to her surprise, a blonde, tidy German girl who spoke nearly perfect English and had a job at the BBC. She was only twenty-one, and already calmly focused on a life plan she probably had set out in a hard-backed exercise book, Katherine thought. She was charming, helpful company, and James looked solicitous.

'Is this serious?' Katherine asked him, out of earshot of Elizabeth and Diane.

He shrugged his shoulders, but only said, 'How do you ever know?'

'Oh, you'll know,' Katherine said.

She still had not re-read her manuscript.

69

On the last night of the year, the Ashes held a party.

'Of course you are going to come, Kathy,' Olivia said. 'First, Joe is bringing all the odd bods from the hospital, including many single men, or at least some working in Oxford and distant from wives ... No, don't be picky. I want to show you off. Second, I want you there myself. Third, could you help with the food?'

Katherine looked fondly at her. She was visibly pregnant, still elegant and bright, with her feathery short hair and pearl and enamel ear-rings. 'Fourth,' Olivia added, 'Dawn and Orlando won't be there.'

'I don't mind about that. It's nothing much, now ... And I actively would like to do food. Cooking is good for me. Tell me what you need, and how many for. Knife and fork? Or standing-up food?'

The Beckley cottage was full and warm and noisy. Katherine carried her plates of food to the kitchen, and returned to find Joe in high spirits among his guests, pouring champagne and moving from one group to another. 'Come on, Kathy', he called, and put his arm around her. 'One of your drinks at least must be for me.' He poured her a glass. She looked questioningly at his own orange juice. 'On duty later,' he said. 'I'm saving my alcohol allowance for midnight.' He was solicitous and flattering. 'You are looking beautiful,' he said. 'Don't get any thinner, will you?' Olivia had arranged big clusters of flowers in silvery jars with '2000' painted on the outside, and a brilliantly formed salmon mousse spelled out the same numbers, in central place on the table. Heather stood squarely beside it, cutting the letters into wobbly pieces and dishing them onto brightly coloured plates. Olivia swirled among her guests, striking in a black strapless dress that swelled out dramatically over her growing shape.

'This is Daniel, from Israel,' she said to Katherine, pulling lightly at her arm. 'Daniel, this is Katherine.' Daniel was a gentle-faced man with very black eyes behind thin, metallic-framed glasses. He had a surprisingly loud, swooping voice. They talked about Olivia's Gallery, and dangerous, dubious millennial tourists in the Holy Land. He was witty and pleasant, and Katherine felt cheered by him.

'You're a historian?' he repeated, as though this was a deeply implausible but interesting suggestion. 'Do you deal in the poetic validity of history, or merely in facts?' He waved his glass around.

'Oh, facts, I'm afraid. Facts and facts, until the pattern reveals itself. The kaleidoscope method, you could call it,' she said, provocatively.

'So facts are of value in themselves, are they?'

'Well, of course.'

'But of course not. Only the means to the end, if it's the pattern you want. If the facts don't fit any pattern you expect at all, if one fact sticks out, what do you do then?' He waved his glass expansively. Joe refilled it, and smiled at Katherine. 'You reject the fact, I'm sure.'

Katherine stared at him. 'If facts don't fit any pattern you know about, what does it mean? Is that what you're asking?' He nodded. She said passionately, 'It means you haven't animated the facts with imagination! The lack is in you, not the piece of information'

Daniel looked at her bright eyes. 'Is that so?' he said, admiringly.

At midnight Joe put on the television and all the radios in the house, and bells and clocks and music filled the rooms and were just audible over their own Old Lang Syne. Katherine held Olivia's hand on one side, and Daniel's on the other, and dragged her hand away from Daniel to wipe tears off her face. 'To the next thousand years!' they shouted, and watched the fireworks stream above the river Thames in London, and then the picture flickered to many other scenes of festivity. Daniel turned to Katherine, but she looked away towards Joe, and his kiss landed on her cheek.

At home in Wolvercote she stood in the dark for a while, and watched more fireworks on Port Meadow. She was overwhelmed by a longing for Richard, like a headache descending. Her eyes felt very dry, and alternately hot and uncomfortably cold. She should do visualisations, she told herself. Visualisations, as she had laughed about with Richard. Visualise that this year was ending, and it was very suitable to celebrate it, and that Richard was still somewhere not too far away, walking and eating and sleeping. And she had written a book for him.

'I have to do something,' she said under her breath the next morning. 'Something to make me let the book go. What am I waiting for? A sign?' Without a conscious plan, she got out her car and drove through the empty holiday streets of Oxford and out to the ring road. South along the river she went, the place-names singing in her mind. Ewelme, Brightwell, Britwell Salome, Dorchester, Benson, Wittenham. She parked her car and climbed towards the top of the Clumps. There was the patchwork of the old territory, with the black winter river snaking through it. The trees blew in their circle at the top. She stood there and looked around her for a long time. The first day of a new century, even a Millennium, if you believed it. Although Ceawlin and Cutha wouldn't, she smiled inwardly. The perspective was different from high up here, the palimpsest of the past flattened out. The old features took their place with the new - the river with the motorway, the farm boundaries with the village streets. None dominated; they were all still there. It was a real place she had found, she thought, a real territory to write about. Our place. She breathed out a long sigh, and raised her arms and dropped them, feeling satisfied, and set off down the track again.

On the way up, a family was approaching, children toiling behind the parents. She recognised the man as he got closer, with a check deer-stalker cap holding down the hair combed over his bald head. She laughed aloud. The sign had arrived!

'Hallo, Piers.'

He looked very red, and was puffing. 'This is a surprise! We're walking off the excesses of last night. How are you?'

'I'm fine,' she said. They spoke for a minute. How could she have thought she might work for him? The book was her sort of history, and she could do no other. 'Happy New Year, Piers. Thank you!' she said, and side stepped him to run on down the track, nodding politely at his family.

'That's the girl from the Gallery, isn't it?' his wife asked.

'It is,' said Piers. 'I've seen her alone around these hills before, just as odd.' For a minute more they watched her figure retreating down the hill, slender and brisk. Then Piers started climbing again, breathing heavily. 'She's entirely unpredictable,' he said. 'I wonder if she could teach, really?'

At home Katherine wrapped and addressed her manuscript, and included a note to Tim.

She put the parcel on her desk, ready for despatch tomorrow. She left both her hands on it for an instant. That sign had come, she thought. It was time to hand the book over. When there was another sign, it would show her how to find Richard again. She needed desperately to tell him about Shimming Lane, and tell him that the worst that could happen to her - that she would grow old and know that she was leaving him and that after her there might be other loves for him - was not as bad as being without him now. She found tears were dripping on to her hands on the parcel, and she shook her head and stood up straighter. She would find him.

70

For three weeks, longer than she expected after his harrying communications, she heard nothing from Tim Rothwell, and then received a long letter and a phone call on the same day.

'I found it so startling, Katherine, and so different from your first drafts, that I got some others to read it for me. I couldn't tell whether it was wildly over-imagined - or wonderful.'

'And?' She was in the Gallery, and turned her back on the bright window end.

'Then we had another meeting about it. We're still not sure.'

'Not sure?' Anxiety clutched at her throat. She had been so certain as she wrote, so carried along in a jet-stream of thought and visions and information. Was it an illusion?

'No, still not sure. But we're bringing publishing along at top speed, and we plan to have it in our general spring list by Easter!'

He obviously meant this to be wonderful news, but she still clutched the phone, and then sat down slowly.

'Does that mean ... ? Is that different to your original plan?'

'Well, yes.' he said patiently. 'Local history is a smaller imprint, and this was going in our Millennium list there. Now you will be in the main list of our parent company, Fox House. Out of my hands, I'm afraid ... Congratulations!' he added, when she was still quiet.

Fox House. The biggest publisher in Britain, she vaguely recalled.

'I don't know what to say, Tim. I'm amazed. And delighted, of course ... '

'In two months we hope. Personally speaking, I'm delighted, too. It's a gamble - but, fingers crossed!'

'Well, yes,' she said, weakly. 'Thank you for telling me, Tim. Good-bye.'

Olivia was standing by her, looking concerned. 'Okay?'

'Oh, Livvy!' she burst out. 'He's still speaking personally! Do you remember, his first letter ... '

'Kathy. What did he say?'

'It's a gamble, and Fox House are going to do it, and they're not sure, and - it'll be out in two months!'

'That's wonderful,' Olivia said, with real relief. Katherine was still thin, and quiet, and preoccupied; but now her cheeks were flushed and she was sparkling as she hadn't seen her for many months. 'We'll open a bottle of that lovely New Zealand bubbly any minute, and, let's be practical, we can talk about boosting your hours here now that you won't be so distracted! It will fit in well with me tapering mine off,' she said, smugly. She hugged Katherine to her bulging figure.

71

Over the next weeks, Katherine willingly worked longer hours in the Gallery, and was there most days. Dawn told her, awkwardly, when they were alone one morning, that she would be away for a fortnight soon. She was going to Rio de Janeiro just before Easter.

'It'll still be terribly hot, in March,' Katherine answered animatedly, to both their surprise. 'Take only the lightest clothes. You'll love it.'

Dawn looked happy and embarrassed.

'It's okay, honestly.' Katherine told her. 'I want you to like it!' Rio de Janeiro with Orlando seemed not only another country but another life, one she scarcely identified with any more. It was mildly nostalgic to think of, nothing more. It could have been a pleasant film she had once seen and only half-remembered.

Waiting for a sign about where Richard might be was much more urgent. In the emptiness which work on the book had filled, the idea of finding find him preoccupied her. This is superstition, nothing more, she told herself, and yet twice, as the days lengthened slowly, she found herself driving out to Benson. She avoided the King's Head, where Eric and Zinnia might have been pleased to see her, and both times ended driving slowly along the road east. There, where Oak Farm House sat, seven roads had met at a place called Roke Elm, and there her life with Richard had begun. The first time, the house was closed, cold and empty-looking. She stopped the car for a moment, and sat looking at it. She glimpsed pale, early blossom in the orchard behind, before leaving guiltily, like someone caught planning an illegal entry. On her way home to Oxford she felt a rush of anger with him, for making her prowl and wait. It faded before she arrived home, subdued with sadness.

On the second occasion, it was obvious that David Freeman had re-let the house. A red Volvo was parked outside and the gate hung open. Matching white curtains framed all the windows, with elaborate ruchings at the top. Everything seemed more finally finished than ever before, and she drove on with her throat and eyes tight with tears, unshed. This time she let herself think the worst, unthinkable thought. Perhaps Richard was nowhere, now?

In April, everything changed. Exactly on time, a parcel from Fox House arrived. With shaking fingers, Katherine pulled the first book from the thick wrapping. More thin green paper covered it, and she put it down again, hesitating. This was public now; no longer her private, provocative, satisfying world. This was a book, and it belonged to Fox House too, and anyone else who cared to try it. She took a deep breath.

First view delighted her. She had discussed the Paul Nash picture of Wittenham Clumps long ago with Tim, and even seen a rough-out of how it might look as a cover, and here it was, a golden view of the Clumps, with the tree-lined path of the Thames beneath, and birds wheeling in a pale blue sky behind. Her name ran along the upper edge, and, much larger, in plain solid letters, black against Paul Nash's autumn cornfield, was the title - *'Benson: People, Time, and Landscape.'*

'Hey!' She said excitedly. 'My book!' She rang her mother and described it to her, and promised to post her off a copy very soon. She had to speak to Diane, too. 'Newspapers already have it,' she said. 'Review copies.'

The Ashes were next, and she got Joe on the phone, not Olivia. Some association in her mind, or confusion connected with his familiar male voice, made her shake as she told him, and speak very fast, not thinking too much.

Then she sat and read it until her eyes ached.

A week later, and Katherine received another envelope from Fox House, a large, A4 sized special delivery envelope. 'Thought you might want to see these before the week-end,' an editorial hand had written laconically. 'Advance copies of the Sunday reviews. Congratulations!'

Katherine unfolded the photocopies carefully, and spread them out. She glanced over the headings, bracing her arms on the desk. 'History as it should be,' read the first. 'A tour-de-force of historic imagination.' 'Figures in a landscape: all our histories', said the second. Katherine breathed out. 'From the front-line: 1066 and everything else, too ... ' began another. She gave a snort, and began reading properly.

'This history has nothing to do with kings and constitutions. Katherine Laidlaw has performed the feat of turning a localised history into the history of us all. Her figures stand before us, bright, real, happy, sad, likeable, dislikeable ... '

'With a magical blend of analytical rigour and imagination, she twists effortlessly between illustration and proof. Take for instance, her heartbreaking image of a Benson father and his family in the grip of the Black Death. The stricken mother trying to breast-feed the sick infant up to and after its death; the father having to pry it away from her and re-open the grave of his other children, in his own garden ... it could be a report direct from the scene. Within pages, though, we have a painstaking analysis of manorial court and taxation records in succeeding years, and hard figures for the numbers of surviving families and even some of their names. Meticulous research and electrifying imagination combine ... '

'Landscape history evolves into human history ... this remarkable book began with an investigation into why seven old roads once met at an obscure point at the foot of the Chiltern hills ... An overall marshalling intelligence assembles a mass of material - from anecdotal to statistical to religious - and sets the past bright and immediate before us. With this dazzling, unusual book, Katherine Laidlaw gives us eyes to see - if we will - that all our history is with us still ... Buy it and read it. This is New History.'

72

Katherine was relieved and elated, and by the end of the day, depressed. She read and re-read the description of her Black Death chapter, and remembered, without needing to look, the ensuing pages where she moved on to the Benson survivors picking up their lives, starting their mills turning again, rounding up orphaned livestock, planting out the surplus furlongs in the fields, and kneeling bitterly and obediently in their churches, surrounded by wall-paintings of doom and the gates of hell. Eventually, some moved away.

She paced around her flat. Some moved away. What had she expected; that the reviewers might include a route-map to Richard? Or perhaps an address, neatly at the bottom of the page?

He might see some of these reviews, if he ... if he was sitting somewhere, reading papers. She resisted an irrational urge to look for him at Oak Farm House one more time.

By Saturday morning, she knew where she wanted to go. It will be a small holiday, a reward, she rationalised it to herself. It was a fine spring day when she set off, but in the western sky a flurry of clouds was assembling. The rolling Cotswold views, different from the sharper slopes and smaller valleys of the Chilterns, grew shorter as she drove.

By mid-afternoon, she was circling around the high lanes above the Severn valley. There was almost no traffic, and the hills felt remote and distant. It was misty. Sheep crowded like clusters of restless white ghosts at farm gates, and crows rose, flapping, as she swerved around the corners. After a few false turns, she came upon the tiny hotel, near the crossroads. The little building seemed to grow out of its patch of land as naturally as a tree. Its Oak Tree sign hung on one end, and tables stood on the patch of grass outside. She turned off the engine and sat for a while, postponing going in, and thinking about their walk here in late summer sun, with ripe fields visible from the woodland edges.

After some minutes she started the engine again, and parked behind the hotel and went in. The landlord looked at her curiously as he showed her up to the small bedroom in the roof.

'I hope you'll be warm enough.' he said, and demonstrated how the single radiator worked. It was beneath the deep window sill on which the vase of hops still stood, pale and straw-like.

'Will you be having dinner?'

The girl was pretty, unwinding a long scarf, and placing it on the bed. She had a white shirt tucked into slim-fitting tan trousers, and a belt with a complicated buckle around her waist. She turned to him as if she had only just heard him.

'Dinner? Oh, yes, I'll be down later. Thank you.'

When he had gone she lay on the bed with her eyes closed, but awake.

She should go for a walk, she supposed, before it was quite dark. But when she reached the little bar downstairs a few customers were already arriving, and it felt warm and convivial.

'Have some coffee, at least,' the cheerful barman said.

'Perhaps I will, after all.'

She took the cup and found a chair with her back to the thick wall. The room began filling up, and she found a local paper and moved to a glass of red wine. As she settled back in her chair with them, the black retriever came running straight towards her. She had forgotten about the dog, she thought, and remembered Richard throwing a quoit for him, and pretending irritation at his importuning. She smiled at the animal's indiscriminate welcome. He had grown a little in the intervening months. He half jumped at her and then sat heavily on her feet, leaning against her and looking up. The tail wagged ecstatically and the bright eyes caught her own. As she looked down, the animal let out a whimper of pleasure and pawed at her. Katherine looked at the dog's wide head, and bent over and touched the flickering ears. The dog pushed back into her hands in a familiar way. Katherine looked harder.

'Bella?' she said incredulously. 'Are you Bella?'

She sank her arms around the dog and clutched the thick fur. She looked around, nearly deafened by her own heartbeat. The room seemed to slant around her. For a moment too many people stood in her way and she could see nothing, and then someone moved, and Richard came through the door.

73

She sat motionless for a moment, holding Bella, until she saw him glance around for the dog, and their eyes met. He seemed to walk the few feet between them very slowly, and she found she had stood up.

'Why are you here?' they said, interrupting each other.

Katherine tried again. 'Why are you?'

'I live near.'

There was a silence.

'Bella found me.'

'Yes.'

Her eyes filled with tears, and at last he touched her arm and said, 'Shall we have a drink?'

'Richard,' she said urgently. 'I found out about Shimming Lane.'

'Shimming Lane?' he repeated, looking bewildered. 'Why is that important?'

She spoke as if he might disappear again. 'Because there is no way anyone could know anything about Shimming Lane. Unless they were there ... I know you were there.'

He looked at her without a word, and without glancing away as a passing couple jostled them.

'Richard?'

The passing couple turned back and bumped them again, and as if they broke a spell, Richard said, 'Shall we sit down? Shall I get us a drink?'

They sat with their shoulders inches apart. Bella skulked around the tables and eventually ambled off outside.

'She'll find the resident dog out there. Do you remember him?'

Katherine nodded, watching his face. Her skin felt very tight.

'You've lost weight,' he said, and caught her wrists. 'Look how thin these are!' He held them between his hands and she felt his hard palms. Still looking at her hands, he said, 'I was beside myself with missing you. But even more enraged about having to convince you about - things. And then not liking myself for making that the most important thing.'

'But it was the most important thing! Everything else was fine!'

For the first time he really smiled. 'You must have been angry, too.'

'I was. But then I found about Shimming Lane.' She told him in detail about the map and the enlargement. He still held one of her wrists, gently.

His eyes never left her bright, intense face, but when she stopped talking, he merely said, 'But why are you here?'

'I needed to be near you, somehow ... ' She hadn't even told him about her book yet, she realised, and had forgotten it herself since she had caught sight of him. 'This is where we talked about ... You know, that talk we had.' She glanced upwards, towards the bedroom. 'It didn't cross my mind you'd be here. How could it? And Oak Farm House seems to be let out again', she suddenly changed track.

'Does it? I suppose I ended up here for the same reason. We had a sort of good time here, didn't we?'

'Sort of, yes.'

They were silent for a minute. Then Richard stood up abruptly. 'Shall we go outside?'

'I need a coat.'

In the small bedroom she pulled a coat on and found she was breathing hard and had to force her arms into the sleeves as though her body were not quite under control. She glanced into the mirror as if a different person might be reflected there.

74

Outside, it was raining hard.

'This is ridiculous. We should have noticed.' Richard said, and at the corner of the building he stopped walking and turned her to face him, holding her shoulders. In the dim light from a window she could see the fair shine of his hair being spattered with raindrops.

'Could you tell me about Shimming Lane again?'

'When the map is blown up ... '

'Not all that,' he interrupted her.

'I believe you. You were there.'

He looked at her for a long minute, as though her words were hard to understand. He stared at her as though he had to memorise every feature of her face.

'Katherine ... ', but she was speaking on, ignoring the rain.

'My book is finished. It'll be out next week. There's lots in it that you told me. Will you mind? Of course you are not mentioned - but you are there. It's your book, too.'

'No!' His white smile flashed at last. He was almost shouting. 'No, of course I don't mind, if you did it.'

'It's very good, apparently!' she said, laughing with happiness. 'I've got some reviews. Do we have to stand out here getting wet?'

She could have floated up through the rain. She gave a little groan, and was in his arms. He gave her an achingly long kiss, and she felt relief and calm run through her body like a river.

'No, we don't have to get wet,' he said firmly in a minute. 'Why don't you show me this book? Inside. Bella's probably there already, very sensibly.'

'Shall we have dinner?' They looked at each other uncertainly.

'I'm not hungry,' Katherine said.

'I need to talk to you.'

She nodded.

Richard walked outside again, taking Bella. 'Come on, you,' he said to her, very gently, and urged her into his car and shut the door.

Back in the hotel, Katherine was waiting at the stairs. He followed her up, and closed the door of the little bedroom behind them. He put his arms around her.

'I really mean it,' he said. 'I want to talk to you.'

'I know.'

'Where's this book?'

She pulled out of his arms and reached to pass it to him. He smiled with pleasure at the golden Wittenham cover, and glanced through the first pages.

'Look.'

She found the chapter called 'Roke Elm,' and he read the opening paragraphs about the odd meeting place of seven roads. 'A search on the ground, reveals, however, that these paths are not lost at all ... '

'I told you your house seems to be let out again, didn't I?'

He closed the book firmly. 'Yes, you did. But we're not only Roke Elm, are we? We are more than that. We are ourselves, now.'

He put the book down and held her again. They lay on the bed. silently.

Eventually she spoke, mouth on his shoulder.

'What's the worst thing that could happen?'

'You die and leave me.'

'The worst for me is that you won't, and you'll get other women after me.'

Neither smiled.

'But this is different! No-one else has known about me. How can that not alter everything? I love you. I will always love you, no matter how ... how it turns out.'

'No one else could know,' she agreed, still into his shoulder. 'Who else has ever wanted to do ... that kind of searching ... in that precise place? I started doing it for me, of course. But then it became ... for you. I so wanted to find you!'

He kissed her head, rubbing his face on her silky, untidy hair.

'I so wanted you to find me. I think I had waited for you for a long time ... '

She pressed her face against his neck as she listened, swept by a confusion of sadness and relief.

'But it had to be you of your own accord ... do you understand?' He pulled her chin gently up to look into her eyes. She nodded, and after a silent moment spoke herself.

'Nothing which happens could be as bad for me as when you were suddenly gone.'

'I didn't trust you. Can you get over that?'

'And I knew you'd gone because I hadn't trusted you ... '

She looked up and kissed him passionately.

'Quite a mess, really', Richard said, in his usual brisk voice, but clearing his throat.

'I always said it was a muddle,' Katherine said, matching him.

They lay on their backs and spoke into the dark again.

'It might change, of course. Your ... condition mightn't last forever. Some year, some decade, you may just start getting grey hair, like the rest of us.' She held out her long plait and scrutinised it.

'True. It will change, sometime.' He thought before adding, 'And, anyway, I have good start on you. How old are you? Twenty-nine?' He smiled, and she responded.

'Years to go. And I love you.'

There were long gaps between their sentences. Every question and every answer had to be dragged from deep inarticulate levels into exchangeable words.

'I could do something ... I could do something to you. If I start dying. When I start dying. If we wanted, I could ... '

'It's an idea. If you still love me then. Or I could do it myself.'

We are discussing terrible things, she thought.

'I'll still love you then. We don't have to decide anything. We can wait.'

There was a pause again.

'We can have a very long time together.'

They turned to each other and she looked into his eyes.

'Are you crying?' he said, sternly.

'No. Yes.'

'Come here.' He pulled her against him, and stroked the long hair without speaking.

'Come here,' he said again, and pulled her harder against him, turning to face her.

There was a last hesitation, before Richard said, spacing out his words as he stroked her, 'I ... have ... wanted ... you ...'

They sighed into each other and breathed each other's breath. At last her arms stretched around him and pulled. His hands found her breasts and she gasped and shivered as if it were the first time he had kissed her, and the first time she had wrapped herself around him. She pressed her face into his chest and smelled his skin.

'Richard', she muttered, and thought she heard him answer in his language she only half-understood. 'Richard,' she said again.

For a moment he was completely still, and then he moved on top of her and looked down. She opened her eyes to look at him, and he groaned as if an enormous weight had rolled off him and he could breathe at last.

When he was nearly asleep, Katherine nudged him.

'Rich,' she said.

'Go to sleep.'

'Do you remember we talked about signs once? Kingfishers and so on?' And Piers Finch, she added to herself.

'Mmmh.'

'Rich, Bella was a sign!'

He raised his eyebrows, silently.

'The sign that I was going to find you.'

'Bella? A sign?'

For some moments, she thought he was asleep again. Then he said,

'Really, for a great historian, Kathy, you talk some nonsense.'

She giggled, and lay closer against him, and closed her eyes.

75

A few hours later, the landlord of the Oak Tree Inn opened up his doors to let his dog out and clear the smoky fumes from his small bar with cool, early-morning air. Outside he noticed a car still parked there, an old Saab with a black dog peacefully in the back seat. That's interesting, he thought. Considering it, he bent to pick up the bundle of assorted Sunday papers left by the newsagent on his step. Soon he would distribute them around the tables for the entertainment of his customers. He lay them on the bar, picked up his mug of coffee, and began to thumb through the top one. He flicked through the book pages, which rarely detained him, and was arrested by a photograph. He studied it closely, a picture of a tall young woman with wide, dark eyes. She was standing near a thatched cruck cottage in a village high street. The label underneath was, 'Katherine Laidlaw: the history of Everyman - and Woman.'

'Well, here's a turn-up,' he said.

The review covered the whole page. 'People, Time and Landscape', it began. 'Katherine Laidlaw has taken these vast themes in hand and effortlessly shaped them into a gripping history ... '

The landlord pulled a face, and looked out towards his car park again, thoughtfully.

'Here certainly is a turn-up', he said again. He took a swig of his coffee. 'And when's he going to appear and get that dog?'

He put his mug down, and began reading. It was more interesting than he expected. The sun rose a little further, and lay mild golden rays across the car. Bella slept on.